MAKE
IT
shine

JESSIE HARPER

Cover Design: Ya'll That Graphic

Editing: Tamara Mataya and Austin Ryan

Print ISBN: 978-1-7350961-8-6

❀ Created with Vellum

ALSO BY JESSIE HARPER

The Finally Falling Series

Fight For It

Forget About It

Fix It

1

Chance

Pushing through the crowd to get to the bar, I can almost smell the money. It's a typical Saturday night out with the typical crowd, which means expensive drinks and giant egos. But the blonde at the bar looks way more interesting than the group of tech investors I'm supposed to be meeting. With her tight dress and thick-framed glasses, she's the kind of girl I've come to expect here. She looks smart in a trashy way—something I've been told plenty of times takes way more effort than you'd think. I'm not about to turn down the opportunity to find out just how smart she is, especially if it means sliding off those glasses when I take her back to my apartment. Buying her a drink will be the easy part; they always let you buy them a drink. The trick is getting them to talk to you for more than two minutes. But I know I'm not hard on the eyes so when she slides over to make space for me next to her, I take advantage of the opportunity. I push the meeting back a little further in my mind. Those guys can wait.

"What're you drinking?"

"Vodka tonic." Her lips come dangerously close to my ear. It's loud in here, but not *that* loud, so points to her for starting out bold.

I move to find one of the bartenders.

That's when I notice the rooster.

He's perched on the bar, pecking around, walking between drinks like he owns the place.

"Is that a...?"

"It's a rooster." She's unconcerned about the poultry on the bar. "Are you going to buy me a drink or not?" She's a little pouty, letting her bottom lip jut out just enough to bring me back to the matter at hand.

"Of course I am." There's a rooster on the bar and no one seems bothered but me. "Let's get you that drink. Vodka tonic, right?"

"Sure." She smiles. "Just ask the rooster and he'll get it for you."

What? This city gets weirder and weirder.

"I'm pretty sure a chicken can't mix drinks, honey," I tell her with more confidence than I feel. Can you train a rooster to make drinks? I don't remember them being that smart. Mean, maybe, but not intelligent. And he doesn't have thumbs. How's that going to work?

As if he feels my doubt, the rooster walks down the length of the bar and stops in front of me. I expect him to try to peck at me, chase me like the roosters used to on my grandpa's farm when I was little. We stare each other down —the rooster not breaking eye contact for even a second despite the chaos of this bar and other people trying to get his attention... to fill their drink orders...? When he finally turns, I breathe a sigh of relief. Getting in a fight with a chicken was not something I thought I'd be trying to avoid tonight.

But the rooster doesn't walk away. Instead he tilts his head back and starts crowing, the feathers on his throat rolling with the sound. He crows and crows, startling me enough to make me take a step back from the bar.

"What the hell?" No one bats an eye. "Why is he doing that?"

"Because it's time to get up?" The girl shrugs her shoulders. "Rise and shine, Chance. Time to get your lazy ass out of bed."

I roll over in the bed I used to sleep in every summer and crack one eye open. The wallpaper's peeling and I feel a rush of irritation. In the dark it had been difficult to see, just like the noticeable sagging going on in the middle of the ceiling. There's obviously been a roof leak. It's dry now, but the brown ring running from the ancient light fixture is all the evidence I need.

I roll on my back and stare at the stain, cursing myself for staying away so long. My grandfather would never have told me how much this house had fallen into disrepair, and since I've avoided coming back here, there was no way to see it with my own eyes. I give the mattress a punch. When my fist almost goes through the fabric, I realize this is going to get me nowhere. This is probably the same mattress I slept on as a teenager when I spent summers on the farm. Just like everything else, it's falling apart.

More crowing from the rooster—a real, regular, non-drink-making rooster—convinces me to get out of bed. My back is killing me and lying here any longer isn't going to do anything to fix that. I need to get up and start looking the house over, deciding what needs to be repaired first. That crowing won't stop until my aunts get around to feeding that bird, so there's no use in trying to go back to sleep. Now that I'm back on the farm, it's going to be farm hours, I guess.

~

After a cup of coffee, I feel marginally better. There's no food in the house, but I had expected that. My grandpa passed away three weeks ago Sunday and dead men don't eat. What I didn't expect was the state of this house and how angry it'd make me. I'm here now, but it's too little too late when it comes to making my grandfather's last days more comfortable.

I push my way through the rickety screen door to sit on the porch. The old rocking chairs are still there, but neither one of them looks like it would hold my weight. I settle myself down on the steps and sip at my already cold coffee. I made it with the dregs of the can that's been sitting on the kitchen counter for who knows how long. A million years, I'm guessing, by the way it tastes. I let the sun warm my face a little. I have always loved Georgia mornings. Even in the worst of circumstances, being on this farm raises my spirits. This time it may take a bit more than just the sound of the bugs gearing up for the day, but I'm willing to give it a try.

I groan at the slap of another screen door. My aunts come bickering out of their house and I know the peace of my morning is probably over for now. From where I'm sitting I can see the front porch of the house my grandfather built for his sisters. Technically they're my great-aunts, but I grew up calling them Aunt Mae and Aunt Sadie. They wouldn't have tolerated me adding the "great" in there. For years I ran between these two houses, hoping for a slice of peach pie or a taste of jam in the summer when my aunts were hard at work putting up all the things they grew in their garden. Now they come down the front stairs to their chickens and I wince as they gingerly put one foot in front of the other, both of them holding on tight to the rail running alongside.

"It doesn't matter when we come out, he's still going to crow at the same time," Mae's arguing. "A rooster crows when he crows, that's his job."

"I don't think that's the case, Mae," Sadie says. "What do you know about chickens, anyway?"

"Plenty! I've been raising chickens since before you were born. I know roosters."

Sadie huffs and I'm not sure if it's in response to her sister or from the exertion of the stairs. "Since before I was born? What, you were raisin' chickens in your crib?"

In my memories they're always like this, younger maybe, but attached at the hip and fighting like it would kill them to stop. Since they never married, building this house on the farm right next to their brother's was less about family closeness and more about convenience. Now that he's gone, they're another reason I'm back. Watching them this morning confirms what I should have already known: two elderly ladies do not need to be living out on this farm all alone.

"Chance?" Mae shouts and Sadie turns to look at me. "Chance Allen, is that you sneaking around over there?"

I'm hardly sneaking, but there's no sense in arguing with Mae.

"Yes, ma'am." I stand, really feeling my lower back. I've got to replace that mattress.

"Did you get in last night? You should've come over to let us know." Sadie's always ready to give me a scolding.

"It was pretty late. I know how you two love your beauty sleep. Not that you need it." Sweet talk usually works with my aunts and I hope today will be no exception. I let a little of my drawl work its way in there for good measure. I no longer sound like I'm from around here, but there are some things not even California can fully erase.

Sadie and Mae preen a little bit, looking more than a little similar to the chickens now gathered at their feet. Mae's got an old coffee can full of chicken feed and the birds are getting anxious for their breakfast. My stomach growls, reminding me that I'm going to have to do something about my own breakfast before too long.

"Did Marlon Brando wake you up? He's been crowing earlier and earlier." Sadie scowls down at the huge red rooster. "He's nice to look at, but more trouble than he's worth."

"What can you expect?" Mae asks. "He's a man, after all." My aunts cackle. "No offense, Chance."

"None taken. Your rooster's named Marlon Brando? Why am I not surprised?" I smile at my spinster aunts and watch feathers fly as Sadie sprinkles out the feed.

"You haven't eaten, have you?" Mae asks, moving away from the bird tornado. "I've got some of that blackberry jam left from this summer's berries. Let me grab you a few eggs from the coop and I'll whip you something up. You want biscuits?"

"Yes, ma'am. I always want biscuits." That is the truth. I always want biscuits, especially here.

"Come on, then."

And I follow her back up the porch steps, putting one arm out to catch her in case she falls.

The third degree begins when I finish my third biscuit. My aunts aren't subtle, but at least they wait until your stomach is full before they pounce.

"So's this just a visit?" Sadie asks as she clears the dishes. She's careful not to make eye contact and I can't help but notice the irritated look Mae shoots her.

"I'm here for a bit." I wipe the rest of the blackberry jam from the corners of my mouth. I won't need to worry about losing weight while I'm here. My aunts tend to keep a steady stream of butter and sugar on the menu. I make a mental note to check the basement of the farmhouse for my old workout bench.

"How long's a bit?" Sadie presses.

Again, Mae gives her the stink eye. "You don't have to answer that," Mae chimes in. "We're happy to have you here as long as you want to stay."

"Well, of course." Sadie nods but glares at her sister. "But I was just wanting to know a ballpark figure, that's all. I wasn't sure when you'd need to get back to California and your job. And your girlfriend...?" The last part comes out like the fishing expedition it is. Sadie's apparently heard just enough about recent events to get her curious but not enough to know what she's talking about.

"The job's on hold for a while," I confess, giving them a little of what they want. "Right now, getting Grandpa's house in order's more important."

"I see." Sadie's not satisfied. She's hoping I'll spend the next few hours telling her all about how my life in California ground to a slow halt. No thanks. That story's way less interesting than people think and I'm not about to ruin my breakfast talking about it.

"Well, if you're staying until that house is livable again then you'd better plan on staying a while." Mae's mouth sets into a frown. "Jefferson let that place go once he got sick. Wouldn't let anybody in to fix things once they broke either." She's obviously still a little angry about my grandfather's stubborn streak.

"He probably didn't want anybody to know he needed the help," I offer, knowing this won't be an excuse for either of my aunts. Family helps each other. Family's there when you need them no matter what. Guilt gnaws at my belly. Great example I've been of what family really means.

"Are your brothers coming to help?" Sadie asks. "Or are you gonna be hiring the work out? There's no way you'll be able to do all of the repairs yourself. You really will be here forever if that's your plan."

"Just me for now." I try to sound confident. I've done plenty of repair work in my twenty-nine years. I'm sure I can figure out what needs to be done to get that house livable again.

"None of those boys are coming to help? Not even Cade?" Mae seems disappointed. Once again, the dream of our happy helping family can't cover up the reality.

"Not even Cade." I shrug. My baby brother's got a degree to finish. I'd never ask him to come out here if it meant messing up his studies. And my oldest brother's not in a position to take much time off work. But Cooper'd kill me if I told that around town. And Charlie? Well, Charlie's Charlie. "If I need them, I'll call them," I lie. I wouldn't drag them into this mess if I was on fire.

"At least tell me your father's paying for your time. Or the repairs. That's the least he could do." Sadie's voice is stern. She's no fan of my father. When she says it's the least he could do, she really means it. My father is the master of doing the bare minimum. Less, if he can get away with it.

"We haven't worked everything out yet. I'm sure he'll do his part." Whatever that means.

My aunts look about as convinced as I feel.

"I should get going." I stand to clear my plate. "I need to make a punch list of the jobs at the house so I can get started."

"You should probably take a look at the barn while you're at it." Mae takes my plate from me and rinses it in the big farmhouse sink. "We've got a little issue over there."

"At the barn?" In all the discussions we've had about the farm no one's mentioned anything about the barn. "What's wrong with the barn?"

Mae looks over her shoulder at Sadie and I catch some head shaking out of the corner of my eye.

"Well..." Mae hesitates.

"It's missing a wall," Sadie blurts out. "There, I said it. When it comes to news like that you have to just get it out there, Mae."

"Missing a wall?" I ask, dumbfounded. That makes no sense. "How's the barn missing a wall?" As far as I know no one's been using the barn for much of anything but storage these past few years.

"Someone took it," Mae says, still hunched over the sink. "Took the whole thing clean off."

"Someone took a quarter of the barn?" I'm more confused than ever. "When? How?"

"We're not exactly sure. Mae and I don't go by there that often. There's no need. And you can't see the back wall from here."

I look out the kitchen window and try to see the barn in the distance. I can barely make out the edges of the gray form through the pine trees. The gravel path leading from the houses to the barn isn't in the best shape. I can see why they avoid walking over there.

"People want the wood, I guess. We've had folks drive up asking if they can buy some. Old barn wood's expensive.

They make tables and things out of it." Sadie's explanation doesn't do much to answer my questions.

"You sold someone a wall of the barn?" I can't believe this.

"No, no, we'd never do that. Your great-grandfather built that barn. That wood's the only lumber we've ever milled from this property," Sadie's indignant. "And we'd never sell a *wall*. The barn's no good without four walls, Chance. We know that."

"Someone came and took the thing down. They took down the ivy and everything. Pulled the boards down whole and hauled them out," Mae tells me.

"While you were here?" Now I'm more worried than confused. "At night or something? They'd have to bring a flatbed to get the boards out. And it isn't exactly a quick job." The barn's two stories high with stables on the bottom and a loft on top. It'd be no easy feat to sneak onto the farm, yank down the boards, and then get the wood out with no one noticing.

"We don't know when they did it. Just one day when Sadie and I were out walking we noticed the far wall's gone."

I blink, fury rising up and threatening to boil over. Who steals part of a dead man's barn?

"I'm sorry, Chance. We had the police out. They said there isn't much they can do. We don't have electricity over there so we don't have security lights. Not sure if that would have made any difference." Sadie pats my arm.

"I'll go over and take a look. Thanks for breakfast," I say, tamping my anger down. Mae and Sadie let me go and the screen door slams behind me. To have the house falling down is one thing, but to have thieves coming onto the property and taking part of a building? It's beyond anything I could have imagined.

I flex my fingers as I stomp along the gravel path, gritting my teeth and berating myself for staying gone so long. As I near the barn the gaping hole in the side becomes more apparent. Not just a hole, but one entire side of the thing stripped clean away, exposing the inside to the elements. Anything in there's as good as ruined now.

"Son of a bitch," I mutter to myself. *Son of a bitch.*

2

Lily

"Lily! Lily! Liiiiily!"

I sigh. "What?" I shout.

"Can you come out here for a second?" my mother yells.

"Right now?" I wipe the sweat from my forehead and hope I can ignore her.

"Yeah, right now."

I groan and get ready to have my morning hijacked. "Give me a second. I'm right in the middle of something." I shake the sawdust from my hands and try to dust myself off. Most of the grit stays put, though, clinging to my sweatshirt. I'm sure I'm going to leave a trail from the workshop out into the store. Not that my mother or grandmother will care. I'll be the only one to notice and the only one to think to clean it up.

I come through the shop doors to find my mother and grandmother both standing with their hands on their hips. That's never a good sign.

"You bellowed?"

"Lily, what the hell is going on in here?"

I look around the huge warehouse space that houses our family business. Southern Comforts is part furniture store, part treasure trove, and part junk heap. My grandmother started it back before I was born and we've been trying to turn a profit ever since. Some years are better than others, of course, but the store has never been the kind of thing that's going to make anyone rich. I scan the tables full of knick-knacks and the bins of everything under the sun. It all looks fine to me. Well, not fine—it's a mess—but that's how it's always been.

"You're going to have to be more specific. It looks normal to me." I keep it to myself that it looks less than fine. No sense in getting my grandmother riled up. We're all trying to keep her blood pressure down since her stroke.

"Look over there. You don't see anything different?" My mother points a finger toward the back of the store where I've been slowly but surely trying to make a dent in the crazy. Busted.

"I see a few vignettes."

"Some vin-whats?" my grandmother demands.

"Vignettes. Like displays," I explain. "I set them up last night."

"I thought vignette was what you put on your salad," my mother interjects.

"That's vinaigrette, Mama."

"Well, whatever it is I don't like it. It looks too much like a department store." My grandmother leans forward onto the handles of her walker. "Our customers won't like it."

"What's not to like? People can see how things would go together in a room. They don't have to pick through all the junk to get to what they want."

The shock on my grandmother's face has me wishing I'd never opened my mouth. She shakes her head and gives my mother a look. "Our customers *like* to pick through the *junk*, as you so nicely put it. They like to come and see what they can find. They don't want to come in here and see this." She gives my work a dismissive wave.

"The customers we have now might not like that, Bunny, but the kind of customers we need to attract to make any money will. Atlanta ladies don't necessarily want to pick through piles of stuff and if they do, they expect to find a bargain. I didn't come home to help you keep doing things the same old way."

Now my mother looks offended as well. Great. I'll never get back to working on the furniture I'm stripping in the back room at this rate. I'll end up spending all day trying to smooth over all these hurt feelings. My family's never been big on change, in the store or anywhere else. That's why when I up and moved to Chicago they were more than a little pissed off. They thought I was trying to get away from this place, from home, when they didn't understand there was just no way I could stay, not without losing more of myself than I already had.

"Well, we appreciate your *help*," Bunny tells me. "But we don't need you running around changing everything. You moved that pile of old windows I had against the back wall and now I won't know where anything is."

I'm not sure how my grandmother knows where anything is in this place, but she does. A customer can walk in and ask her if we have some esoteric item from a million years ago and Bunny'll know that, yes, we have one, and it's back there in that bin on top of that shelf underneath the collection of hats. She's good, Bunny. Her body may be giving up the ghost, but her mind's sharp.

"You could at least let me use some of the things I know to see if we can make a little more money," I protest. I didn't give up my life to become my grandmother's helper. Not that I had much going on in Illinois anyway, but they don't need to know that the thing I'm missing most is the freedom to binge watch television without anyone's comments. "I know a little about this."

"You know a little," my mother concedes. "But your Bunny and I have been running this shop for a long time. I think we know what works."

"I'm not saying my way is better, Mama. I just think we should try a little bit of both to get things rolling. We could always use a little extra money." I try not to look at my grandmother when I say this. We all know I'm talking about her mountain of medical bills. They keep coming and we can never catch up. That's the only reason anyone even told me about Bunny's stroke. It's the reason I moved back to Mint Springs. Temporarily, I said, but watching my grandmother hobble around I know I'm going to have a hard time leaving again.

Bunny coughs into her hand and steadies herself on the walker. "I guess it couldn't hurt," she says in that voice that tells me she's pretty sure it will. "Just keep it toward the back of the store. And don't move too much around, you hear?"

"Yes, ma'am."

Bunny moves back over to her stool behind the counter. She's been sitting there for as long as I can remember, waiting on customers that only appear every now and then in the big front window.

"Aren't you hot in that sweatshirt?" my mother asks, startling me out of my reminiscing. "It's at least ninety degrees back there in the shop."

"I'm fine." I pull the sleeves of my old hoodie farther down my arms. "It keeps me from getting scratches while I work."

"If you say so. You're pretty bundled up for springtime."

I shrug. Avoiding the subject usually works the best but eventually my mother will notice something's up. My uniform of men's sweatpants and oversized shirts works better in a colder climate. Summer in the South is going to be a challenge for me.

"I need to get back to work," I say, hoping to make a quick getaway and be able to return to the quiet of the workshop.

"What've you got going on back there today? Anything we can see yet? That last one was so pretty."

"Nothing yet, but the lines on this one are really unique. Hopefully it'll sell as quickly as the last piece." I'm exceptionally proud of this find even if Bunny isn't likely to appreciate it.

My mother nods. The fact that all of the furniture I've painted has sold quickly is the one reason she's started taking any of my advice.

"Well, get back there and get to work. What color are you thinking about this time? More of the blue?"

I make a move toward the workshop door. "Not sure yet. I'm going to mix up a few things. Maybe a green this time? I'll let you and Bunny vote once I have a few options."

"Okay, Lily. That sounds nice." She brushes her hand along my arm and I stiffen at the contact. My mother frowns, but doesn't say anything. "You let us know when you're ready."

"Of course, Mama." And I let the silence of the workshop wash over me as I shut the door behind me.

3

Chance

Getting the old truck to start was a challenge. After finally finding the extra set of keys in the kitchen junk drawer, I pulled the tarp from the ancient green Chevy and tried to start it up.

Nothing.

An hour later, covered in grease, I managed to get the engine to turn over, but it took me another hour of tinkering to get the thing running for more than a few minutes at a time. Add the truck to my list of things that could use a little attention around here.

My plan to head into town to grab groceries and possibly a new mattress was now delayed by a few hours. Showering left me cleaner but with a crick in my neck. How did I ever manage to bend myself under the sprayer in that old attic bathroom? I guess the last time I had to use it I must have been a foot shorter. I had contemplated using the shower in the master bath, but made a hasty retreat when confronted with the evidence of my grandfather's illness. The counter still holds more medicine than any one man should have a need for, and the smell of his aftershave still lingers in the room. I'll take squeezing myself into the upstairs clown car of a bathroom any day if it means avoiding the flood of emotions downstairs keeps stirring up.

Smelling slightly better and looking considerably less greasy, I slide behind the wheel of the truck and hope like hell it won't decide to break down on one of the less traveled roads on the way to town. The Chevy had been my grandfather's for as long as I can remember. There'd been newer trucks for hauling things and farm work, but this old truck had always hung around. It was the first one my grandfather had been able to buy free and clear and even when he could afford something newer he'd kept this one. I learned to change the oil and check the fluids on this very truck when I was about twelve. Now I put my backside into the groove in the seat where my grandfather once sat and ease the truck off the gravel road and onto the pavement that means I'm heading toward civilization.

If you could call Mint Springs civilization, that is.

But things do look different than the last time I was here. This sleepy little town has woken up a bit and I can't decide if I like it. Instead of the old corner store where my grandpa used to send me for his chewing tobacco, there's a big new supermarket. The old gas station has been replaced with some kind of coffee shop. If I'd been looking for landmarks I'd be pretty lost right about now. But some things have stayed exactly the same. Sullivan's Nursery is still five miles down the road, its hand-painted sign chipped and faded. The beauty parlor where my aunts get their hair done is right where it's supposed to be and when I make the left to head to the town square, the front window of the junk shop still glints right in my eyes. It's a little dusty, sure, but the glass is still clean enough to have me pulling down the visor to block the light.

"Shit!" My grandpa's old key ring slides from the visor and lands squarely on my forehead. That solves that mystery, I guess. I'd forgotten how Grandpa used to stow the keys up there. If you needed to borrow his truck, no need to hot-wire the thing. That had come in handy more than a few summer nights when my brothers and I needed to make a midnight run to the river or into town for more beer.

I slide my thumb along the edge of the plastic keychain, remembering all the times I'd seen my grandfather do the same. There's a groove worn in one side from all the absent-minded swipes of his fingers. In my nostalgic haze I almost miss the sandwich board propped up in front of Southern Comforts.

Almost.

I slam on the brakes and wince when the Chevy skids and slides to a stop. Horns honking behind me remind me that I'm not on some back road, but coming to a complete stop in the middle of town. I'm lucky no one rammed into the back of me with a maneuver like that.

"Sorry, sorry," I mumble and wave out the window in what I hope looks like an apology. Easing the truck over to the side of the road, I reread the sign to be sure my eyes aren't playing tricks on me.

There it is in fancy curlicue lettering: *Barn Wood.*

My hands tighten around the steering wheel. Another mystery solved. I'm like the goddamn Sherlock Holmes of this town right now—only our stolen property the police were sure they couldn't find is being advertised in broad daylight. The anger from earlier comes flooding back over me and before I can stop myself, I'm slamming the truck into park and marching myself through the double doors of the store. The bell jingles as I yank the handle so hard I imagine the door coming off the hinges. I'd slam it behind me for effect, but it's one of those glass doors that eases itself shut. This frustrates me more, especially when the two customers milling around inside turn to stare at me.

"Can I help you?" an elderly woman asks me. I turn to where she's seated on a stool, her face quirked into an almost amused expression. I hadn't planned on yelling at someone who looks so much like my aunts, but if she's somehow responsible for the theft of the side of my barn, then by God she's going get an earful.

"Where'd you get the wood?" I demand.

"The wood?" Her face mirrors the confusion in her voice.

"The barn wood. From the sign." I cross my arms over my chest and prepare to argue.

"Oh, that's Lily's thing," she tells me before leaning back in her seat and screaming toward the back of the store. "Lily! Lily!"

A muffled "What?" comes from the back.

"There's a young man here to see you." The woman smirks and runs her eyes over me. After she finishes sizing me up she yells again. "About your sign!" She lowers her voice. "She'll be out soon."

But whoever she was screaming at doesn't come. We stand facing each other and I can feel the seconds ticking by. The woman eventually goes back to staring out the window as I shift uncomfortably from foot to foot.

"Is she coming or not?" I'm irritated now, not only about the wood, but about the waiting.

"She should be." The woman reaches for a magazine and licks her index finger before beginning to turn the pages. "You'll just have to be patient, I guess."

Patient?

I fume for two more minutes, shoving my hands in my pockets with enough force to have the woman at the counter look up from her reading. She cocks an eyebrow, but does nothing to help me, not even attempting to call again to her mystery colleague in the back of the shop.

I should leave, walk out with the same amount of force I came in with, but my anger keeps me glued to the spot, steam most likely visibly coming out both my ears. What feels like an eternity passes with not a peep from the back of the store. She knows I'm here and she couldn't, apparently, care less. The older woman just keeps right on turning the pages of her magazine. She's not big on customer service, from what I can tell, and she doesn't seem like the kind to worry about whether or not I'm going to buy anything.

The other customers in the shop steal sideways glances at me from time to time, no doubt wondering why I'm planted here by the counter waiting for someone who seems unlikely to bother coming to the front to see what I want. The feeling of being some sort of a spectacle starts to get to me after a while and I lose whatever hold I had on my cool. What the fuck am I doing waiting around here? I've got plenty of errands to run and projects to start. And I've got my pride, which is what finally propels me toward the back of the store, ignoring the warning from the woman behind the counter.

"I wouldn't do that if I were you," she calls after me, but I'm done waiting. This Lily person can't manage to get out here to answer my questions about stealing my barn? Then she's about to have an unwelcome interruption.

I push the door open and feel some satisfaction as it shakes on its hinges. It's almost as dramatic as my entry into the store and it startles the woman I find behind it. She's lying on her back, half of her positioned under a giant china cabinet. She's got the thing propped up on blocks to raise it up off the floor, but there's barely room underneath it for her to fit, and she's wedged herself in pretty tight. She startles a little when she sees me, pulling her head to the side to get a better look. Her brown eyes go wide and then narrow as she slides herself out from under the furniture. She's sweaty and covered in sawdust. Flecks of it stick to her long brown ponytail and the side of her face.

"You can't come back here." She wipes her hands on the front of her sweatshirt.

"I had a question and I got tired of waiting. From the looks of things, you weren't planning on coming out front for a while." I want her to feel guilty and I wait for her apology but her face doesn't change. If anything I can see her harden her resolve. She puts her hands on her hips and widens her stance, tips her chin back. She's familiar somehow, and I have a fleeting memory of this same look being given to me before.

"I was busy, obviously."

"Obviously."

We stare each other down, neither willing to be the first to break. In the end she speaks first, but I don't feel like she's anywhere near surrendering. "What's so important that you thought you needed to barge on in here?"

"I saw your sign out front."

"That's not a question."

"Where are you getting your barn wood?" I fold my arms over my chest.

"Are you looking to get something made or do you have wood to sell?" She doesn't move from her original pose.

"To *sell*? No, I don't have any wood to sell but someone's stolen some from me, and I think I might have just found it."

She reacts to my accusation as I would have expected.

"You think I stole your barn wood?" Her eyes glint. She's nearly as angry as I am. "Like I snuck out to wherever you live and hauled it off in the dead of night?"

"Well, someone did."

This surprises her. She blinks a few times before scowling at me. "Well, that someone wasn't me. I bought this wood from Dan Rayborn. He's tearing down his old barn and building a new one. You can ask him yourself."

"Believe me, I will." I know Dan Rayborn. If she's lying it'll be easy enough to catch her in it.

"I hope you do. Now, if you'll excuse me." She turns her back to me and moves to slide back under the cabinet. When I don't move she stops, pointing toward the door. "I assume you can show yourself out."

She's dismissing me. On principle I decide to stand here a minute longer. This earns me another scowl and a dismissive wave of her hand. "Don't let the door hit you on your way out, Chance."

"Thanks for your help," I bark back over my shoulder as I shove my way out the door. I move toward the front of the store, still feeling the frustration from earlier pulling me down. As I yank the front door open and hear the tinkling of the bell I'm tempted to reach up and rip the thing down. I keep my hands balled into fists instead and dig my fingernails even deeper into my palms when I hear the woman behind the counter singsong, "Hope to see you again soon!"

Over my dead body. I'm never setting foot in Southern Comforts again. Not if I have to deal with any of those women, especially the one in the back. I'm all the way in the truck before it hits me.

Don't let the door hit you on the way out, Chance.

She knew my name.

4

Lily

"I heard one of the Allen boys came into the shop today."

I keep as still as possible.

"Don't act like you didn't hear me, Lily. I know you're not asleep."

"Well, not anymore," I protest, rolling over to face my roommate. As grateful as I am not to be living back at home with my mother and Bunny, living with Hadley can be just as exhausting.

"Is that true? Was there an Allen sighting at Southern Comforts today?" She's way too excited for her own good.

"And where'd you hear that?" There are multiple people who could have blabbed this bit of gossip. Small town life means everyone's in everyone else's business. Even with only a few witnesses it can take about five minutes for a juicy story to circulate.

"It's true? Which one was it?" Hadley flops down on the couch next to me, moving my feet to make room for her butt.

"Not the one you're hoping for," I deadpan.

She purses her lips. "Why would you think I was hoping for a specific one?" Hadley tries to give her most innocent face. Just like when we were younger, she fails miserably.

"Oh, I don't know, maybe because your red-hot love for Cooper Allen is the stuff of legends." I smirk. Hadley's been in love with Cooper since the first time she saw him and even if it took him years to notice her, she's never gotten over the fact that they didn't live happily ever after.

"That was a million years ago." She shifts over to face me. "I've been over Cooper forever now."

"Liar."

"Fine. There was a little glimmer there." Hadley frowns. "But it really wasn't Cooper?"

"Nope."

"Which one then?"

"Chance." I try not to let my face give too much away. After he'd stormed out it had taken me a good ten minutes to stop shaking. I'd done everything I was supposed to, I even managed to put myself in a power stance, but having him bust in and then tower over me nearly made me have a panic attack. When I'd heard the door open Chance was the last person I'd been expecting. He looked the same—angrier—but the same. Sixteen-year-old me would have been more appreciative of the way he still managed to make a pair of blue jeans and a T-shirt look like something a model would wear, but today's Lily knew better than to go there. Those hazel eyes or the memories of a million summers past wouldn't influence today's Lily.

"Ohhh, I see."

I give Hadley a punch in the arm, which she pretends hurts more than it could have. "It wasn't like that. He came in all angry, accusing me of stealing wood from their farm."

"Really? That sounds crazy." Hadley settles back into the couch cushions. "But he was still hot, right?"

He was, but I don't tell Hadley. She'll start again with the pushing and I'll have to disappoint her. "If you like a lot of yelling, I guess. I don't even think he knew who I was." That had been slightly disappointing, but there's no sense in feeling badly about something that doesn't really matter. If I didn't make that much of an impression on him, then that's that.

"But you told him who you are, right? You reminded him?" The hope in Hadley's voice makes me want to lie, to tell her what she wants to hear. It'd be easy and she'd probably never find out. But I like to keep things honest, especially with the few friends I've kept.

"No, I didn't even bother. It didn't seem worth it."

"Didn't seem worth it?"

Of course Hadley doesn't understand. Bold, vivacious Hadley doesn't have a timid bone in her body. If Cooper Allen had walked into Hot House Flowers—the beauty salon where Hadley works—she would have made sure he remembered who she was. Hell, if it had been Chance she'd have done the same thing. But that's because Hadley's the same as she's ever been and I'm... not. Reminding Chance of the girl I used to be would mean reminding myself, and that's not something I'm willing to do.

"I was in the middle of something. I was actually on the floor, Hadley, and he just busted in and started yelling. There was no point in trying to take a walk down memory lane."

"You make it sound like you're a hundred years old. You didn't see him in the retirement home, Lily."

"I know, but maybe he's changed. He didn't seem all that nice. I don't have time for that."

"You don't have time for anyone. He could be the nicest, most reasonable man on the planet and you'd still act like there was something wrong with him." Hadley slides my feet from her lap and stands. "It wouldn't kill you to put yourself out there a little bit."

But it might, and I'm not willing to take that risk.

I shrug and let Hadley's disapproving face linger long enough for her to feel some satisfaction.

"Have you eaten?" I ask just to change the subject. My run-in with Chance has left me so shaken up I'm not actually sure I can eat. I even contemplated swiping one of the beers from the fridge in an effort to try to calm my nerves. "We could order something. Unless you want to cook."

Hadley groans. "When are you going to learn to feed yourself, Lily? How did you survive in Chicago, living alone?"

I shrug again. "I ordered a lot of takeout. You want to give me another cooking lesson?" That'll keep Hadley busy with something other than grilling me about Chance Allen.

"Maybe. What do we have in the kitchen?" Sure enough she heads toward the fridge and starts rifling around. "We could do a veggie pasta. That's easy. Come in here and I'll help you get your Julia Child on."

I follow her into the kitchen without hesitation. Time to put this day and the sudden appearance of Chance Allen behind me. "On my way, boss."

5

Chance

It's days later when I realize who she was. Who she is, really, since she obviously still exists and still lives right here in Mint Springs. It should have been easier to put two and two together. She's a Gentry and Southern Comforts has been in the Gentry family for years. But she didn't look the way I remember her, at least not until she started giving me attitude. If there's one thing I remember about Lily Gentry, it's her smart mouth. That and the way she used to look in a bikini on those hot afternoons down by the river in the summer. She was usually with my cousin Riley, hell bent on having a good time. That girl under baggy sweatpants and a giant hoodie barely resembled the one who used to be the first off the rope swing and the last out of the water.

But it's definitely her.

I watch her lift a French fry to her lips and I can almost see a trace of the playful smile that used to drive me wild. The same brown hair that used to shine when the sun hit it. The same dark eyes that sparkled whenever someone would get a harebrained idea we all should have ignored. Lily

Gentry of so many of my teenage summer fantasies. She's the same girl but somehow she's different. Less bright. Missing her spark. And still wearing an outfit that would have looked reasonable for Alaska instead of Georgia in April.

I stare through the front window of Ham & Eggs and watch her eat, like some kind of stalker. She's sitting at the diner's long counter, her feet swinging in her paint-splattered work boots. She's small enough that her feet barely touch the floor. There's a mountain of a sandwich in front of her and she's happily munching away, unaware that I'm fixated on her every move. Why didn't she call me out on my crazy the other day? She put me in my place, but she didn't bother to reintroduce herself. Of course, the way I treated her didn't exactly deserve her kindness or respect. She didn't need to go out of her way to use her manners when I couldn't be bothered to use mine. Still, the fact that she let me stomp off like a stranger that way bothers me.

There's an empty seat next to her when I finally move from the window and into the restaurant. Sure there are a million other places I could park my butt, but I ignore them all and slide in next to her. I'd intended to grab a sandwich to go, but now I'm contemplating staying right here, right next to Lily Gentry.

She startles a bit when she feels me sidle up beside her. I get a quick flash of a face I remember before her new one comes back down. I smile in what I hope is an invitation, but Lily's expression stays the same. I clear my throat.

"Hi," I start and then falter.

"Hello," she says without any warmth there. I owe her an apology and she knows it.

"Lily, right? Lily Gentry. I'm—"

"I know who you are." She doesn't take my outstretched

hand, only looks at it like I've presented her with a dead fish or a court summons.

"You do?" I can't hide my surprise. "Then why didn't you..."

"Why didn't I what? Stop you from making an ass of yourself?" She swivels in her seat. "That's not my responsibility."

I run a hand through my hair. "No, I guess not. Look, I'm sorry for the way I acted the other day. I'd just found out about the barn wood and then I saw your sign. I shouldn't have busted in like that and I certainly shouldn't have yelled at you. I checked with Dan and he told me you bought that wood so I'm clearly in the wrong."

Lily nods her head. When the waitress comes by with a menu for me Lily stops her. "Can I get a box for the rest of my sandwich, Debbie?"

"Sure, Lily. Be right back," the waitress drawls. She slides her gaze over to me and gives me a frown. "I'll be right back to take your order."

"Take your time," I tell her and actually hope she does. I focus my attention back on Lily. Still no smile, but I'm hoping I can change that. "You don't have to leave. Let me buy you lunch. We can catch up." But Lily's already standing up and getting her things together.

"No, thank you."

"Please? At least let me pay for your sandwich." I start to reach my hand out to touch hers, but she pulls her hand away from mine like I'm the town leper.

"No, thank you," she says again with even more conviction. "I don't need you to pay for my lunch."

Right on cue the waitress appears in front of us with Lily's bill and a box for her leftovers. She waits while Lily puts a few bills in her hand and dumps the rest of her food in the cardboard container. "Thanks, Debbie. Keep the change."

Lily's on her way out the door before I can make my brain communicate with my legs. "Lily, wait!"

She pauses in the threshold and I have a moment of hope, but she doesn't turn around. She's leaving and I'm still the ass who came back into town only to scream at her. I jog toward her thinking only of how I can fix this, how I can clean this slate before I've lost what could be my only chance.

"Lily!" I reach forward and touch her shoulder only to have her spin around like I've slapped her.

"Don't touch me!"

She yells it loud enough to have all the restaurant patrons turning to gawk at us.

I pull my hand back and keep it up where she can see it. I manage a startled, "Sorry," but it does nothing to change her expression.

"Just leave me alone, Chance," Lily snarls at me before striding out into the parking lot, the cardboard box nearly flattened in her hand. "Leave. Me. Alone."

I watch her fumble with her keys as she tries to unlock her car. Once she's inside she guns the engine and then peels out of the parking lot. This isn't the Lily Gentry that I remember.

Not at all.

"Damn it!"

I yank my thumb out from under the hammer and watch as blood starts to pool under the nail. As much as it hurts now, I know it'll hurt even more once it starts to swell.

I'd take a break and try to ice it, but there's no ice inside the house. The old fridge never had an icemaker and I can't remember to buy a bag of ice at the store. Mae suggested I use those ice dish things, but I haven't remembered to fill the ones she gave me. This house, and the work it needs, takes up all my mental space. In a way I'm happy. It keeps me in the moment, keeps me from thinking too much about the past. But it's also taking forever. Another blessing and a curse because once the work's done who knows where I'll go next and what will happen to the house and the farm. I doubt my father has plans to use either of them, which usually puts him in the mood to move on.

I haven't mentioned it to my aunts, but I know they have their suspicions. They've been around my dad enough to know that he doesn't have the soft spot for the farm the rest of us do. He may have met my mother in this small town but now he's big time. At least too busy to waste time with a visit to Mint Springs. Not like I have the right to throw stones. *Just like you were. Too busy making money to take a week to check on your dying grandfather.* I scowl down at my swelling thumb. Mae and Sadie own the land their house sits on and a little more, but with my grandpa's passing it's my father who owns the rest. He's the one calling the shots. Even if I'm the one putting in the sweat equity.

I grab my last cold beer from the fridge and stomp out onto the porch, holding my throbbing thumb against it. Yep, I'm definitely going to lose that thumbnail. That should be great for all the paint stripping and wallpaper removal I've got planned. I flop down on the steps and try to organize myself for the rest of the day. It's already four o'clock and I haven't even gotten through the first few things on my list.

Sadie comes around the corner carrying a trowel. "Calling it a day?" Dirt's smeared across the front of her apron and some of it's gotten into the white poufs of her hair that have escaped from under her wide-brimmed hat.

"Just taking a break," I tell her and let the cold bottle take some of the sting out of my thumb. "I've got too much to do to quit this early."

"It's not that early," Sadie protests. "And I know you've been at it since before the sun came up. You should go into town. Have a little fun."

"Not tonight." Especially not after I've smashed my thumb all to hell. There's no bar in the world that'll make my mood better after that.

"Fine, then. You comin' for supper? Sadie's baking a hummingbird cake. We'll need your help to eat it."

"You two don't have to feed me every night." Not that I haven't been appreciating it, but I can't keep taking advantage of my aunts' generosity forever. They know I've already started working on the kitchen here in this house and I'll be reduced to frozen dinners if they don't take pity on me. Frozen dinners alone in my dead grandfather's house is as close to torture as I can imagine.

"We know we don't have to. We want to. There's a difference." Sadie shifts the garden tool from one hand to the other and wipes her palm along her apron. "How does six sound? Too early?"

"No, ma'am. I can be cleaned up by six."

"Okay then. How's the kitchen coming along?"

Sadie can see into the kitchen behind me and knows full well that there's been little-to-no progress on the kitchen today. I keep starting to pull down some cabinets or wrestle with the linoleum and I get stuck. It's not just the memories of my grandfather making my breakfast over that stove, or the images of my brothers and I at the kitchen table for dinners after hauling hay, it's that I lack any vision. I'm good at tearing it all apart, and clueless at figuring out how to put it all back together.

"Slow." It's the best answer I can give her.

"Can I give you a little advice?"

She's not really asking, so I just nod. When Sadie wants to give you some advice you'd best just listen.

"I know you want to do the work yourself, but maybe you could use a little help."

I set my jaw. This is the kind of advice I hate to hear. It's something I already know to be true but I'm too stubborn to accept. Just the kind of advice Sadie's been giving me all my life.

"It doesn't have to mean hiring out the work, Chance. It could be something as simple as getting an opinion on how to reconfigure that kitchen."

"I can figure that out." *Eventually.* "I asked you and Mae for suggestions. I'm not doing it alone."

"Sure, but Mae and I know what *we* like, not what everybody else likes. This house needs to be more livable. You need to bring it into this century, Chance. The kind of thing everybody would like, not just us." Sadie leaves out the reason we'd want everyone else to like it and I'm grateful that it lets me avoid thinking about some other family making this house their home for a little while longer.

"Well, who do you suggest I ask to help me? If I decide to get another opinion, that is."

"If I was the one doing the asking, I'd probably ask that Gentry girl."

"Which Gentry girl?" I keep my fingers crossed that Lily's got a long-lost sister.

"Lily."

"You want me to ask Lily Gentry to come over here and help me?"

"Sure. You don't think she will?"

I know there's not a chance in hell Lily's going to help me. "Pretty sure she won't. I don't think Lily'd pee on me if I was on fire, Sadie."

"Why not? Because of your little argument the other day? I'm sure we can smooth over whatever that was and there's no need to be vulgar, Chance Allen. I don't need to hear about urine, thank you very much." Sadie gives me a glare.

"You heard about us fighting?"

"Of course. This is Mint Springs. I knew about it before you made it home. You're lucky you didn't get yourself shot rushing into Southern Comforts like that. You do know that shop got its name because that's what Maggie Gentry used to keep in her coffee cup."

"Seriously?" I make a note never to cross Lily's grandmother.

"Well, that's just gossip, but you should watch yourself. Those Gentry women do not like to be pushed around."

I sigh, remembering the way Lily pulled back when I touched her arm. "I guess you know about her yelling at me in the diner too, then."

"Sure. But I still think Lily'll come around under the right set of circumstances. She's had a rough go of it, I think, but I'm pretty sure she's still the same girl she used to be. When you come over for supper, I'll give you something that's sure to help convince her to help you with this house."

"Hummingbird cake?" I ask because what else could it be?

"Hardly." Sadie turns to make the short hop over to her house. "You'll see. Finish your beer and get cleaned up. I'll see you at six."

6
———

Lily

"You have got to be kidding me." I put the stack of plates I've been carrying down on the closest table.

"Lily!" my grandmother yells. "Your friend's back."

"I see him, Bunny, and he's not my friend." Through the front window of the shop I see Chance crossing the street, a bouquet of wildflowers in one hand and a jar in the other. He looks both ways before he steps out into the road and the breeze blows the edge of his T-shirt up just enough to show me a sliver of stomach. I look away.

"Well, friend or not, he's comin' in here and I'm pretty sure those flowers aren't for me."

"You don't know that." It comes out sharper than I intend but Bunny just laughs. She's still laughing when Chance pulls the door open, a rush of springtime air following him.

He's nervous, tapping his work boots on the concrete floor as he waits for Bunny to pull herself together. "Ladies," he says and I watch Bunny's eyebrows shoot up. Very few people call Bunny a lady, for obvious reasons. He leans forward and hands the bouquet to my grandmother. She takes it hesitantly and cocks her head to the side.

"What are these for?" Bunny demands, even though her tight grip indicates there's no way she's giving those flowers back no matter what Chance says.

"They're to say I'm sorry for the way I acted the other day. I was rude." Chance says the words like he's rehearsed them and I can't help but imagine this is the kind of thing he'd have done as a kid when he put a baseball through some neighbor's window.

Bunny examines the flowers, letting the corner of her mouth perk up a little. It's not quite a smile, but I know he's already got her. Apology accepted. Traitor.

"Well, thank you!" Bunny exclaims in the voice she uses almost exclusively with Mr. Sims at the liquor store. "I'll go and put these in some water." And like that Bunny's scurrying off with the flowers crumpled against the handle of her walker, leaving me with Chance and no excuse to get away.

"These are for you." He hands me the Mason jar and I get a look at what's inside. "My aunts said you'd prefer this over flowers. They're from last summer." I watch his fingers come dangerously close to touching mine. His hands are surprisingly clean, the nails cut short, his thumb a deep purple color.

I stare at the yellow rounds inside the jar. Pickles. But not just any pickles. Squash pickles. Homemade.

It's so much better than flowers. But maybe not enough to convince me to be civil. Chance may be cute—more than cute, if I'm being honest—but I know being nice to handsome men leads to nothing but trouble.

"Thank you." I make my mouth form the words. Let them make it past my lips. But I don't smile, not even a little.

Not even though the weight of the jar in my hand has my lips begging to curl up.

Chance looks less than pleased with my reaction. He's probably used to getting more than the cold shoulder when he delivers a gift. Hell, he's probably used to getting a standing ovation just for showing up. He's even charmed Bunny a little with nothing but some flowers he picked from the side of the road. Even if he's managed to get this present pretty damn near perfect, I'm not about to make things easy for him.

"Please tell your aunts I appreciate them sending them over. I'm sure they'll be delicious." My mouth actually waters when I let myself think about opening the jar, something I can't do until I get rid of Chance. I let the silence get awkward, just standing there. This is my signature move—making people uncomfortable enough that they run the other direction. It usually works like a charm—and fast—but Chance seems immune. He just stands there, his eyes locked on mine.

"You really like pickles?" he asks.

"Yes."

"More than flowers?"

"Yes." You would think he'd take the hint from my one-word answers that I want him to move along. But again, he refuses to go, just stares at me and keeps his boots planted where they are.

"I actually came in here today because I need to ask you a favor."

I should have expected this. No one gives anyone something for free.

"I'm working on my grandpa's house out at the farm, trying to get it back in shape. He passed away a few weeks ago."

"I'm sorry for your loss." I'm overly formal and momentarily regret it, especially since I can see the difficulty Chance has even saying those words. The old me wants to reach out, to touch his arm, to give him a smile that shows him I understand. But the new Lily keeps all that from happening. My spine stays straight, my face blank.

"Thank you," Chance says, his politeness a rote reaction to mine. "The thing is, I'm having trouble. Not with the work, just with the design part."

"Design?"

"Yeah. Like, I need to remodel the kitchen, but between the way my grandpa built the place and the fact that I've never really used a kitchen... well. You can see the problem, right?"

I blink at him, making him work for every look, every acknowledgment of understanding. "I'm not an interior designer, Chance."

"I know," he says in that way that lets me know he really doesn't have a clue. "But this is you in here, isn't it?" He glances around the store, looking at the displays I've put together. "You painted that." Chance points to the china cabinet he found me working on before, now angled into a corner and loaded down with antique dishes. It does look fabulous with the shiny new pulls and the deep green paint job I gave it. A giant sold tag already hangs from the top cabinet door.

"Yeah, but I've never done anything like design a kitchen." And I've never really wanted to either.

"But you have good taste. You know what people like."

"I know what I like. It's accidental if other people like it too."

Chance gives me a look. "All this is accidental?"

He and I both know it isn't. It's the result of research and my previous work in other people's stores, in other people's studios, the art classes I took when I thought that was my dream. Now I'm combining those things to try to make Southern Comforts into something else—something that I can be proud of while I'm here.

"Look, I'm not asking you to commit to anything. Maybe just come out and give me your opinion. I'd pay you, obviously." He gives me a hopeful smile.

"You'd pay me?" I have zero interest in redesigning a kitchen and even less interest in spending more awkward time with Chance. But money? Money is something I'm interested in. Something my family needs.

"Sure. We could do an hourly rate or a one-time fee. I don't know how it usually works but I wouldn't expect you to do it for free. Tell me what it'll take, and I'll make it happen."

He'll make it happen. This is less reassuring than he thinks. Still, when he keeps looking at me with that *what do you say?* expression on his face I start to waver. A big job like that might make us some significant money. It would mean time away from the store, but it isn't like I'm filling my free time with exciting adventures. I'd be able to help make a dent in Bunny's medical bills, and the faster that happens the faster I can get my life back. Or what's left of it.

Chance sticks out his hand. "So, do we have a deal? You can come by whenever you want to see the place. I'm always available."

Sixteen-year-old Lily knows that Chance won't be available for long, not once one of the local girls gets her claws in him, but as older, wiser Lily, I tell myself not to care. I'm busy bracing myself to touch Chance's hand and that's taking all my brain power anyway. It's just a handshake. I can do this.

I slide my palm over his and relax enough to let him close his hand over mine. It's over in two seconds, but I hold my breath just the same. His hand's a little rough and he doesn't pull away as quickly as I'd like, pinning me with his eyes as he touches my hand.

"Any idea when you might want to come by?" Chance is more relaxed now that he's convinced me, leaning against the counter like he owns the place. I frown at the space where his hip makes contact with the wood and he straightens back up.

"I can't today." Today I'll need a few hours to get my head wrapped around being with Chance in his house, most likely alone. "Tomorrow?"

"Sure. How about you come by once you're done here? Or I could come and pick you up."

"To be clear, this isn't a favor. This is business. I can get myself there." While I'm firmer than I need to be, the sudden thought of being alone with Chance in his truck has me shuddering. "Is five too late?"

"Nope. Five's perfect. I'll be ready."

Watching him leave through the double doors I'm surer than ever that I won't be.

7

Chance

Gravel crunches in the driveway at exactly five o'clock. Lily might not be friendly, but she's punctual. I've got the house as organized as possible, which isn't saying much. The sun's still too high in the sky to hide any of the wear and tear this place has taken. But if the work that needs to be done scares Lily off, then so be it. Although, according to my aunts she might be the only game in town for something like this, and I desperately need another set of eyes around here.

I'm desperate enough that I've got another jar of bribery pickles—bread and butter this time—and I've put on a shirt with actual buttons and a collar. I debated for thirty minutes about rolling the sleeves up or leaving them down, even testing out the possibilities in front of the bathroom mirror. I settled on rolling them up to the middle of my forearms. I fidget with the cuffs as I wait for Lily to make her way out of her car and up the front steps, trying to keep myself from rushing to the front door before she has a chance to even hit the stairs.

When she rings the doorbell, nothing happens. The old chime is refusing to do anything to let me know she's standing there. I mentally add *replace doorbell* to my list. I consider waiting until her knuckles rap on the wood, but decide to go ahead and give myself away. I'm standing here like an idiot already, might as well go ahead and make it official.

Lily's mouth opens into a surprised *"o"* when I pull the door open. Her little fist is primed for knocking, and luckily, she stops it before it makes contact with my chest. Her brown eyes are startled, like one of the deer I see in the woods around the house. She's still wearing one of her baggy gray outfits, but there's no hiding her pretty face.

"The doorbell doesn't work," I confess and try to usher her into the living room. She resists, planting herself firmly on the stoop. "You have to come in, Lily," I remind her. "All the work's in here."

She scowls at me but comes inside when I move as far as possible away from the doorframe. Even then Lily slides along the edge of the wall as if touching me in any way would expose her to some horrible germ.

This girl's impossible and here I am trying my damnedest to convince her to spend time with me. She doesn't even bother trying to hide the fact that she's not excited to see me and even less excited to be walking into my living room.

But it isn't really my living room and I can see the exact moment Lily remembers she's in my grandpa's house. His work boots still sit by the door and she nearly trips over them in an effort to put more space between us. She turns her head and the shiny brown ponytail slides over her shoulder and onto her back. The place is dark, the furniture old, and the memories palatable. I haven't changed anything in this room since I arrived. Like the master bedroom, it's a shrine to my childhood and I can't bring myself to do anything but look at it. I'm sure there's a layer of dust on the coffee table, and I've left the framed photos of my grandma right where they were—next to my grandfather's chair so he could see them better.

"Wow," Lily says as she takes in the room.

"Yeah," I manage before succumbing to the overwhelming need to get her out of here. "The kitchen's this way."

I don't need to shepherd her into the kitchen but I do it anyway, putting my hand on the small of her back to encourage her to move forward. She resists, of course, shooting me a look over her shoulder as she stiffens under my palm. I pull my hand back with a mumbled, "Sorry," and let her lead the way.

She's still quiet as she surveys the kitchen cabinets and countertops, taking in the ancient appliances and the peeling linoleum floor. "This isn't so bad," Lily finally says. "Depending on how much work you're planning on."

I nod and wait for her to continue, but she just stares at me with those big eyes until I forget what we were talking about.

"Chance?"

"Huh?"

"How much work are you planning on doing in here? I mean, what's the end result supposed to be?"

"The end result?" I stare back at her, more than a little distracted by the way her mouth puckers as she listens to my answer. And who the hell knows what the end result of all of this will be? For now I'm focused on doing the work and avoiding the future, not thinking about what's going to happen to this house or the rest of the farm once my father makes his final decision.

"Is this supposed to be for you? Who's going to live here?"

"I'm not sure." It sounds ridiculous and Lily's face lets me know she agrees. "That's not up to me. We might keep it, but my father might decide to sell it, so it needs to be ready for both those options."

"I see." Lily's all business now, running her hands along the cabinet fronts. I cringe thinking of the dirt that must be there under her fingers, but she doesn't seem too bothered by it. "We could leave these cabinets if you like the layout now. This wood is nice and they're pretty sturdy."

"My grandpa made those," I tell her, moving closer. "I'd like to keep them if you think we can." I'd love to leave the house as is, but I know that's not an option. If Lily says we can keep some of the sentimental things then I'm going to follow her advice.

"I think we can fix them up, change out the handles, maybe paint them if you're okay with that." She moves to the window over the sink and looks out over the pasture. "This view is incredible. I think we could make this kitchen really beautiful." The last part comes out a little breathy and I have a flash of Lily doing dishes at that sink, having that view every day. I shake the image from my head.

"You'll help me, then?"

"I'll try. I really haven't ever done this kind of work before so I can't give you any references or show you any examples." Lily leans a little against the sink. "I can work up some options and price some things. And we should talk about my rates."

I try to keep my grinning to a minimum, but judging by the displeasure I see on Lily's face, I'm failing miserably.

"Whatever you want. Seriously, Lily, you're doing me a big favor here."

"It's not a favor, remember?" Lily chastises me. "This is business, Chance."

"Of course." We're not friends, and I don't think I'd really want to be. We're going to be working together. Nothing more.

"Do you mind if I take some pictures?" Lily asks. "It'll help when I go to put together the design boards."

I have no idea what Lily's talking about but I nod my head all the same. "Sure. Take all the pictures you want. I'll get out of your way. Do you want a beer or anything?" I reach into the fridge, accidentally bumping Lily's hip as I pull two bottles out. They clink together as my forearm grazes her side.

Lily's face freezes for a minute but then her manners kick in. "No, thank you. I'll just take a few photos and then head on home." And then she's pulling out her phone from the side pocket of her oversized pants with a shaky hand and clicking away. She's finished in two minutes and basically racing toward the front door.

"I'll write up a proposal and send it to you," Lily nearly shouts over her shoulder at me. She's pulling her keys from her pocket and holding them so tight in her hand that the knuckles have whitened.

"Whoa, slow down. I'll have to give you an email address or something, right? Unless you want to come back over here. I could come by the store..."

Lily's flustered face has me going quiet.

"Here." I put out my hand and watch her jump. "Give me your phone and I'll put my contact information in there. Then you can shoot me a text or something when you're ready."

Lily gives me the phone like she's expecting me to reach out and grab her. I take it and type myself into her contacts before handing it back. I move slowly, the way I would with a wounded animal until the whole thing's finished. "My aunts also left you another jar of pickles. Let me get those for you and then you can get home." I grab the jar from the counter and put them into Lily's other hand. Slow and steady with no sudden movements. She bolts as soon as I give her the opportunity, flying down the front steps.

As I watch her drive away, tires nearly screeching as she rounds the corner, I know one thing for sure: something is seriously off about Lily Gentry.

I try to keep my Lily confusion to myself during dinner with my aunts, but Mae and Sadie aren't dumb. In between bites of fried chicken, I watch them shoot looks across the table at each other until there's nothing left to do but confront the issue.

"Lily Gentry came over to look at the kitchen."

Mae feigns surprise. "Did she?"

"Today?" Sadie asks like they both weren't probably over here with their noses pressed up against the window the second Lily's car came into the driveway.

"Uh huh." I put some more mashed potatoes on my fork and swirl it around in the puddle of gravy I've got going on in the center.

"How did that go?" Mae's concentrating on cutting into her chicken and pretending she's not dying to know.

"Fine, I guess. She's going to put some suggestions together." I put the potatoes in my mouth and chew. Not that I need to, there are never any lumps in Sadie's mashed potatoes.

"Did you give her those pickles? That girl loves pickles," Sadie tells me excitedly. She's been telling me this since I asked about Lily the first time. According to Sadie, pickles hold the key to all things Lily Gentry. After this afternoon I'm not so sure things are that easy.

"I gave them to her. She told me to tell you two thank you."

Mae looks at Sadie, her brows furrowed.

"What?" I look from one concerned face to the other.

"Well, she didn't seem to stay very long." Mae's comment all but admits they were watching the whole time.

"She looked around, took some pictures. Then she got uncomfortable, I guess."

"What do you mean 'uncomfortable'?" Sadie asks.

"Lily sort of freaked out. Then she ran out of the house like a bear was chasing her."

My aunts look at each other and seem to communicate using some sort of telepathic mind meld that I've never been able to understand. Finally, Mae goes back to her dinner. "I think you have to be a little bit gentle with Lily," she says before she pops a green bean in her mouth, her chewing keeping her from telling me anything more.

"I don't get it though. When we were younger Lily was always fearless. Maybe a little crazy." I smile at the memory of Lily as a teenager. "But fun. She smiled. Now..." I shrug.

"You have to have a little patience with her, that's all," Sadie tells me. That doesn't clear anything up as far as I can tell.

"You've both said that."

"Well, it's true. Lily takes a little time to warm up to people since she's been back."

"Since she's been back from where?" It's like Mae and Sadie have pieces of the puzzle, but they won't give them to me. Lily isn't my business and whatever cryptic message they're trying to send is lost on me.

"Since she came back home." Mae can't hide her frustration. "Before that she was in Chicago, I think."

"Art school," Sadie supplies. "She's an artist."

"Okay, but that doesn't explain..." The way she's acting. The angry outbursts. The way she seems to hate me. "What are you two not telling me?" Around here gossip is an Olympic sport and my aunts are gold medalists. If there's something to know, my aunts have heard all about it.

"After high school she started out at the university, but she didn't finish." Mae gives me a look I can't begin to understand. "I just think she could use a friend."

"And you two were thinking I could be her friend?" My previous infatuation with the girl aside, there's no way Lily would have any interest in that.

"Maybe. If you two end up working together on the house, try to be nice."

"I'm always nice, Mae." My aunts' faces let me know that they aren't buying that. "Okay, I promise to be nice to Lily."

"And patient," Sadie reminds me.

"Fine, and patient." Whatever patience I have left after this dinner I'll be sure to reserve for Lily. Which won't be much.

8

Lily

"How long are you planning on sitting there like that?"

I look up from my phone to see Hadley watching me from the living room. I've been so engrossed in this text I'm writing—or trying to write—that I hadn't even noticed her come home.

"I'm just..."

"Looking at Chris Pratt's Instagram? Because that's the only thing on your phone that I can think of that would have you making that serious face." Hadley smirks. She thinks she's hilarious, obviously.

"I'm trying to finish this text." I go back to looking at the screen, but my fingers just hover there.

"What you're doing is giving yourself a giant wrinkle on your forehead. Who are you texting? It's lucky whoever it is can't see that sour face you're making." Hadley's long legs eat up the distance between the living room and the kitchen before I can move to close the open window on my phone. "Chance Allen? Why are you texting him?"

"It's business," I tell her as she rolls her eyes.

"Sure it is, Lil. I'll bet Chance's got a big order coming in tomorrow at Southern Comforts. Probably a million of those ancient windows with the messed up paint. That sounds like something he'd be into."

"It *is* business!" I protest, pointing to the pile of fabrics and paint samples on the kitchen table. "I'm finishing up the design boards for his kitchen and I need to set up a time to let him see them."

Hadley's eyes scan the mess on the table as her fingers roam over the tile samples. "This is actually coming together, Lily. I love this combination here." She pulls my favorite board away from the others. "I like these blues."

"Not too girly?" I ask. Not knowing whether I was designing for Chance or some mystery buyer made me second guess a few of my decisions.

"I don't think so. He's going to love all these ideas. They're all great." Hadley plops in a chair. "When're you going to show them to him?"

"That's what I'm trying to set up now." I sigh. "But I'm not having much luck."

"Is he super busy or something?" Hadley asks, absent-mindedly. She's forgotten how much my anxiety spills over into all sorts of things.

"No... I'm just dreading it, I think."

"Dreading it? Why? This is good work, Lily. Chance'll be impressed."

"I know he will." My work stands on its own, it's the personal part of this that has me spooked. "I just wasn't all that professional last time I saw him." And I've been communicating via tortured texts ever since. Texts that take me forever to compose and even longer to manage to hit send. The sight of those little bouncing bubbles as he types a response has me sweating every time. Meeting in person will most likely kill me.

"You didn't tell me that." Hadley's her usual mix of annoyed and concerned. Not sure if she should be pushing for more information or letting things slide.

"I was too mortified to share it." I can't make eye contact when I confess the molehill I made into a mountain last time I was with Chance. "He accidentally touched me and I jumped out of my skin."

"That's not so bad. Lots of people don't like surprise touching."

"And then I peeled out of his driveway like it was an episode of *The Dukes of Hazard*."

Hadley winces.

"And in between I acted like I was in some horror movie and he was the monster."

"Sweet baby Jesus, Lily. What did Chance do?" I can see Hadley holding her breath.

"He started acting like I was broken, obviously. And he's been sending me all these attentive texts about taking my time. He thinks I'm a crazy person." I put my head in my hands. "And he isn't wrong. How can I walk things back from there?"

"Look, you're a business woman, right? You handle it. Set up the meeting and apologize. Just say you're sorry and you hope it won't affect your working relationship. You don't have to go into any details."

Hadley seems so confident that I wish I could put her in my pocket and carry her around all day. She'd be like the little angel on my shoulder. She'd probably be the devil sometimes too, but I'd welcome even that if it meant I could get through normal human interaction without making a fool of myself.

"Hand me that." Hadley reaches for my phone and furiously starts typing. "Look at that and see what you think."

I stare at the text it's taken Hadley five seconds to write.

Design boards are done. When are you available to get together to take a look?

It's simple and straightforward and Chance starts responding as soon as I hit send. That boy must keep his phone in his pocket at all times. I watch the bubbles move along the screen, hoping he tells me he's busy from now until doomsday. Of course he's not. He's free all the time because nothing's more important to him right now than getting to work on that house.

"He wants to meet tomorrow." I stare at Hadley. "I can't be ready tomorrow."

"Yes, you can," Hadley assures me. "Meet someplace you feel comfortable and show him the work."

It's good advice except for one tiny detail: there's no place in the world where I feel comfortable anymore. And if I can get through this meeting then I'll have to work out how to be in that farmhouse with Chance to actually make this kitchen a reality.

"Lily, you can do this. Meet him at the diner. I know it's hard, but he's not one of those boys." I can see that Hadley regrets bringing it up. We don't talk about those boys for a reason and I try not to think about them unless I have to. She gives me a tight smile and plows on. "This is a good opportunity and around here you aren't going to get too many of those."

Hadley's right. I can't let my fear keep me from doing things. I fight the churning of my stomach and the shaking of my fingers to respond to Chance. When he texts back I get a shot of adrenaline that can't be the best way to feel about a business meeting.

"He's going to meet me for lunch tomorrow," I tell Hadley who immediately puts her palm up for a high five.

"You've got this, Lily," she tells me.

I hope she's right.

Chance stands when he sees me coming through the door at Ham & Eggs. I'm loaded down with multiple bags and he's next to me in two seconds, reaching for the things I'm carrying and grabbing the top of the glass door high above my head. I notice how hard he works not to touch me. My cheeks flame with embarrassment but after our last meeting I can't exactly blame him.

"Here, hand that to me." Chance stretches out his arm as far as it will go. Luckily his arms are long, so he's still a million miles away. He manages to take the bag I have in my hand and waits for me to slide the one I have on my shoulder a safe distance away before taking that one too.

"I got us a booth. Will that give us enough room?" Chance moves toward the back of the restaurant and I'm treated to the sight of his broad back, muscles bunching under the weight of the bags. "How were you carrying these?" He sets the bags down on the table top. "They're heavy." He wipes imaginary sweat from his brow.

"I'm stronger than I look." I mean it as a joke, but Chance barely cracks a grin.

"I don't doubt it," he says and slides into his side of the booth. "Do you want something to drink? Or to eat?" Chance signals for Debbie, who zips right over. She's been lingering since I walked in, pretending not to be paying attention.

I spread the design boards out over the surface of the table. I've done four different looks for the kitchen, each with coordinating paints and fabrics. I'm surprisingly nervous as Chance starts to examine them. He pulls one closer to him to get a better look and I have to sit on my hands to keep from snatching it back.

"What've you been up to, Lily?" Debbie asks as she looks over Chance's shoulder.

"She's redoing my grandpa's kitchen," Chance tells her, still engrossed in the things I've put together. "I'm the first customer for her interior design business."

Debbie gives me an impressed look. "Interior design? Well, well." Her hand shoots forward to touch one of the fabric samples. "Ohhh, I like this one."

"I like that one too," Chance agrees. "But I think I like this one even more." He angles the board he's holding toward Debbie who gives it an appreciative nod.

"That one's nice, too. I like the floor. Is that wood?" Debbie runs a finger over the sample.

"It's tile, actually," I say, feeling some of my confidence start to come back. "It'll be more durable than wood."

"Hmmm." Debbie's impressed. "Well, can I get y'all anything while you work over here?"

"Whatever Lily wants," Chance tells her, still looking through the things on the table.

"I see," Debbie answers, giving me a raised eyebrow. "Well then, Miss Lily, what can I get for you?"

"I'll just have a glass of sweet tea." I hesitate and Debbie waits with her pencil poised over her tiny order pad.

Chance looks up and meets my eyes across the table. "Is that all? I was thinking you might like something else. Maybe..." He scans the diner menu but I'm sure he'll never be able to guess what I'm dying to order. "How about a plate of those fried pickles?"

Chance looks to Debbie for confirmation.

"Looks like you know Lily pretty well," she says as she scribbles down the rest of our order.

"Not as well as I'm going to if this work is any indication," Chance says and I feel my face flush again. "These are better than I could have imagined. We're going to be spending a lot of time together when Lily holds my hand through all this."

"There are worse things I can think of." Debbie gives me a wink.

I look at Chance's hands and try to imagine actually holding one. My own palms start to sweat at just the thought of it. But he's right; we are going to be spending plenty of time together if we decide to work together. I'm going to need to work on my deep breathing if he decides to hire me.

"I like them all, but I think this one's the winner," Chance announces and holds up the board I'd thought he'd choose. It's slightly more masculine than the others with darker fabric and flooring, but still the modern farmhouse look people are loving right now. I haven't even had a chance to give him the little presentations I'd planned for each look and he's already jumping in.

"Okay," I stutter. While this is going better than

expected I'm still out of my element. I'm not an interior designer, and I'm sitting across from Chance's giant grin. Those two things alone have me flustered. Noticing the frequent stares of the other Ham & Eggs patrons has me wishing I'd had the nerve to ask for this meeting at my apartment or at the farmhouse. Chance gets his fair share of attention just being himself. Add that to the whispers I always get behind my back and there's plenty to talk about. The two of us sitting together, business or not, will have tongues wagging. I try to ignore the shudder that gives me.

"When do we start?" Chance asks just as Debbie slides my glass of tea in front of me.

"You're hiring me?" I take a giant gulp of my drink and wish it was something stronger.

"Yeah, I'm hiring you. Can you start tomorrow or is that too soon?"

"Well, I'll need your help ordering some of the materials. I could come by tomorrow and we could double check the measurements. Talk about schedules." I take another giant gulp. Am I really doing this?

"Perfect!" Chance reaches forward to grab one of the fried pickle slices from the plate Debbie's depositing in front of us. He pops it in his mouth and chews. "These are actually pretty good."

I grab a slice, myself, if only to have something to do with my hands. I bite down into the saltiness of the pickle and close my eyes. Pickles might not solve everyone's problems, but they always make me feel better. I open my eyes to find Chance staring at me, the corners of his mouth turned up just enough to have me checking the corners of mine for crumbs.

"What?" I wipe at my chin.

"I just haven't seen you smile in a long time. I'll have to feed you pickles more often."

I school my mouth back into a frown and Chance barks with laughter, tilting his head back so that I can see his throat working. If everyone wasn't looking at us before, they're certainly looking now.

"Lily Gentry," Chance whispers to me as he leans forward and wipes his eyes. "This is going to be fun."

9

Chance

"Lily!" She jumps when she hears me shout. "Shit. Sorry. I didn't realize you were right there."

After working together for the past few days we're getting used to each other, but we're still not comfortable enough for abrupt yelling. I'll never get used to seeing Lily startle the way she does when I accidentally get in her space or appear unannounced. She's like a little rabbit, hopping out of her skin when something unexpected happens. No surprise parties in Lily Gentry's future, that's for sure.

"It's fine," Lily tells me, her hand dramatically resting over her heart. "I just didn't hear you come back in." She's down in front of one of the lower cabinets in the kitchen, still trying to pry the old handle off. That's exactly where I left her when I went to pick up lunch.

"No luck?" I put the paper bag filled with our takeout salads on what's left of the kitchen counter.

"No. These things are wedged on tighter than a..." Lily trails off before she can finish what I'm assuming was going to be a colorful sentence. I've learned that she's got quite the vocabulary, especially when she gets frustrated.

"Here, I'll help. Move over." I give her time to slide out of the way and sit down next to her. I can smell her shampoo as she moves out of reach, careful not to get too close. There's a hint of vanilla making her smell like one of Aunt Mae's fluffy cakes.

"I think the screws are all stripped and maybe there's some glue or something in there. Would your grandpa have glued these handles on?" Lily seems to think this is a crazy idea, but she didn't know Jefferson Allen the way I did. If the handles had been wobbly he'd have stuck them on with tar rather than deal with that annoyance. He was about functionality, not appearances.

"There is a high likelihood that we have some glue involved here." I try unsuccessfully to turn one of the screws in the back of the cabinet door. "I think these screws are just for show, unfortunately."

When Lily's forehead crinkles to match her scrunched up nose, I know she's thinking, trying to work out a solution to this new problem. It's one of many we've run into as we try to take this kitchen apart and put it back together again.

"How about we take a break for lunch and think about what to do next?" I suggest. Lily's stomach growls, and I catch the tail end of a grin she can't fully suppress. "It'll be easier to think on a full stomach."

"Okay." Lily gives in and we scramble to our feet. I offer her my hand before I can think it through. The gesture's automatic and so's Lily's reaction to it. She stares at my hand for two beats before she ignores it and hoists herself up.

"I've got it." Lily wipes her hands on the front of her jeans. They're loose, of course, although she does have on a short-sleeved T-shirt today. It's the first time I've seen her elbows. The skin on her arms is creamy white but there are unmistakable muscles there.

"I'll wash up and meet you back here at the table." I don't give her the opportunity to argue. I take my time washing my hands in the back bathroom before I make my way to the kitchen. I'm sure Lily's going to try to ditch me for lunch again. The last few times she's stayed through the afternoon she's waited until I was already organized—my sandwich unwrapped and already mid-chew—before she came up with an excuse to bolt out the door and eat by herself. She needed fresh air, she'd said. Or she wanted to wait to eat a little later and needed to stretch her legs. Anything to get out of sitting alone with me at the kitchen table like two normal people.

So I'm more than a little surprised to find Lily sitting, hands neatly folded in her lap, her butt in one of the kitchen chairs when I come back. She's put the salads out, one in front of her and one across the table like it's no big deal.

"That one's yours, I think. There's no cheese on it."

I grunt, trying to act casual about her staying, too. "Does yours have extra?"

"Looks like it. Thanks for making sure to tell them." Lily waits patiently while I sit and reach for my silverware. We're using plastic now that I've pulled out the dishwasher and disconnected it from the water supply.

Lily clears her throat. "Are you okay with me eating in here with you today?" She acts like I haven't been inviting her every damn day. Like it's putting me out to have company instead of eating in silence by myself.

"I'd be thrilled to have lunch with you."

Lily's cheeks redden and she fumbles with the napkin

wrapped around her plastic knife and fork. "Okay, then." It's barely a whisper.

For the next fifteen minutes we eat in silence. I can literally hear every bite I take and it's way too late now to reconsider the salad idea. Lily crunches away across from me, barely even looking up from the plastic container. Did I think eating alone was the worst option here? This is ten times more excruciating. I focus on cutting my lettuce into the smallest pieces possible.

"I heard you were living in California."

Lily's head's still bent over her food, but I'm sure she spoke.

"Did you say something?" I can't imagine that Lily's going to be the one to make the first move here.

"I said that I'd heard you live in California." Lily raises her head and her eyes meet mine.

"Um, yeah. I used to, I guess."

"You don't anymore?" Lily gives me a quizzical look. She's expecting more information, but there's not much more to tell.

"I guess not."

Lily wrinkles her brow. As much as I want her to talk to me, this is a subject that can't really go anywhere.

"I mean, I did. But now I don't."

"Does that mean you're planning on living here?" Lily puts another bite of lettuce in her mouth and goes to work chewing it.

"No," I answer too quickly. "Not that there's anything wrong with living here."

Lily stabs another bite with her fork and lets me fumble around for the right words. Her expression tells me she'd be happy to watch me put my foot in my mouth all day.

"I guess I'm between places right now," I finish. "I'm still figuring things out. I heard you were living in Chicago." Now it's my turn to pop a bite of lunch in my mouth and wait for her to answer. But Lily's not going to give me any more information than I've given her, I guess.

"I used to," she tells me and starts crunching more lettuce. We sound like a herd of horses.

"Does that mean you're planning on living here?" *Because two can play at that game, Lily.*

She pretends to consider the question as she pushes the rest of her salad around. "No. Not that there's anything wrong with it."

I roll my eyes. "I guess you're in between places right now, too?"

"I guess."

Stalemate. Again.

The sound of a car in the driveway has us both turning toward the front door.

"Were you expecting somebody?" Lily asks right before we hear the unmistakable sound of heels click-clacking up the steps and a futile attempt at ringing the broken doorbell.

"Nope." Other than my aunts, everybody I have any reason to see is already sitting here at this table. I pull my napkin from my lap and go to open the door. Standing at the top of the stairs is a blonde in the shortest shorts I've ever seen. She's clutching a brown box and her blue eyes light up when she sees me. Her bright red lips pull into a smile that makes her look like an ad for toothpaste.

"Is Lily here?" the woman asks as she tries to peer around me and into the house. "I'm Hadley." When I don't respond to this in the way she was apparently expecting, she lets out a sigh. "I'm Lily's roommate."

"She's here." I push the door open wider and let her see inside. "We were just finishing lunch."

Hadley pushes past me and heads straight for Lily. "Isn't this cozy?" she asks no one in particular. "You two are eating together?"

"Not anymore," Lily says, more than a little irritated.

"Well, I don't mean to intrude but I thought you might want these. They were delivered to the apartment and I didn't want you to be stuck without them." Hadley holds out the cardboard box, her red fingernails glinting against the package. Lily takes it from her more aggressively than expected, and Hadley's eyes widen a fraction.

"You drove forty-five minutes out of your way just to be sure we had the cabinet pulls I ordered." Lily presents this as the most absurd thing she's ever heard.

Hadley just smiles. "Well, that, and I wanted to see how things were going." She walks toward the kitchen. "Lily's been telling me all about the work you're doing in here. Looks like things are coming along."

"Yep," Lily grinds out. "Coming along. Speaking of that, we should get back to work. And I'm sure you've got places to be, Hadley. Things are going just fine here." Lily manhandles Hadley back toward the front door. Lily might be smaller, but Hadley's shoes make it hard for her to fight back. "Thanks for bringing those knobs by."

"You're welcome," Hadley says as she wrestles her elbow back from Lily. "Just wanted to be sure you didn't need them."

"If I needed them, I would have texted you." Lily's voice tells me we're talking about much more than hardware for the cabinets.

"Just making sure." Hadley's all fake sugar and smiles. "Always looking out for my bestie. Good to see you,

Chance." I give her a nod as Lily drags her back out onto the front porch.

As Lily's hands fly around her face during an animated discussion with her roommate, I watch from the safety of the living room. That is one thing I never plan on getting in the middle of, and I'm sure Lily will never explain to me. Things have been awkward, sure, but nothing requiring the cavalry or a babysitter. I congratulate myself on keeping things all business and drama-free even as I notice the pretty flush of Lily's angry cheeks and the curve of her neck.

When Lily stomps back in I pretend to be extremely concerned with the wallpaper.

"Sorry about that," she says. "Hadley means well."

"She was nervous about you being here?" I try not to take it personally, but it puts a little burn in my chest that Lily might have said she feels unsafe with me.

"Sort of. It's complicated." Lily looks away, refusing to meet my eyes. "Like I said, she means well."

"I hope she knows that she doesn't have anything to worry about while you're here." I hope *Lily* knows this. I couldn't care less about what her roommate thinks, but I'm finding it hard to keep from worrying about how Lily sees me.

"She knows." Lily's big brown eyes finally meet mine. "She was just checking in. And now she's mad that you don't remember her." She gives me an almost-smile.

"*Should* I remember her?" I try to think back to summers here but don't come up with much for Lily's friend.

"*Everybody* remembers *Hadley*."

"Would she have been standing next to you?" I ask.

"Most of the time." Lily tells me, her brows knitting together over those chocolate eyes.

"Then that's why I don't remember. Probably never

noticed her. Hardly ever took my eyes off you." I shrug and turn my back on Lily's shocked face, the red starting to creep down onto her neck. She'll be blushing for the rest of the day.

10

Lily

The door's wide open when I make it up the front porch steps, which is lucky because I could never have managed the two coffees I'm holding, the bag of cinnamon rolls, and the doorknob. As is, I can barely manage the coffee and pastry because my hands are shaking so badly. Stopping by the bakery was a stupid idea, one that Hadley will laugh about once I get home this afternoon and tell her. I stopped at Patty Cakes on my way into work for no other reason than Chance mentioning how much he loves cinnamon rolls. He probably doesn't even remember saying it, which will make me showing up with baked goods at seven in the morning even more regrettable. I'll have to do that thing where you pretend it's nothing when you both realize it's probably more like something, and Chance will know I've been thinking about him enough to make an unscheduled stop at his favorite bakery to buy him breakfast.

In reality I've been thinking about him all weekend. I could blame Hadley because she kept bringing him up. That girl cannot believe that she isn't the subject of discussion at all Allen family dinners and holiday get-togethers. How could Chance *not* remember her? Doesn't his brother talk about her all the time? Hasn't Cooper Allen been lamenting the one that got away? Hadley had been sure she'd have come up in conversation *at least* once a month. Holidays for sure. Reminding her that it's been years since any of those boys have laid eyes on her didn't do any good. That's no excuse. Not when you're Hadley. And so we spent all Saturday night and Sunday morning dissecting what Chance might have meant when he claimed not to remember her.

But I left out the most important part.

If I'd told Hadley about what Chance had really said I'd have never heard the end of it. That Chance hadn't noticed Hadley because he'd been noticing me? My stomach had done that traitorous flip when he'd said that and even though I have no interest in anything more than a working relationship with Chance Allen, here I am less than forty-eight hours later with cinnamon rolls fresh from the oven. The only thing worse would have been if I'd made them myself. Which—who am I kidding here?—I had considered.

The wall of heat and humidity hits me the second I walk in the living room. It's a good thing I don't care what my hair looks like most of the time because the inside of this house is rivaling any South Georgia heatwave. I can feel the sweat starting to trickle between my breasts before I even make it all the way to the kitchen. I've got on a T-shirt today but the sweatpants I pulled on when I rolled out of bed are making for a nice little mini sauna for my legs. Whatever Chance has going on in here has turned this house into a steam room.

And this hot sticky mess apparently comes with music—loud Johnny Cash to be exact. Chance is belting out his own version of *I Walk the Line* from somewhere farther in the house. I pick my way along the edge of the kitchen, careful not to step on any of the bits of debris that have ended up scattered around. It looks like Chance has been up for a while and has been doing some of the demolition we need to get to our next steps. He's got a fan running in the hallway that connects the kitchen to the rest of the house, not that it's doing much to cool things down, and I have to step over the long extension cord he's used to plug the useless thing in.

I follow Chance's horrible singing deeper into the house but when I finally find him, I nearly drop the breakfast rolls on the floor. Luckily there's a wall to hold me up because the sight of Chance when I finally lay eyes on him nearly knocks the breath out of me.

There is no kind of advance warning that could have prepared me.

He's straddling the top of the ladder, wedged in at the end of the hallway with the wallpaper steamer in one hand and one of those metal scrapers in the other. He loosens a piece of wallpaper with the steamer and then uses the scraper to free it from the wall. It hangs there for a moment until he slides the steamer lower and goes to work on the next section. The muscles in his back bunch and tense as he moves around along the wall, something that's easy to see because Chance isn't wearing a shirt.

He's naked from the waist up and covered in sweat. It drips from his elbow as he changes the position of his arm and trickles down his back when he shifts on the ladder.

My brain is telling me I should turn and run; this is a definite *alarm bells* situation. But my feet stay where they are and my eyes keep raking over the expanse of skin in front of me. Chance's jeans sit low on his hips and it doesn't take much imagination to go just a few inches lower. I watch a bead of sweat make its way from his shoulder all the way down to his waistband. It twists and turns over muscles normally hidden by the fabric of one of his worn T-shirts. When it finally disappears, I come to my senses and clear my throat. The music's loud and Chance doesn't hear me at first, leaving me ogling him for a minute longer as I try to get his attention.

"Chance!" Yelling his name turns out to be the only option.

He turns, wide smile already pulling at the corners of his mouth. But that smile is the last thing on my mind as I get a full view of Chance's glistening chest. Is it possible to have more than a six pack? Because I have never seen that many muscles on a real person before. Teenage Chance may have been something to see in a swimsuit, but he's got nothing on the man in front of me this morning.

"You're early!" Chance yells as he scrambles off the ladder. "Is that coffee?" He grabs his phone out of his back pocket and lowers the volume on the music playing from the portable speaker on the floor. Johnny Cash slowly fades away and Chance moves too close to me.

Suddenly I'm claustrophobic, the air too stifling for me to breathe. I imagine shoving a Styrofoam cup at Chance's midsection and plowing back out onto the porch. I can see myself gasping for breath as I hit the front door, my chest heaving as I struggle to get air in my lungs. But instead of running I make myself stay where I am. I fight the panic. This isn't fight or flight time. Chance is just a man—a sweaty, shirtless one, sure—but he's not a threat. I tell myself this on repeat as I hand him his coffee. My heart is pounding like a kick drum in my chest, but I'm not dying. My therapist would be so proud.

Chance is careful to keep his fingers from touching mine as he takes the cup from me. "There's sugar in what's left of the kitchen," he tells me as he eyes the bag I've got mangled in my other hand.

"I already put sugar in yours," I confess. "I hope that's okay. You take it with two sugars, no cream, right?" I don't know what possessed me to go ahead and fix his coffee like that. I was on autopilot in the bakery doctoring up our drinks like I do it all the time. I've seen Chance drink plenty of coffee by now. The early mornings are adding up. But this feels too familiar, too much like friendship and it's too late to take it back.

Chance juts his lower lip out for a second before he answers, obviously considering his next move. He wants to tease me, that much is sure, but he's being cautious about it. I hate that it takes this much effort just to be around me.

Chance is probably thinking the same thing.

He moves the cup to his lips and takes a swig, his throat moving as he swallows. His tongue darts out to catch the last drops of coffee from his lips. When he finally makes a move to speak, I don't have time to look away when he quirks up one side of that mesmerizing mouth and quips, "Thanks for giving me some sugar, Lily."

I groan. Is he *flirting* with me? It's just this side of dirty, the way he's thanking me. "You're welcome," I manage, trying to put things back on even ground.

"What's in the bag?" Chance asks and I know I'm really done for now. Once he finds out the extent of my breakfast purchases, he'll think I'm in love with him.

"Cinnamon rolls." I loosen my grip a little on the top of the bag. I hold it out to him and he takes it greedily, opening it up and sticking his nose inside. He closes his eyes and I get a second to freely look at him. Square jaw, dark blond hair in need of a trim, the kind of nose you find on statues in a museum. His mouth stays in that perma-smirk as he opens his hazel eyes to stare back at me.

"These are still warm," Chance whispers like it's the most reverent thing he'll ever say to me.

"Patty had just finished putting the glaze on when I bought them," I answer back in the same hushed voice.

"Let's eat them on the porch. Give me two seconds to wash up." Chance looks down, forcing me to do the same. His sweaty abs wink up at me. "And grab a shirt."

We eat the cinnamon rolls and drink our coffee, sitting in the sunshine. The pastry's still warm and we both end up covered in melted butter and sugar, licking our fingers. In between bites Chance moans like they're the best thing he's ever eaten. It's more theatrical than I expected and after the fourth outburst I find it impossible to hold in the laugh I've been fighting off. It bubbles up and over my lips before I can stop it. Chance halts mid-groan, and I cover my mouth with my hand, but once I start, I can't do anything but keep giggling.

"Sorry," I say from between my fingers.

"If I didn't know better, I'd think you were laughing," Chance tells me, a cocky grin on his face. "I mean, you're laughing *at me* so it hurts a little, but I'll take it." He leans forward on the steps and announces, "Do you hear that, chickens? I made Lily Gentry laugh!"

I shrug, smiling. It's his own fault for being so ridiculous. "You are pretty funny."

"Don't say, 'But looks aren't everything' because that joke is too middle school even for me." He smiles again, full teeth, and I have to remind myself not to be sucked in by the dimple in his chin.

"Too middle school even for you?" I'm grinning back at

him, forgetting to keep my face blank, forgetting to keep my distance.

"Yeah," he says. And then sits for what feels like eternity, looking at me.

"Do I have something on my face?" I wipe my chin with the back of my hand, looking for errant bits of cinnamon and sugar.

"Yeah. That smile again." Chance keeps smiling back at me like a maniac. "You should do that more often. The laughing, too. It's nice."

I blush and duck my head, something I used to hate to see other girls do. I used to be able to take a compliment and run with it. Now, the mere hint of one and I'm hiding.

"Sorry." The regret's already messing with the happiness on Chance's face.

"Don't be." I wave him off and try to keep my mouth from turning back down into its predictable frown. "You decided to take down the wallpaper?"

He seems relieved to change the subject and I'm kicking myself again for not being able to be normal. I should be able to joke around with him, give him a playful shove or something, but I'm still not there yet. Not with anyone.

"We have to paint the kitchen, right? But when I was looking at the walls last night, I realized that wallpaper goes all the way down the hall. I figured it wouldn't be that big of a deal to steam it off. I think I've bitten off more than I can chew, maybe." He looks at me like a kid who's been caught with his hand in the cookie jar. "There may have been whiskey involved."

I laugh again, surprising myself. "It's easier with two people. I can help you, if you want."

"Don't you have to be at the store? That wallpaper's a bitch. It's going to take us all day to scrape it off. I think it's stuck on there with regular glue or something." His words are meant to warn me off, but his face says otherwise. He wants me to stay, needs me to help.

"I don't have to go into the store today," I lie. I've been spending less and less time at Southern Comforts and more and more time out here. Bunny's made a few cracks about it, but I know she and my mother are secretly happy I'm able to keep the panic at bay long enough to socialize at all.

"Not at all?"

"Not at all. I can help you with the wallpaper. It'll go faster with two."

Chance pumps a fist in the air. "Too late to take it back now, Lily. You're stuck with me for the whole day." He leans forward to yell at the chickens again, "Did you hear that, Marlon? Lily's promised to help me all day."

I'm beginning to wonder about Chance's mental stability. "Marlon?" I'm almost afraid of the answer.

"Marlon Brando. He's the rooster," Chance clarifies, standing and brushing the crumbs off his jeans. He holds out a sticky hand to help me up. "Come on, partner, time to get sweaty."

11

Chance

"Cat or dog?"

"What?"

"Cat or dog? Like, if you had to choose?"

Lily peers up at me from the space underneath my armpit. Unfortunately for her she's been stuck there all afternoon. Taking down this wallpaper is requiring us to get way closer than I imagine she ever expected. We take turns steaming and scraping, steaming and scraping and even though we've made progress there's still plenty of work left to do. A hiss of steam nearly hits me in the face and I pull back enough to keep from getting a nasty burn. This is hot, sweaty stuff and not in the way I pictured myself getting hot and sweaty with Lily. Not that this situation really lends itself to any kind of sexy thoughts. By now we're both drenched, looking more like drowned rats than centerfolds. Although, somehow, Lily still manages to smell like a cupcake. I notice because her ponytail has spent a good deal of time pressed against my nose.

"As a pet?" Lily asks me, bringing me back to the game.

"Well, maybe not as a pet. More like a general preference, I guess." I catch some of the hot water dripping down the wall before it can land on Lily's hand. Now I'm holding a steaming hot towel, trying to keep from burning my own fingers. It's one of the unforeseen dangers of this wallpaper fiasco that we've learned the hard way. Boiling water, horribly sticky glue, and idle chit chat. We've been working for hours and, still, I'm doing most of the talking. That works great for operation make Lily smile—I'm up to five and a half genuine smiles and two laughs before lunch—but not so well for getting to the bottom of what's turned Lily into some shy little turtle. Every now and then I see her start to poke her head out of her shell only to have her pull back in again.

"Oh." She finally understands. "Dog? I guess?"

"You don't sound very sure." I slide the handle of the steamer over and let her start scraping the blistered spot I leave behind.

"I'm not really into animals so much."

"Hmm, okay." There's one interesting Lily fact. "Beach or mountain?"

"Beach, definitely," she answers without taking any time to think. "Are you not answering these questions too?" Lily frees another corner of the wallpaper and tugs. A big section comes off in her hand, ripping along a seam.

"That was a good one. I wish we'd been keeping track of the big pieces. We could've made it a competition."

"Why does it not surprise me that you'd want to make pulling down wallpaper a competition?" Lily shoves the paper into the giant garbage bag we're dragging around with us. "So, beach or mountain?"

"Me?" I pretend to think. "Mountain. I think I've had enough beach for a while."

"Because of California?" Lily doesn't look at me, just keeps working the scraper along the wall. Globs of wet glue come off and she has to wipe it on one of the old towels we found in the laundry room.

"Yeah, I've had enough sand in my shoes to last a lifetime."

"That's too bad. I love the beach." Lily's voice goes small but her hands keep moving, pulling paper and scraping glue. There's interesting Lily fact number two.

"And dog. Definitely dog." I nod my head like I've just confirmed some major issue.

"Why did you leave California?" Lily's question catches me off guard. One of the good things about Mint Springs is the lack of questions. My aunts might spend some time digging into my sudden departure from my dream job and all the things that went along with it, but no one else here really cares. I'm sure people'd gossip about it if they had even a shred of information, but for the most part I'm flying under the radar. But now here's Lily asking questions, and I'm the one who opened the door. I can't exactly shut it without stopping the momentum, so I keep moving the steamer along the wall and just tell the truth.

"Things got complicated."

"That isn't an answer."

She's right so I try again. "My business partners and I had a little bit of a disagreement."

"Ah, so you got fired?" Lily keeps scraping, not looking at me.

"I didn't get fired. I walked away." I sound more indignant than I should. If I'd walked away without any hard feelings, I'd sound less angry, less upset. But my ego's still bruised from the battering it took when I realized things weren't up to me.

Lily hones in on a tiny speck of paper that refuses to budge. The blue floral wallpaper has been hanging in this house for as long as I can remember. For all I know my grandmother picked it out. Lily wrinkles her brow and picks at the paper with her fingernail.

"But it was your decision?"

"Sort of." I let out a sigh and just decide to spill it. "The short version is I started a company with some friends from college and we had different ideas about where we wanted to go, so I left." It's more complicated than that and Lily knows it, but she doesn't try to argue, doesn't contradict me.

"What kind of company?"

"Tech." I'd explain the specifics but just that one word makes Lily's entire face change. If I didn't know better, I'd think she was smirking.

"You had a nerd fight?" She *is* smirking. "Did anybody's glasses get broken? Any protractor injuries?" Lily turns to me with a raised eyebrow.

I laugh in spite of myself. "Was that a joke? Did you just try to be funny? I'm both wounded and impressed."

Lily shrugs. "I'm here all week."

I secretly hope that's true.

"The only thing hurt were nerd feelings, so there was a lot of emailing." I also punched a hole in a wall. Becoming the Hulk in a room full of Bruce Banners didn't help my cause.

"Sounds high drama. Lots of big words, I'm assuming." Lily's mouth quirks back up on one side.

"Indeed. We all needed to get out our thesauruses. Our thesauri. What's the plural of thesaurus?"

"I have no idea." Lily's smiling now—number six—and I

feel my own mouth imitating hers. She's loosening up a bit with me, and I can't help but celebrate that win a little. I'm mentally high-fiving myself when I bring it all crashing back down.

"So why did you leave Chicago?"

Lily's smile fades and I'm kicking myself.

"My grandmother had a stroke." Lily says it like it's no big deal, but all the ease of before gets sucked out of the room, and she turns back to scraping the wall.

"I'm sorry." I am. And I'm sorry for ever bringing it up.

"She can't do as much at the store, so I'm here for a while to help out."

"You don't sound too excited about that."

"It's fine. It's temporary." Lily shrugs. "Move the steamer a little."

I push my arm forward on auto pilot, wisps of steam escaping from the pan before the machine sputters a bit, the last of the hot water evaporating. We'll need to refill the empty tank and then wait for the water to heat up again.

"Break time?" I suggest. Not that there's any choice, really. We move away from the wall, bending and stretching. I know my back will be sore tomorrow. We're both covered in sweat and glue and the house has become a sauna, but Lily's still dressed like it's a chilly fall day. She has to be broiling under those sweatpants. I've kept my shirt on, but I'm dying.

"Porch?" Lily asks. "I could use some water. Whose idea was it to take all this wallpaper down, anyway?"

"Yours! And you said it had to come down 'ASAP.'" I throw in some air quotes that earn me an eye roll.

"I was talking about the part in the kitchen. Not the whole house. If it was winter maybe it wouldn't be so bad. It's hot as hell in here."

Lily has a point. It is miserable in the house. The *cooler* porch still leaves us baking in the sun.

"We could take a river break." I watch Lily's face as I suggest it. Instead of wholehearted enthusiasm I get a blank stare.

"The river?" She looks at me like I have two heads.

"Yeah, we can swim. Jump off the rope swing."

"It's barely May. The water will be freezing," Lily counters. "And we don't have swimsuits." Her cheeks pink up a bit.

"Do we need them?"

Lily folds her arms across her chest. "I'm not going skinny dipping with you, Chance."

"We don't have to get naked." I don't remind Lily that there was a time when the mention of skinny dipping would have had her already peeling her top off. Granted it was usually late and dark out, but it's still burned in my memories of summers here. "What have you got on under there?"

Lily shifts from foot to foot uncomfortably. "None of your business."

"I bet it covers as much as a swimsuit." I think back to Lily's teeny tiny bikinis.

"I'm not swimming in my underwear, either." Lily eyes me like I'm some kind of pervert.

"Fine. Then leave your T-shirt on." That thing comes down almost to her knees. I cut her off when Lily opens her mouth to protest. "Then you can borrow a dry one from me when we get back. Or you can swim in one of mine if you don't want to get that one wet. Once you're in the water there's nothing to see anyway."

Lily doesn't look convinced, but she stops arguing. "Do you have towels?"

"I'm sure I can dig some up. Go get in the truck."

Lily hesitates.

"Look, we're dying in here and I know you're roasting in those pants." I cast a glance down at her fleece-covered legs. "We'll go for five minutes. If you hate it, we'll come right back." But I know she won't hate it. Who can hate a jump in the river on a hot day, especially after the work we've done?

"Fine. But we come back when I say so. You have to promise."

"I promise. Hop in the truck and I'll get the towels."

Lily turns and trudges out to my truck like she's headed to the electric chair. The screen door slams behind her, and I scramble around grabbing towels and the cooler. There's barely anything in the fridge now that I have it rigged up in the living room, but luckily there are a few beers and bottles of water. I shove them in the cooler with the rest of the bag of ice I have in the freezer. I probably won't remember to buy another bag, but it will be worth it to burn through this one if it means getting Lily to enjoy herself for even five minutes.

A horn honks. Lily's getting impatient. And surprisingly bossy. I bust through the front door and sprint to the truck. No way am I giving her a chance to change her mind. I've got the thing started in two seconds and we're driving down the road, gravel spitting out behind us, before she can make a crack about how long it took me.

It isn't far to the river, but the pasture's so overgrown that I have to slow down and make my own path to get us to the spot where the brush is cleared enough to make it to the water. I make a mental note that there's work to be done down here as well, and my to-do list grows again.

I'll worry about taming all this later, because once we're close enough to see a sliver of the water and hear the sound of the river rushing past through the open truck windows, all I can think about is getting cold and wet.

Lily seems almost as excited as me, yanking open the door and clambering down from the cab of the truck. We pick our way down to the edge of the water and I can feel myself go back in time. I'm suddenly sixteen years old with nothing to worry about except being able to shake the cobwebs out of my head in the morning so I can put my butt in the seat of the tractor. After baling hay or painting fence posts we'd all pile in the back of someone's truck and come straight here, all four Allen boys ready to whoop it up a little. We'd head back down after supper most nights to yell and splash around. My brother Cooper would always have his arm slung around some girl's shoulder and the rest of us would have been hoping—and usually failing—to do the same. There'd be a fire going, which my grandpa hated. We had to be careful to put the entire thing out to "keep from burning the whole place down" and even if we acted like we ignored those lectures, we always made sure to completely douse the embers before trying to sneak back up to the house. Then we'd tiptoe up those creaky stairs to get ready to do it all again the next day.

I wonder if Lily remembers nights at the river the same way, if it has the same memories for her. She was what my aunts call "a spitfire" so maybe her river nights were even wilder than mine. I was too chicken shit to even talk to her then, terrified of her bravado. I smile as Lily scans the river bed, watching the water slosh and dance over the rocks. The leaves of the trees block some of the sunlight and splash patterns over her face. She's more relaxed now, less concerned with whatever is always eating her up, but I know she'll get uncomfortable again if we stand around for too long. The wheels will start turning and she'll go wherever it is she goes when she puts her guard back up.

"Let's go," I say more to myself than to Lily. I reach behind and pull my shirt over my head. I can feel Lily's eyes on me, but I don't turn to look at her. Instead, I focus on stripping down to my boxers and barreling toward the water.

The river's not deep until you hit the middle, something my grandpa always kept reminding us. There are spots deep enough to jump in, but you have to test them first. The river's a living thing, changing all the time, and you can't assume you know what to expect just because you've been here before. It takes some wading until you're up to your neck; there's no cannonballing off the bank. I push against the pull of the frigid water's movement, mud squishing between my toes until it turns to silt and then something closer to sand. I dunk myself under and come back up to Lily still fully dressed and standing high on the bank.

I raise my arm and motion for her to come in, but it's like she's frozen, watching me stuck here in the middle of the river. Water drips from my hair, my eyelashes, my chin as we stare at each other. Slowly, I turn around until I have my back to her, and the image of Lily exists only in my mind. In my imagination I see her peeling off her oversized sweatpants and sliding her T-shirt over her head, the neck catching her shiny ponytail for a second until it swishes back down against her spine. I imagine her easing into the water, the current rushing around her body on its way to the ocean. I'm sure none of that is happening. I'm giving her a little privacy, but I doubt she took me up on it.

"Okay."

Her whisper comes from close behind me, making all the hair on the back of my neck stand up. I turn and the smile that takes over my face threatens to crack the whole thing open. Lily's come down into the water. The tip of her ponytail grazes the top of the tiny eddies that form around her shoulders. Her bare shoulders.

Because Lily's taken off her T-shirt.

12

Lily

"Well, look who finally managed to drag herself away from her boyfriend to come to work!"

I scowl down at Bunny from the top of the ladder. I'm arranging vases on top of one of the cabinets I've painted. If they weren't so pretty, I'd sacrifice one and drop it on my grandmother's head. But we can't afford to be breaking merchandise, even for the noble cause of revenge.

"He's not my boyfriend," I tell her and go back to sliding glassware around.

"Sorry to hear that." Bunny gives me a *tsk, tsk* and shakes her gray head. "I was hoping you being out at that house for so long would lead to a love connection." She smiles up at me and I frown back. My grandma knows that I'm not looking for any kind of a relationship. I could barely handle being alone with Chance when I first took the decorating job he offered me.

"It's work, Bunny. Just work." I try not to picture water sluicing off Chance's muscular back as I tell her this, but I can't help myself. I've had his nearly naked body on repeat for the past few days. Between the shirtless wallpaper removal and the river swim I have more than a few suggestive images of Chance Allen rattling around in my brain. It's one of the main reasons I'm here at the store instead of out at the farmhouse. I needed a little distance.

"He didn't need you out there today?" Bunny fishes.

"I decided you guys probably needed me here more. I have a few things I need to get done this morning and then I'll probably head over to the Allen place," I try to keep it all matter-of-fact. I can be nonchalant when I need to be, right?

Wrong.

"Well, don't let us keep you." The edges of Bunny's mouth turn up a touch. "I'd hate to make that boy less than pleased with your performance."

I growl down at Bunny and she lumbers away cackling. She's getting worse at her quick escapes, even with the walker. I miss the days when she was the spry old lady with the razor-sharp tongue. Her sassy retorts might be the same, but her body is definitely starting to betray her.

And I can't blame her for teasing me. I have been spending more time than I planned with Chance. After the initial freak out period I went through at the beginning, we've kind of settled into an easy work relationship. I've surprised myself by managing to keep calm and even enjoy myself some of the time. Our impromptu swim party is a good example of that. Before, I would never have put myself in that situation, especially not if it required removing clothing. But for some reason I trusted Chance. He's figured out my quirks and works around them with respect, so I let my guard down.

Not that I'm broadcasting all over town that I stripped down to my underwear and went swimming with Chance Allen. If my mother or Bunny got even a whiff of that story, they'd be all over me with questions. I didn't even tell Hadley. Once Chance and I dried off and made it back it was late enough for dinner. Chance tried to convince me to stay and join him at his aunts' house. I declined, of course, because I'd never show up for dinner unannounced, and never wearing a filthy shirt.

And if I'd gone to Miss Sadie and Miss Mae's house for dinner, they'd have taken one look at me and known every filthy thought that was running through my head. There'd be no way to hide it from those two. They'd see that even though I was looking at Chance's face I was thinking about him toweling off his chest, remembering the way his muscles rippled when he launched himself off the rope swing into the clear water underneath. They'd be able to read my mind and see it was full of stolen glances at Chance's wet thighs, at the way the fabric of his boxers clung to the rest of him. They'd see because it's been so long since I've had any thoughts even remotely close to as scandalous as these, that my face can no longer hide it. I would have been drooling all through dinner and it wouldn't have been because of anyone's blackberry cobbler.

I avoided dinner, insisting that I needed to get home. And I'm avoiding Chance because I need more time to pull myself together. I need time to figure out what's happening here and how to stop it. Because I can't afford to mess things up with this job and I can't afford to take the armor I've been wearing off yet. Not if I want to keep myself safe.

"Lily!" my mother calls from somewhere in the front of the store. No wonder I can't ever get anything done when I come in here during business hours. My best work happens in the studio once the front doors are locked for the night and my family's long gone. I've been coming in late after I finish up at the farmhouse, painting and arranging so that certain sections of the store look like they could be in *Southern Living*. I've kept my hands busy, now I have to find something to occupy my increasingly distracted brain.

I climb down from the ladder and follow the sound of my mother's voice. Maybe I should suggest we get walkie-talkies or something. Anything to keep from hearing this shrill screaming all day. When I finally find her, I stop short. My mother's standing near one of my more recent pieces, one hand smoothing the surface of the cabinet and the other patting Chance's solid forearm. She smiles up at him and he grins down at her like it's the most normal thing in the world for the two of them to be all buddy-buddy. I watch as they finish their discussion, my mother never letting his attention waver.

I clear my throat and my mother gives Chance one final pat, this one firmly on his chest. She's always said this was one of her superpowers. Just the tiniest touch and she has men eating out of her hand. It was something she passed down to her daughter.

Too bad now it's more like my kryptonite.

"There she is!" my mother exclaims, all but shoving Chance in my direction. "Look who stopped by to see you!" From over his shoulder I see my mother raise an eyebrow. I'm sure I'll be explaining this later. I feel a bubble of annoyance start to rise in my chest, but the huge smile Chance gives me has it bursting, a small flutter of something else taking its place. That look can't be for me, can it?

"Thanks, Mama," I say as sweetly as I can.

"Always happy to help," she answers back nearly as saccharine. "Chance was telling me all about the work you've been doing over at his house."

"Was he?"

"I was bragging on you a bit," Chance confesses. "I told

her you're a genius when it comes to putting things together. I don't even know how to match socks but you're able to coordinate an entire room in two minutes."

I feel myself blush a bit and watch my mother blink at Chance's compliment. "Well," she sputters. "I'll let you two talk." She seems as confused as I am by Chance's overzealous appreciation for my skills.

As she retreats to the back of the store to undoubtedly fill my grandmother in on everything she's just seen, I turn to look at Chance. He's the same as he was two days ago, but somehow he's different. More, somehow. And he's holding another jar of pickles.

"Sorry just to drop by," he begins, extending his arm and offering me the jar. "I did bring these to apologize for the intrusion." He shifts in his work boots, feet scuffling on the floor.

I take the pickles, ignoring the spark I feel when his fingertips brush mine. I see him brace for my reaction, waiting for the inevitable shudder or wince.

We're both surprised when it doesn't come.

"I, um, wanted to maybe see if you could show me some of the pieces you were talking about the other day. You know, the ones you thought might look good in the living room instead of what I've got in there now."

I nod, watching Chance's throat work a nervous swallow. His Adam's apple bobs up and down as he continues to explain himself. "And maybe you could show me those paint colors we were considering for the kitchen cabinets. If you have anything painted with those."

"Over here—" I begin before he cuts me off.

"And then I thought maybe I could take you to lunch." He hesitates. "If you're free."

I blink. There are a million reasons to say no, but then

he smiles again and I'm done for. He gives me a nervous little shrug, the kind that tells me he's hopeful but not counting on anything. By now he knows me a little, knows I'm likely to bolt to the back of the store and hide under something rather than let him be nice. He's not sure why and I can't ever tell him, so I surprise us both when I feel my head nodding yes.

"I'd like that," I hear myself saying before my feet turn to lead him through the store. "The things you want to see are back here, mostly." I can feel Chance's eyes boring a hole through me as I walk away, but the familiar creepy-crawlies that usually come with a moment like this—the awareness of a man watching me—don't start to wander up my back.

Something's changed and we both know it. How I decide to handle it is going to be up to me.

13

Chance

"What've you got planned for the rest of the day?" It should be an easy question, one that would be small talk for anybody else. But Lily isn't just anybody, so when she shifts a little on the bench seat beside me, I take my eyes off the road to look at her. She's managed to slide all the way to the other end of the truck, about as far away from me as possible. "I'm only asking," I assure her. "I'm not trying to hijack your time."

Lily shoots me a sideways glance. "I know." She goes back to looking out the window.

This isn't what I expected after our easy lunch together. And there wasn't any of this weirdness when she showed me around Southern Comforts. You can really see her stamp over there now, and she beamed when I told her so. She had seemed pleased that I could easily pick out all the things she'd arranged and decorated. But after spending so much time together I can easily identify her style. It's farm but modern. I'm sure that having her around the store has translated into more sales. She's talented and I don't mind telling anybody who'll listen, even if it means I embarrassed her in front of everyone at the diner. Which I did. Even then she looked more surprised than genuinely mortified. Now, alone in my grandfather's truck, she's back to the silent girl I thought I'd been able to banish.

"So, where to now? You headed back to the store?"

"I actually have a favor to ask you," Lily says to the farmland passing by outside. She's rolled down the temperamental crank window and has one hand dangling outside the frame. The wind whips the hair from the edges of her ponytail around and nearly swallows her words.

"A favor?" I can't help teasing her, drawing it out. I know I shouldn't do that. Whatever's made Lily timid isn't something that needs taunting. She needs people who'll say yes to her asks unconditionally, without a second thought, but I can't bring myself to be perfect just yet. I keep waiting for that unguarded smile, the one from years ago, and I can't get over the fact that it doesn't just wash across her face automatically the way it used to.

"Yes, but I don't want to put you out." Lily turns her head and I get a glimpse of those brown eyes before I focus back on the road. She's like Bambi transformed into human form in the front seat of this Chevy and there's no way I'm about to say no. It doesn't even matter what she needs from me, after looking in those big brown eyes I'm going to say yes. I'm probably always going to say yes, something that has me really concentrating hard on the dotted yellow lines unfurling in front of me. I cannot afford to get this attached to Lily, not when neither of us is making anything permanent. Not when whatever's hurt her still hovers always in the background.

"I was planning on going to the flea market."

I blink. Where's the favor in that?

"I could really use a strong back and a truck to haul the stuff I've bought back to the shop."

"How much stuff are we talking about?" I drive on, already prepping to make the turn toward the fairgrounds where the local flea market is constantly in operation.

"Not much. A few dressers, a set of these cane-back chairs that are going to look so good once I get the cushions recovered." Lily cuts those eyes over to me again. "But I also like to browse, and I'd hate to make you do that."

"You want me to lift a bunch of furniture into the bed of this truck, unload it at Southern Comforts, *and* walk around with you while you shop?" I try to act annoyed when I'm anything but.

"You could stay in the truck," Lily offers. "You wouldn't have to walk around with me. And I know I'm asking you to do some heavy lifting. I could pay you. Or we could knock a little off my bill. Then we'd be even." Her voice is so hopeful it crushes me.

"Like I'd let you wander around at the flea market by yourself," I scoff. I can almost hear Lily roll her eyes, and the corners of my mouth twitch up in response.

"What are you worried about? Everyone there is ancient." She looks at me with a hint of a smile on her lips.

"And they're all out to take your money. What kind of a friend would I be if I just let you walk into that all alone?" I give Lily my most astonished stare, eyes wide, mouth open. "Consider it my moment of chivalry for the day. No charge."

"I'm going to regret this, aren't I?" Lily asks, but she's relaxing against the back of the seat, letting her hand dip in the breeze as we drive along. Her fingers catch the wind and wiggle and I think about reaching across the seat to thread my own fingers through the still ones on her left hand.

"Probably," I tell her, keeping my hand to myself. "But I'll try not to be too embarrassing."

"That should be interesting."

What turns out to be interesting is watching Lily work her magic. I park the truck as close as possible to the entrance to the warehouse, hoping that will make it easier to drag whatever she's buying back out and into the bed. Lily's already grinning with excitement before we can even make it through the giant double doors, her ponytail swinging behind her and her steps quicker than I've ever seen them. From the minute we get close to the vendors, people start calling out their hellos to her, waving wrinkled hands in the air like they've been waiting all morning to see her. And that might not be too far from the truth if all the huge smiles on some of those older faces are any indication. Lily pushes through the stalls like she knows exactly where she's going and I have to jog along behind her to keep up.

"Do you want to go ahead and load the furniture first or are we browsing?" I stretch out the word to make it sound like something I'm dreading.

Lily barely gives me a backward glance as she maneuvers around a rusty piece of old farm equipment. The place is littered with junk like that: rickety furniture, dusty kitchen utensils, old doors from houses no one's lived in for years. It makes Southern Comforts look like Bloomingdale's. Lily doesn't seem bothered by the random things on every table or the layer of dust that covers most of it. She reaches out a few times to touch this thing or that thing, never stopping for too long. She's still greeting everyone and giving them that easy wave that looks so strange on the end of her arm.

When she finally slows down in front of one of the ramshackle stalls, I think the wizened little senior citizen inside is going to have a heart attack from the excitement.

"Miss Lily!" he almost shouts as he hustles to the front of his little makeshift shop. "I was hoping you'd come today." He gives me the once-over before returning his gaze to Lily. "I have those chairs all ready for you to take home, and I have a special surprise you might be interested in. Lucky you brought a friend."

Lily smiles that big smile for him as she pats me on the arm. "This is Chance. He's the one I'm helping with the farmhouse." She gives me a little tip of her head. "Chance, this is Clifford. He finds some great pieces for me."

Clifford blushes a little underneath all those wrinkles. "It's all Lily's eye. She really could turn a sow's ear into a silk purse. And she's a serious negotiator; don't let that pretty smile fool you." He extends one weathered hand and I shake it. "You Jefferson Allen's grandson?"

"Yes, sir," I answer, although I'm not sure if this will be a positive or a negative for Clifford. I can't imagine my grandpa hanging around the flea market and he could be a son of a bitch at times.

"Knew him from high school," Clifford tells me. "Was sorry to hear he'd passed."

"Thank you." If Clifford went to school with my grandfather then he's even more geriatric than I would have guessed. Lily wasn't kidding that some of these guys are relics.

"Glad you came with Lily to help her. She's stubborn enough to think she can haul some of these things around all by herself. I've told her a million times that I'd be happy to have my grandson deliver things to Southern Comforts. He'd be happy to do that for her." The twinkle in his eyes tells me that he's got more in mind for Lily and his grandson than just furniture delivery, but I try to keep from looking at Lily and raising an eyebrow.

"There's no need for that," Lily tells him.

"I'm more than happy to take care of it for her," I say, a little more possessively than I intend. Lily furrows her brow.

Clifford gives me another long look and shakes his head. "Have it your way. Are you planning on looking around some or should we bring the chairs out for you now?"

"I did promise Chance some browsing before we leave, so we could go ahead and load the chairs to get them out of your way. But you mentioned a surprise..."

Clifford's face lights up again. "Yes, yes! Something I think you're going to love. I don't know if it's right for what you're working on, but once I saw it, I knew I had to show it to you." He's nearly bouncing up and down. "Follow me."

Lily chases after him without a second of hesitation, following him back to the edge of the stall. I tag along like a third wheel, hoping whatever Clifford has to show us isn't too far back in the bowels of this place. The stall is surprisingly deep and leads all the way to the wall of the building. There, pressed in with a few broken-down bookcases and the spindles from someone's long forgotten staircase, is something that makes Lily squeal. She claps her hands together and spins to look at Clifford like he's just given her a unicorn.

"You didn't!" she screeches. "Where did you find it?"

"One of those old houses down the road. They were just going to take it to the dump. I convinced them to let me have it. It was sitting out on the porch. Still works. It just needs a little love."

I stare at the hulking piece of metal in front of us. "Is it a stove?" I ask and both Lily and Clifford turn to glare at me.

"It's a Chambers," Lily tells me, like that clears anything up. She runs her hands over the top, tracing along the raised logo. "From the fifties."

"A '52, I think," Clifford says.

"1952." Lily sighs. "It is beautiful."

"Could go in that kitchen once it was restored. I found a guy who could do it for you and everything."

Lily lets out a breath and turns to me. "We'd have to talk about it first," she tells Clifford. "It's my dream stove, but it might not work for someone else."

Clifford's face falls. "I won't be able to hold it for you forever. If you want it, I'd need to know."

"I could buy it and keep it at the shop, maybe. Give me a little time to think about it." Lily worries her bottom lip between her teeth. "Or I could see if I could convince Chance." She gives my arm a squeeze and I nearly empty my wallet just like that. But she's right, a vintage stove might not be the best bet for a house I'm going to sell, even if it makes Lily's eyes shine.

"Alright, you just let me know. But be quick about it. I could get quite a bit for it if I move it out on the floor."

"I know," Lily says wistfully. "I appreciate you thinking of me first."

Clifford lowers his head and I swear I see him blushing again. "Anything to make you happy, dear."

And that's the theme of the day as we wander around the flea market. Lily sweet talks just about everyone to the point that her cut-throat bargaining starts to feel more like friendly conversation. I'm carrying around all sorts of crazy that she's planning on selling at the store in addition to receipts for several pieces of furniture I'm going to have to go back to get. Still, I find myself grinning like a fool the entire time, watching Lily bounce through the market, letting her load me down with junk. She's in her element and I'm not about to cut this trip short, even if I can hear the farm with all its repairs calling my name. One afternoon of having Lily brush up against me when she asks for my opinion more than makes up for the hours I'll have to put in later.

14

Chance

I'm sitting on the front porch when the car pulls into the drive. Lily's already left for the day and I'm not expecting anyone, so I'm more than a little surprised when it comes to a stop and my older brother Cooper unfolds himself from the driver's seat. Despite wearing a pair of ridiculous sunglasses, he still shades his eyes with one hand while he scans the front of the house. It takes him all of two seconds to see my tired ass parked on the steps, and then he's grinning that crazy grin of his that can only mean trouble.

"Little brother!" he yells. "The cavalry has arrived!"

Only Cooper would describe himself in such chivalrous terms. The cavalry he most certainly is not. He strides over to the porch, steals my beer, and parks his lazy butt next to mine.

"I was drinking that," I say without heat in my voice. I'm actually a little happy to see Cooper. I'm sure the feeling won't last, but for now it's nice to have him here, even if it is unexpected and unannounced.

"Well, now I'm drinking it." Cooper takes another swig

from the bottle. "That was a long drive." He stretches out across the top step, arms above his head.

"What the hell is on your face?" I peer into the reflective surface of Cooper's giant sunglasses.

"Oh, these?" Cooper slides them off and I finally get a good look at him. It's obvious we're brothers—same nose, same eyes—but Cooper's a little taller, his hair a little darker. He's a little wilder too and way more interested in pretending he's still seventeen. "I forgot my sunnies. Had to buy some at the Kwik Mart."

"You look like one of those TV housewives."

Cooper's unfazed by my attempt at a dig. "It takes a confident man to pull this look off. And I am confident in my masculinity."

I snort and steal back my beer. "If you say so." My phone vibrates next to me and I move to silence it before Cooper can take a look at the screen.

"California still calling?" he asks me.

"But I'm not answering."

We sit on the porch like this for a while, alternating sips of my now-warm beer, ignoring the fact that Cooper should be a million miles away right now and not hanging out on grandpa's porch. When he finally breaks the silence, it isn't to clear up any confusion.

"When's supper?" he asks. "I'm starving. Are we eating with Mae and Sadie? I've been looking forward to cornbread since I got in the car."

"I was planning on going over there, but you best give them a warning. They're liable to have a heart attack if you just show up."

"True. I'll go over now and give you time to finish whatever you were doing. After dinner you can show me all this work you've allegedly been doing out here." Cooper gives me a smirk and if he wasn't already ten steps away, I'd probably be trying to smack that look right off his face.

"Looking forward to it." I'm not. I don't need any more opinions around here and that's all Cooper's usually good for. He's almost certain to say something that rubs me the wrong way. After working for weeks, if he's an ass I won't be able to handle it well.

Cooper saunters off to the hero's welcome that probably awaits him next door, and I secretly hope there's no cornbread on the menu tonight.

"So did Chance show you the new kitchen?" Sadie asks as she piles more cornbread onto my brother's plate. "It's starting to look real nice."

Cooper barely slows down from shoving food in his mouth to manage a shake of his head.

"He hasn't come inside yet. He wanted to head straight over here to tell y'all hello first," I tell my aunt, knowing full well I'm giving Cooper undeserved points for politeness. He winks at me over our plates and crams another bite of macaroni and cheese into his maw. His table manners certainly haven't improved since the last time I saw him.

"I've been dreaming about this dinner for weeks now," Cooper says, nearly groaning in appreciation of my aunts' home cooking.

"How can you have been dreaming about it for weeks if you just decided to drive up here today?" Mae asks. She's unconvinced that Cooper just decided to pay us all a visit on a whim.

"Maybe those dreams are what made me decide to get in

the car this morning. The pull of this cornbread cannot be underestimated." He takes another bite to prove his point.

"Well, if you're going to be staying a while, I'm sure Chance could use an extra hand with the repairs. He and Lily can't be expected to do it all on their own."

Cooper's eyebrows lift and I cringe. I was hoping to be able to leave Lily out of things for a bit. Once Cooper finds out about Lily, he'll be merciless. I'll never hear the end of all the "help" he's sure Lily's been giving me since I came back to town. I don't want him running his mouth about things he knows nothing about, and I don't want him slowing down the progress I'm making next door. Or the progress I'm making with Lily.

"Who's this Lily?" Cooper asks, knowing full well that in this town there's only one Lily of consequence for me. Those summers I was a little less careful with what I told my brothers and frequently lived to regret it. He knows my soft spot for Lily Gentry and he's getting ready to poke it.

"You remember Lily Gentry, right?" Aunt Sadie asks. "Pretty little thing. Dark hair?"

Oh, Cooper remembers and he cuts his eyes over at me with just enough intrigue to let me know he does. But he pretends to think about it for a minute, mulling it over in his brain like he can't quite pull up a face to match that name.

"I think I might remember a Lily." Cooper puts more mac and cheese in his mouth. "Hmmm."

"Oh, I'm sure you'd remember Lily." Mae isn't helping things here.

"I'll have to let Chance, here, remind me which one she is. So many pretty girls here in Mint Springs, you know." Cooper grins at my aunts and they eat it up. He's always been the smooth one. He's the oldest and he always saw himself as the leader of our little band of brothers. When we were kids that was undoubtedly true, but I'll be damned if I'll let him tease me about a girl now, especially about my friendship—if you can call it that—with Lily.

"And how did Lily end up working with Chance, anyway? I thought he was a lone wolf over here." Cooper acts like I've had any choice in the matter, as if he's been begging me to let him come here to offer me a hand. I scowl over at him and he responds with more grinning.

"Oh, that story's not one you want to hear." Mae piles more food on our plates. "There was initially some fighting because Chance accused her of stealing our barn wood."

"Stealing our what?" Now she has Cooper's attention.

"The wood from our barn," I explain. "Someone came and liberated a wall."

"What do you mean 'liberated'?"

It's not until we're standing in front of it that Cooper understands what I'm saying.

We both stare for a minute, Cooper taking in the sheer audacity of the situation and me trying not to let my anger get the best of me again. The dishes are washed and the sun's near setting, the resulting shadows highlighting the gaping hole in our grandfather's barn.

"Holy shit, Chance. This is so much worse than I thought it would be." Cooper's solemn, and I can feel the agitation starting to roll off of him.

"I know. The whole thing's a shit show," I concede because there's no other way to put it.

"I'm sorry I left you here to handle all this. Dad made it seem like..." He doesn't have to tell me anything else. I already know a million ways he could finish that sentence. Dad made it seem like it was no big deal, like it wasn't important. Like it wasn't a priority.

"Wait till you see the house." If Cooper thinks the barn's

bad, he's going to lose his mind over the work that needs to be done to the house.

"It can't be worse than this." Cooper frowns when I don't answer. "It's worse than this?" He gestures with his arm, waving at the violated barn and its water-logged contents. "Shit. And you've been dealing with it all? Dad hasn't even come to see it?"

I shrug. Dad couldn't care less, and the only reason he hasn't just sold the whole thing off is the issue of Mae and Sadie. That, and wanting to get top dollar, which necessitates more than a shell of a barn and a rickety house.

We walk back to the house in silence and it isn't until we're back in our childhood room, the darkness enveloping us, that I hear Cooper clear his throat.

"I can come on the weekends," he tells me in the pitch black of the dilapidated bedroom. "That'll give you an extra pair of hands."

I don't say anything from my side of the room. I know Cooper can't afford to drive back and forth just to help out with the repairs here. I know he's volunteering to make a sacrifice that will eat into his bottom line. I'm about to tell him no, to let him off the hook when he opens his big mouth again.

"I mean if you *need* another pair of hands, what with Lily being here and all. You've probably got your hands full most of the time."

I can feel his smirk from all the way across the room and I find myself feeling more than a little satisfaction that I've given him the bed with the ancient mattress.

15

Lily

"I think this is a terrible idea, Hadley."

Hadley ignores me and continues fiddling with the radio. We're driving in her little sports car out to the Allen place despite the fact that Chance texted me this morning to tell me not to come. His brother's in town unexpectedly and they were going to spend the day working out at the barn. The pang of disappointment I'd felt had come as a surprise. After last week I should be pulling back more than I am. I should be happy that Chance had given me an excuse to get a little distance. Instead I'm pouting about missing our morning together.

I should have been more careful with the moping, though, because Hadley can sense the need for a cheer up from a mile away. She latched onto my little grain of disappointment and grew it into something much larger.

"You're pouting because you can't go to work? Because even if you love your job that's a little extreme, Lils."

"I like routine. And there's lots of work that needs doing over there." I tried not to make eye contact, but even that wouldn't deter Hadley. I know these things and yet I didn't fake an aneurysm or something to keep her from sniffing around.

"You like routine or you like something else?"

"What else would I like?" Stupid move, because Hadley thinks she knows what I should like and it's shirtless Chance Allen. Not that I've told her about that, or about the tiny little butterflies starting to form in my belly when I think about him.

"Um, Lily, I'm going to pretend you didn't say that." Hadley's got her hands on her hips, which means she means business. "Why'd he cancel?"

I pretended to be extremely interested in the edge of the tablecloth. "No reason. He's just got other things going on today, I guess."

"What aren't you telling me?"

I can never lie to Hadley even when the fib is for her own good. I knew what would happen the second she heard Cooper was in town. She'd move heaven and earth to get her ass over to wherever he was as quickly as possible. She'd get herself all dolled up and try her damnedest to get him back in her pocket. Hadley still thinks of him as the love of her life, so if he's in town you can bet she's going to be trying to get him back on the hook. Happily ever after, here we come.

I try to reason with her as we speed down the back roads out to the farm. "They aren't expecting us, Hads. We should at least shoot Chance a text or something. They might not even be home."

"You said they're working on the barn, right? They'll be there. And they'll be happy to take a break once they see we've brought snacks." In an effort to quite literally sweeten the deal, Hadley's loaded down the back seat of the car with multiple kinds of pastry and an entire blueberry pie. How we're going to eat that, I have no idea.

"I just want you to consider for a minute that this might not go the way you've been imagining." I try to temper my warning with as much love as possible. After all, Hadley's been sitting here in Mint Springs this whole time and not once has Cooper come looking for her. Chance acted like he didn't even recognize her and even if that was just a ploy to throw me off guard, he didn't give me the impression that Hadley comes up much in conversation with his brother.

"What do you mean? You act like Cooper won't be happy to see me." Hadley takes her eyes off the road long enough to give me the full force of her lower lip.

"I just want you to be prepared. They're working and they might be too busy to sit and chat, you know?"

But Hadley doesn't know because Hadley's not used to being ignored. She flips her glossy blonde ponytail over her shoulder and checks her make-up in the rearview mirror for the millionth time. When we pull to a stop in front of the old Allen barn, she turns to give me a full smile. "You'll see. They're going to be glad we stopped by."

I groan as I ease myself out of the passenger side. Hadley's gone all out—short shorts, sky high wedge sandals, and a tight T-shirt. She wobbles a little as she navigates the overgrown gravel path that leads to the barn. She's definitely not dressed for manual labor. The plastic bag of treats dangles from one wrist while the other arm holds the pie. As she picks her way to where the boys are working, she teeters dangerously side-to-side. If we get out of here without her breaking an ankle it will be a miracle.

Once we're closer I can see Chance up on one of the tall ladders they have leaned against the side of the weathered, gray barn. Cooper's on the ground, one hand holding onto the ladder and the other shielding his eyes as he yells up at his brother. At least I assume it's Cooper. It's been years since he's been around and, like the rest of us, I'm sure he's done some growing up.

Even from this distance I can see Chance's eyes narrow as he takes us in—Hadley in her ridiculous outfit with her arms loaded down with stuff and me in my usual baggy sweats and loose shirt. He's probably annoyed, especially since he texted specifically to tell me I wasn't needed here today. I've never seen Chance angry. Frustrated a few times, sure, but he's pretty good-natured from what I've witnessed. I'm worried that, for some reason, interrupting this barn repair session isn't going to be very easily forgiven.

Cooper turns to face us and Hadley lights up like a Christmas tree. Whatever it is about him that drives her crazy he's apparently still got it. He's obviously Chance's brother, the similarities are plain to see, but he's nowhere near as handsome if you ask me. He's got a baseball cap pulled low over his eyes, and his T-shirt's stretched tight over a chest that probably still looks impressive underneath all that cotton. Hadley's virtually humming with nervous energy and I half expect her to drop the food and launch herself into his arms. She manages to fight the urge, however, and gives him a little half wave with the hand holding the bag. It's one of her practiced and perfected moves, and poor Cooper doesn't stand a chance in this little ambush.

"Can you hold the goddamned ladder?" Chance yells from up above us. "I don't want to break my neck because you got distracted." His voice is harsher than I've heard it, even when we spent an entire afternoon pulling off those cabinet handles.

"Sorry," Cooper mutters. "Come on down. I've got it." He

grips both sides of the ladder in his hands. "I guess we'll be with you in a second, ladies."

"Take your time," Hadley tells him in one of those breathy, come hither voices. I roll my eyes so hard I'm afraid they might get stuck. She's dead set on giving him the whole routine, apparently, even if he's got his back to us.

Chance shimmies down the ladder and I brace myself for a confrontation, but he's nothing but cordial once his feet hit the ground. He takes off his work gloves and wipes his palms down the front of his jeans. He's filthy and it's barely ten a.m.

"Sorry to interrupt," Hadley starts before I even have the opportunity to say hello. "We thought you boys might want a snack."

Chance raises an eyebrow. "That looks like more than a snack you have there." He gestures toward the obvious overkill Hadley's balancing in her arms.

Hadley titters. It's more of a reaction than Chance is expecting and the corners of his mouth quirk up just a bit. He's opening his mouth to say something else when his brother decides to join this conversation. Cooper sticks his hand out, aiming it directly at me.

"I'm Cooper. Chance's big brother."

I brace myself for the contact but Chance rescues me, sliding up beside me and all but blocking Cooper's access. Chance doesn't touch me, but the gesture is the same. There's no way his brother's going to get any closer unless I tell him otherwise.

"She knows who you are, dumb ass," Chance says. It's not entirely playful and Cooper stiffens. "This is Lily. Remember her?"

Cooper stares at me for what feels like an eternity. I should be used to it by now. I'm not as easily recognizable as people think I should be. Still, the scrutiny has me shifting a little on the balls of my feet and I'm about to break out my inner mantra of *relax, relax* to keep myself from running back to the car.

"I wouldn't have recognized you." Cooper pulls the ball cap off his head and squeezes the bill. "Good to see you again." At least he's diplomatic. He moves like he's about to pull me into a hug, and again Chance puts himself in the middle.

"Nope. Hands off. She's not a hugger." He gives his brother a look that keeps Cooper from arguing and has him lowering his arms back down to his sides.

"You got one of those for me?" Hadley bats her eyelashes at Cooper, more than ready to take my place and probably already imagining herself pressed against his chest.

"Um, sure." Cooper hesitates and then does the unthinkable. "I'm Cooper."

Hadley's blue eyes go wide as saucers and her mouth falls open. She wordlessly blinks as Cooper's hand comes out for a shake. Hadley's shaking her head at the offered hand, not that she has a free hand of her own to offer back. She's got the first signs of an angry blush starting to creep up her neck when Chance moves to take the pie and the swinging plastic bag from her. Once she's got a free hand Hadley takes an index finger and jabs herself square in the chest with it.

"I'm Hadley," she says as if she's talking to a dementia patient. "Hadley Crawford."

Cooper has the good sense not to answer right away. We all watch as he flips through whatever filing system he's got for old girlfriends in his brain and comes up empty. He blinks and tries again but still comes up with nothing.

"Oh my God!" Hadley all but yells. "Are you kidding me, Cooper? Hadley! From the hay loft."

Cooper's face goes completely white as Chance doubles over. He's laughing so hard I'm not even sure he can hear Cooper's mumbled apologies. When Chance comes up for air, he jerks his head toward the house.

"Maybe we should leave these two alone for a bit and go get something to serve this pie." Chance is grinning as big as I've ever seen, maybe even bigger than after our river swim. "Sounds like they have some catching up to do."

We leave them standing by the barn, Hadley with arms folded and hip cocked and Cooper already a dead man. Chance continues to chuckle as we walk to the house, swinging the plastic bag between us.

"Can I carry some of that?" I'm already sure Chance isn't about to hand anything to me. "I'm sorry about showing up unannounced. Hadley insisted, and you can see how stubborn she can be."

"No problem." Chance gives me just enough of a glance to send a tiny shiver up my spine. "This is the kind of break I like to take. She's going to hand him his ass on a platter, isn't she?" There's no mistaking the glee in his question.

"Probably. She was convinced he'd remember her. Don't tell her I told you, but she's been obsessed with him since tenth grade. She's convinced he's the one that got away and she's made their whatever it was into some epic love story."

Chance winces. "And then he barely remembered. Ouch."

"Exactly. I warned her. I didn't mean to tell her he was here. You told me not to come by, I wasn't trying to complicate your day."

"You never complicate my day, Lily," Chance says just as we reach the front door. He pulls it open for me and leads me into the dismantled kitchen. "And to tell you the truth, I told you not to come today because I didn't want to share you. But it looks like I'm still getting you all to myself, so I say we cut this pie in half and eat it on the porch. I'm pretty sure Hadley won't mind. I think we can probably hear them fighting from here. It'll be the entertainment."

Chance washes his hands and then fishes around for forks and knives while I try to catch my breath. Chance Allen doesn't want to share me? I never complicate his day? I can't remember the last time anyone has been this sweet to me, let alone a man. Certainly not one who looks like he does. One who doesn't seem to have ulterior motives.

Chance takes the big butcher knife and cuts the entire pie straight down the middle once he gets the plastic cover off the top. "Blueberry?" he asks, incredulous. "Cooper's favorite."

"I told you. She's obsessed." I follow Chance out onto the porch where, sure enough, we can hear shouting from the vicinity of the barn.

Chance pulls two of the camp chairs he's put out there closer together and settles himself in one. He pats the seat of the other and hands me a fork once I put my behind in the mesh fabric. Then we take turns digging into the pie until our faces and fingers are sticky and there's barely any left.

"God, that was good." Chance groans. "Cooper's gonna be sad to have missed that." He licks the back of his fork.

I drop mine into the empty metal pie tin. "I don't think I can eat another bite."

"Good thing." Chance puts his fork in with mine. "There isn't much left. Two bites for Cooper." He gives me a wink as he licks the last of the filling off his fingers. "We just ate a whole pie."

I lean back and try to savor the feeling of sitting here in the sunshine, my stomach overly full with sugar and pastry. Chance stretches his legs out in front of him and pats his belly. I don't think either one of us will be moving much in the next few minutes. We don't say anything for a little while and I'm surprised by how easy it is, not awkward at all, to be sitting here with him in absolute silence. Well, almost silence since we can still hear Hadley yelling from down by the barn.

"Now would be a good time for a river nap." Chance stretches and yawns.

"A river *nap*? What the hell is that?" I'm pretty sure that isn't a thing.

"It's where you go with one of my grandma's quilts and take a nap in one of those shady spots by the river. It's at least ten degrees cooler down there and that, plus the sound of the water, makes for the best naps ever. Well, that and a belly full of pie." He smiles over at me and I can almost picture myself saying yes to this plan, letting him grab a blanket, and jumping in the passenger seat of his truck. Almost.

"I think you're making that up," I say, just a hint of teasing in my voice. "And I don't think our friendship has really gotten to the napping stage quite yet."

"Too bad." Chance's smile never leaves his face. "I'm a pretty proficient snuggler." The fact that I can't look him in the eye has him leaning in closer. "But I'm glad to hear you admit that we're friends."

"Yeah, we are, I guess." It comes out more like a question than a statement and Chance laughs outright at my hesitation.

"Looks like the party's over, friend."

Hadley's car whips up the driveway and slams into park.

She doesn't even bother getting out, just rolls down the window and motions for me to get in.

"Looks like I'm leaving," I say as Chance straightens up.

"You can stay if you want. I'll drive you back home. That nap offer still stands."

"No, I should go. I think Hadley's going to need me even more than I need a nap." I start the walk back to the car. "Tomorrow?"

"Sure. Cooper's only coming to help on the weekends so the coast should be clear. Just make sure Hadley knows to lay low on Saturdays and Sundays from now on." Chance is joking, but he has no idea the can of worms he's opening. Cooper here every weekend? Hadley will die.

"Bye, Hadley from the hay loft," Chance yells and she frowns back at him. She's definitely going to be in a mood all afternoon.

"Wish me luck," I yell over my shoulder, catching one last glimpse of Chance before I slide myself into Hadley's car. She's revving the engine and hightailing it out of there before I can even get my seatbelt buckled.

"You will not believe that ass!" she screeches as we barrel down the road toward home.

This should be a fun afternoon.

16

Chance

"More chips!"

"Seriously? You think more chips is going to be the answer to this?" I thrust another bag of potato chips at my brother, hitting him squarely in the chest.

"Well *these* chips won't fix anything," Cooper whines. "Don't we have corn chips? We should have gotten some of that cheese dip. Girls love that shit."

"Why do you care what girls like?" I give Cooper a sideways glance.

"I just want to be a good host," he sniffs, like I've actually hurt his feelings. "And I'd like to at least pretend I have the possibility of getting laid." Ah, there's the brother I know and sometimes love.

"Poker night isn't about getting laid. It's about playing cards."

"Then why did you even invite Lily and her friends? If this is about cards, we shouldn't even have those girls around. They're distracting." Cooper keeps rearranging the chairs around the card table he's set up in the living room. "And there's probably not enough space for everyone."

"You're the one who wanted to have people over. There's only so much I can do about the remodeling." I slide some of the boxes that are scattered on the floor closer to the kitchen. Things are a mess, but you can see there's a light at the end of the tunnel. The tile for the backsplash came yesterday and Lily and I'll be painting the cabinets soon.

I really should have put a stop to this little get together Cooper insisted on organizing. Although, *organize* is a strong word for what Cooper actually did. He's basically rounded up a few cousins and some other local idiots and made a stop at the liquor store. I'm not even sure he's checked to make sure we have a full deck of cards. Being out in the country makes Cooper go a little stir crazy and he's always been all about manufacturing his own fun. He's the reason my brothers and I have all had at least one broken bone and countless stitches. Cooper isn't a planner—he jumps first and hopes there's something there to break his fall. Putting together poker night to help him get through another quiet Saturday evening is one of his tamest ideas. I couldn't say no.

And it gave me another excuse to see Lily outside of work. Cooper's right that adding girls to poker night might be a terrible idea, but she's really the only person I'd want to spend Saturday night with. Not that I'd ever tell her that, or Cooper either. She's warming up to me, but my attempts at flirting haven't met with much success. Although, Lily never seems to spend time anywhere but at Southern Comforts and my house, which doesn't leave her much time to be dating. This little nugget of information is the thing that's been keeping any hope I might have of ever kissing Lily Gentry alive. Because at the end of the day, even if we're just friends, I can't stop thinking about how it would feel to be able to put my lips up against the pouty, pink ones Lily's got.

And that's an inconvenient thought to be having as my recently repaired doorbell rings and Cooper lets Lily in. She's wearing something other than her sweats for the first time in forever, and my eyes rake up and down her body before I can stop myself. She's got on a pair of jeans that actually fit and I can see the curve of her ass in them when she turns to greet my brother. I have to remind myself that I've technically seen her in her underwear—the flashes of her I saw when we were swimming have become my go-to fantasy these days—but even just the hint of her body makes the hair on the back of my neck stand up tonight. Her shirt's not fitted exactly, but again it's four sizes smaller than what I've gotten used to. Anyone who's here tonight will be able to see Lily's impressive rack. That thought has me considering locking the front door and turning off the porch light. I have all the guests I need here already, thank you very much.

Lily's brought lemonade and Hadley's brought a glare for Cooper. He has the good sense to at least pretend to be contrite. I have no idea what happened during their fight, but Cooper came back from the barn shell-shocked. Suffice it to say he's now terrified of Hadley, and the past few weekends he's been staying close to home to avoid her. Now he's got nowhere to run.

"Are we the first ones here?" Lily asks. "I thought you said eight."

"Eight?" Cooper glowers at me. "I told everybody nine."

I shrug. Lily told me she didn't want to stay late and I sure as hell didn't want to overwhelm her with all the guys my brother's invited. So did I "accidentally" tell her the wrong time? You bet I did.

"Can I get you ladies something to drink? We've got a million kinds of beer and Cooper's restocked the liquor cabinet."

Hadley's eyes light up. "Whiskey?" she asks, and Cooper tries to hide his smirk.

"You hoping for a whiskey sour or something? One of those blackberry lemonade things?" He's already rifling through the mixers he picked up at the Piggly Wiggly.

"I'm hoping for *whiskey*," Hadley tells him. "You've got ice, don't you?" And then she's pushing past him to pour herself a drink. Cooper follows along behind her like the helpless puppy he is, knocked off balance by Hadley and her assertive Southern charm.

That leaves me with Lily. She gives me a smile that knocks me off balance a little as well. I still can't get used to seeing the corners of her mouth easily tilt up after weeks and weeks of seeing her scowl. We stand there like nervous teenagers until I remember my manners and offer her a drink.

"I've got this." She lifts the plastic bottle of lemonade. "Designated driver. Hadley likes to drink when she's mad and I'm pretty sure she's going to be angry drinking tonight." Lily looks over at her friend, already verbally sparring with my brother as they try to pour drinks.

"Good planning, I guess." I have to give Lily credit; she is a planner.

"Thanks, though," she says and then gives me a little bump with her hip. It's the most innocent kind of contact, more friendly than anything, but she shocks me both literally and figuratively, the little jolt of electricity I get from her touch surprising me only slightly more than the touching itself. Lily seems surprised, too, and I'm hoping that's because I'm not the only one who got a little zing when we were hip to hip.

I clear my throat. "Do you want some ice for that, or a glass, maybe?" It's a literal jug of lemonade.

"No, thanks. I like to drink it out of the container."

I laugh, thinking that Lily's joking, but her face doesn't show any hint of amusement.

"What? This way I can keep everyone else out of my drink." Lily shrugs and looks away. That seems pretty OCD, but I'm learning not to question her quirks.

"Fine. Suit yourself. Do you mind if I get a drink?"

"Knock yourself out."

I wander to the bar Cooper's set up, always aware of Lily. I don't have to be looking at her to know where she is, which should probably freak me out a little bit. Instead, I find it calming, like hearing the reassurance of my own heartbeat. Strong and steady, that's Lily. Once I've got my drink in my hand I go straight back to her, every muscle in my body straining to be closer to her even if I know it's useless. Lily's not interested in me. Not in any way other than friendship. Not in more than the working relationship we've got going.

It isn't ten minutes later that Cooper's guests start spilling through the front door. I'm sure he's texted a few of them with an SOS. *Please save me from my scary former teenage hook up.* And I'm sure more than one of our cousins would be happy to take Hadley off his hands. Lily too, for that matter, so I stay close to her. Hopefully more protective than stalkerish, in her opinion, because that's the only opinion I care about.

Once the cards come out it's easier for Hadley and Lily to blend into the background. A few of their friends stop by and that makes it more of a party. Cooper makes the mistake of flirting with one of Hadley's high school friends—an error he won't soon repeat after the tongue lashing he gets from more than one of the ladies. But that's the only drama as we deal hand after hand of poker, pouring drinks and trash talking like we're back ten years.

More than one of my cousins gives Lily a look when she slides in the seat next to me. They're local boys I haven't bothered to reach out to before Cooper decided to show up. No one mentions anything about my lack of contact or about the way I angle my chair toward Lily's, letting her look at the cards in my hand, but their faces tell me everything I need to know. They're curious, and once she leaves there are going to be questions.

"I think we're heading out," Lily eventually says, yawning more for effect than actual tiredness, I'd bet. Hadley doesn't look ready to leave and gives a little pout. It turns out she's kind of a shark when it comes to poker. If we'd been playing for money, Hadley'd be the one holding all our wallets. If we'd been playing strip poker like my brother suggested she'd be the only one with her pants on.

"Thank God!" one of my cousins yells. "Take your girl here so the rest of us can win a hand." He winks at Lily.

Hadley gives him a playful smack on the arm. "Even if I'm not here it won't be you winning, Travis."

Travis rubs the spot where Hadley hit him, the look in his eye more mischief than anger. All my cousins have been giving Lily and Hadley a wide berth tonight, so when Travis jumps up and throws Hadley over his shoulder it takes a beat to register what's happening. One second she's standing on her own two feet and the next she's hoisted in the air. The screech Hadley lets out has Cooper knocking his chair over, grabbing at her waist until she's off Travis' back and wobbling back and forth again, the soles of her super high heels firmly on the ground. She's ruffled and furious, nostrils flaring and hair sticking out in every direction.

"What the hell was that?" Cooper demands.

"Just playing around. Calm down," Travis pants. Picking Hadley up and then being forced to put her down has him winded.

"Are you alright?" Cooper's looking Hadley over like she's been in a car accident. He keeps putting his hands out like he might touch her and then pulling them back like she might burn him. The look he gives Travis is one of pure murder. Only Hadley's nod has him turning away from our cousin instead of punching him in the face.

"I'm fine," Hadley says but she's not paying attention to Cooper now. She's looking directly at Lily who's most certainly *not* fine. She's white as a sheet and looks like she's seconds away from throwing up all over the hardwood floor we just recently decided to refinish. "I'm fine," Hadley says again with more conviction. "Let's go."

When Lily doesn't move, Hadley gives me a pleading look. Wordlessly, I reach for Lily and slide my arm around her shoulders. She looks at me like she's not quite sure what's happening, but she doesn't flinch, doesn't recoil the way she used to. I give the top of her arm a squeeze and she comes back into herself, blinking.

"Why don't I walk you ladies out, now that Hadley's back on the ground."

Lily gives me a nod and the smallest *okay* and I'm putting my hand on the small of her back and leading her toward the door. Hadley follows behind saying their good-byes until we're all outside and our feet are crunching through the gravel to Lily's car.

"What an ass!" Hadley shouts once we're far enough away from the house. "Do me a favor and make sure Travis doesn't ever win a hand tonight. Not one." Hadley shakes a finger at me and then goes to work smoothing her hair. "Thanks for walking us out. I've got it from here."

"It's no trouble." I mean it. I've still got one hand touching Lily as I open the car door and tuck her inside. "Are you okay to drive?"

"I'm okay now," Lily says, finally finding her voice. "I think I just got startled, that's all." She's embarrassed, her eyes shifting around, looking anywhere but at me.

"I shouldn't have screamed like that," Hadley tells her. "Sorry. I overreacted a bit. He didn't hurt me." She's reassuring Lily and buckling her seatbelt. "Thanks for the invite, Chance. Kick your brother for me."

"Right after I kick Travis." I'm only half joking. "See you tomorrow, Lily?"

She nods. "Afternoon, right?"

I nod back and remind myself not to lean in the open window and kiss her. Instead, I pat her head like she's a puppy, and Hadley rolls her eyes.

"Drive safe, okay?"

"Okay." Lily puts the car in drive and eases out of the driveway. I stand there watching until their tail lights disappear around the first curve.

I'm debating texting Lily to make sure she lets me know she's home as I push my way through the front door and back to the loud laughter of the poker game. My brother's scowling in his chair, obviously losing again, and my cousins are getting rowdier by the minute. Alcohol and my cousins almost always leads to bad decisions. It's the peanut butter and jelly of my teenage years, and I can't imagine one without the other. Now they're all a couple of drinks in which means the night's still young.

"What's the deal with you and Lily?" Travis asks, losing interest in his cards. "You fucking her or something?"

The blood in my veins goes cold. "Excuse me?"

"I'll take that as a yes." Travis gives the nearest cousin a shove. "Told you she'd eventually get back on the horse. She was just waiting for an out-of-towner. It's like summers all over again."

"We're working together. She's helping me with the house," I explain like that will make any difference to any of the guys around this table.

"I'm sure that's not all she's helping you with." Travis snickers. "It's alright. Nobody here's got dibs or nothing. You just have to be careful with Lily, that's all."

"What are you talking about?" Cooper asks.

"You know, the stuff that happened with the frat guys." Travis says it like it's common knowledge and Cooper and I exchange a look.

"What stuff?" Already, the uneasiness in my stomach grows. This is a story I know I don't want to hear, but I can't keep myself from asking.

"I don't know all of it, but she accused some of Riley's fraternity brothers of a bunch of stuff. You'd have to ask him for the details. She had to leave school because of it." Travis shifts his cards around in his hand, his face smug. His brother Riley's not here to flesh out the details, not that I'd want him to. He and Lily used to be thick as thieves in the summertime, but now he's off in South Carolina or somewhere and Lily hasn't mentioned him once.

"Just you gotta be sure that after she opens her legs she doesn't open her mouth." Travis looks ready to high five anyone who'll offer him a raised hand. "And you with Hadley." He points to Cooper. "Wouldn't have thought you'd come running straight back to that."

I can see Cooper's hands flex under the table and realize that my hands have been doing the same thing. If Travis keeps talking I'm likely to put my fist where his mouth is and Cooper's likely to let me. Hell, Cooper's likely to hit him *before* I get an opportunity.

"I think it's time to call it a night." I rise and shove my chair out behind me. "Card game's over."

"What? Because I told you something you didn't want to hear about your girlfriend? Lily's no angel, Chance. It's no secret." Travis keeps his butt planted in the chair and I resist the overwhelming urge to drag him out of it and throw him down the front steps.

"You keep her name out of your mouth. You hear me?" I'm only adding fuel to the fire, but I can't stop myself. "You don't talk about her, don't look at her, don't even think about her."

By now the room's gone quiet, everyone looking from me to Travis and back again. Cooper slides his chair back and starts picking up the bottles and cans that litter the floor.

"You heard him. Time to go." Cooper moves closer to where Travis is still stubbornly sitting. He may be our cousin, but that won't stop us from getting physical if need be. Cooper picks up a bottle and lets it swing dangerously close to Travis' face. "And don't touch Hadley again."

"We were just horsing around," Travis protests, but he's lost some of his bravado.

"Well, she didn't like it, Trav. Don't do it again. I don't care if she's fucking begging you to throw her over your shoulder, if you mess with her again..." Cooper lets the rest of that threat go unspoken.

"Thought you didn't even remember her," Travis says as he grabs his keys and ball cap from the table.

"Why don't you let me worry about that?" Cooper

motions toward the front door with the bottle. "Have a good night."

There's general grumbling as everyone makes their way to the door. I have a feeling there won't be many takers if we decide to entertain again. Not that we will. Not after tonight. I feel like there's a fifty-pound weight on my chest even after Cooper slams the front door shut and turns off the porch light, leaving our guests in darkness. I hear a bottle smash and know that even though I'm going to be pissed tomorrow cleaning up the glass, at least we all avoided a trip to the emergency room or the police station.

"What hell was that?" Cooper asks. "You know anything about any of that?"

I shake my head. The pebble of a story Travis just spilled rattles around in my brain.

"Well, it doesn't sound good."

"No, it sounds fucked up. Lily's never said anything about any of that to me." And why would she?

"You gonna ask her about it?" Cooper reaches into the fridge and grabs out two more bottles. I wave him away when he tries to hand one to me. I think I'm going to need something much, much stronger than beer as I mull this over.

"I can't ask her about that. It's some stupid rumor. Travis is trying to start shit." I grab the bottle of whiskey Hadley's left conveniently on the table and fish around for two glasses. I end up with two jelly jars and consider that good enough. "What would I even say?"

Cooper considers this while I pour us two extremely large glasses of booze. "You could ask Riley," he suggests before taking a big gulp of the amber liquid in his glass. "But you might not like what he tells you."

"Riley's not even fucking here," I protest. There's no way

I'm calling up my cousin to ask him about something that already has my jaw setting tight. "And it sounds like something I *know* I'm not going to like."

Cooper finishes his glass and pours us both another. "Then you gotta wait for her to tell you, or be okay without knowing. But Travis isn't going to stop bringing it up."

"Then I'll stop talking to Travis." I let the whiskey burn its way down to my stomach.

"Good luck with that."

"What? Just because he's technically family doesn't mean I have to be his friend." I can avoid Travis the same way I have been. We hardly ever see my mother's side of the family and I'm fine to keep it that way. Cooper's always been the one to reach out to them. I can keep to myself.

"Mint Springs is too small for you to avoid them forever." Cooper's right about that, but he's forgotten one important thing.

"I'm not planning on being here forever."

Cooper laughs. "Like you're gonna be able to walk away from this farm. That'll be the day." He finishes his drink and pours another. "I'm not drunk enough yet to believe a lie like that, Chance."

He has a point. Leaving Mint Springs means leaving the farm, letting someone else live in this house, saying goodbye. It means leaving Lily, something that suddenly seems like the hardest part in all of this.

I down my whiskey in one gulp and motion for Cooper to fill my glass again.

"Here's to you getting your head out of your ass." Cooper raises his jar to clink with the edge of mine.

"Same to you."

17

Lily

"All right, young lady, you've got some explaining to do."
Hadley leans farther over me and I know I'm stuck here. Not
that I could really run from her. She's got her fingers in my
hair and I'm covered in shampoo.

"I thought this part was supposed to be *relaxing*, Hads," I
offer, even though I know I'm only delaying the inevitable.
My head's dangling over the sink as Hadley washes my hair
but she prefers to use this time with me to interrogate rather
than invigorate. I'm not going to leave today's haircut feeling
anything less than wrung out.

"Don't try to deflect. You'll get your scalp massage when
you tell me what's going on with you and Chance."

I close my eyes and release a sigh. What's going on with
me and Chance? I have no idea. How can I explain to
Hadley the way he's become someone I simultaneously
dread seeing and can't wait until I'm with again? How can I
tell someone else about the conflicting feelings bouncing
around in my belly when I can't even make sense of them?

"We're friends, I guess," I tell her and her fingers stop

moving.

"Friends?" Hadley asks and when I open my eyes, she's staring right at me. "Lily, I saw you the other night. You two are more than friends." She turns on the sprayer and rinses the soap from my hairline. "You let him touch you. More than once. And not in that oops, so sorry, that was an accident, way."

I snap my eyes shut. Thinking about Chance touching me has the tiniest smile threatening to break out on my lips. There's no smiling about Chance Allen in front of Hadley—not yet. If ever there was a time to go to my happy place this would be it.

"He touched you, Lily, and you were okay with it. That's big news. Great news, if you ask me." Hadley's voice has gone soft and I keep my eyes closed so I won't have to see the inevitable look of pity she's going to have in hers.

She cuts off the sprayer and pulls the excess water from my hair. I can hear the familiar sounds of Hadley reaching for additional bottles and squirting conditioner into her hand. When she touches me again it's with the familiarity of someone who's done this countless times. Hadley's been cutting my hair since before I ever should have let her. She's a professional now with her own chair at her family's salon. When her grandmother started Hot House Flowers years ago, I'm sure she had no idea it would end up being a family business. Hadley works beside her sister most days and their mother sees her own clients at one of the stations across the room. There are other girls working here now, but when the doors first opened it was literally an extra room in Hadley's determined grandmother's house. Now that house is an actual salon. Hadley's grandmother lives in another house out back so she's never far from the action. Even at eighty years old she still drops by most days to give unsolicited advice and hairstyle critiques. It's all very Steel Magnolias around here.

"I don't know, Hadley," I confess. "It's confusing. Chance is..." I sigh again. "He's patient."

"Oh nooooo. *And* hot."

I scowl and she gives my hair an unnecessary tug.

"You can't deny he's easy on the eyes, Lily. Not that that has anything to do with your *friendship*."

"We really are friends," I protest, leaving out the part about how I can't stop thinking about Chance's naked chest every five seconds.

"Um hum." Hadley works the conditioner through my hair. "So, there's nothing else there at all? I've seen the way he looks at you, Lily. That's not the way a man looks at someone he thinks is just his friend."

I look at Hadley with wide eyes. I've been entertaining some pretty lustful thoughts about Chance, but I'm pretty sure he hasn't been having those same thoughts about me. I've done my best to make sure no man thinks of me in those terms, protecting myself with my baggy clothes and an angry attitude so no one gets close enough to see past them. But with Chance I've relaxed that a little, trusting him at the river to get a glimpse of my body and trusting him enough at other times to see me without all my bravado. Even with the chinks in my armor I can't imagine that he sees me as more than a friend.

"Come on, Lily. You're going to deny you're attracted to him?" Hadley turns the sprayer back on, giving me five lucky seconds to gather my thoughts. Those feelings get all jumbled up inside me when I think about anything more happening with Chance. I can't imagine kissing him without my brain screaming to stop, reminding me that I'm not doing that anymore, can't do that anymore, and I won't be able to take the risk. By the time Hadley stops rinsing I'm surer than ever that I'm headed down a slippery slope.

She shuts off the water with a definitive click and begins to towel off my hair. "I'm waiting, and I haven't heard a denial yet, Lils."

"That's because I can't give you one. Yes, I'm attracted to him, but I haven't felt those feelings since before..." I give that the five second pause it deserves knowing Hadley will understand and won't make me fill in those blanks. "I'm not sure what to do."

Hadley sits me up and wraps the towel around my head like a turban. She's gentle with me and I can see the wheels turning as she mulls my predicament over.

"He doesn't know, does he?" she finally asks and I shake my head.

"He's figured out the touching thing and he knows I get spooked easily. He's made a few cracks about the sweatpants but unless someone else has told him, he doesn't know why. I'm not exactly running around town telling everyone all my business."

"Would you tell him?"

"I don't know. If we were more than friends I'd have to. I haven't really been with anyone since it happened. I'm not sure how I'd react and that's not fair to Chance. This is prime therapy stuff right here."

Hadley manages to crack a smile, but I can see the way she's thinking it through, trying to come up with the best advice for this impossible situation.

"I guess you'll have to just take it slow," she finally says. "See if you can trust him."

"Sure, but that takes time, and I'm not sure I can trust my instincts where that's concerned. They've failed me before." I think back to some of my oldest friendships.

Hadley's never let me down but I've misjudged before, and that's a big part of how I got here. Trusting people to look out for me who only had their own interests in mind. Trusting people to protect me who were only interested in protecting themselves.

We finish the rest of the haircut in silence. Hadley knows what I want and we don't need to talk about it. Even more importantly, she understands I don't need to talk about the rest of it, that we don't need to fill the silence with small talk. She works with the scissors to give my hair a trim and then pulls out the blow dryer to finish. Once my hair's in shiny waves, she fluffs the edges a bit and I see the old me staring back in the mirror.

"You could leave it down for a bit. Not pull it back right away," Hadley says. "I hate for all this work to be wasted on one of your ponytails."

I think about it. The ponytail is one of my major lines of defense. No sexy hair for Lily Gentry. No flowing waves for anyone to run their fingers through or imagine spread over a pillow.

"Where are you going now? To the store?" Hadley smoothes an errant strand and pulls out the hairspray. "I could give it just a little spritz and it would stay all day even with this humidity."

"I'm going to the farm." My eyes meet hers in the mirror.

"Oh." Hadley holds the hairspray up like its own question.

"Go ahead," I tell her, giving her permission to cover my head in aerosol.

Hadley shields my eyes with her hand and sprays away.

"Sorry, I overdid it a bit there." Hadley laughs. "I didn't mean to make you so flammable."

And here I am getting ready to play with fire.

18

Chance

There's no way I can concentrate on painting.

From the moment Lily walked in today all I've been able to think about is that hair, the way it keeps sliding over her shoulders and down along her back. Even swimming, she kept it up tight and I haven't seen any deviation from that style since I've come back into town. Now she's suddenly got these loose waves going on and with every swish of that chestnut brown hair I'm going crazier and crazier.

It doesn't help that I've been thinking about nothing but Lily since Saturday's poker night debacle. Long after the place cleared out Cooper and I sat up, just drinking. He knows better than to say much when I'm thinking something through and all I could manage to do was replay what Travis had said. All I know for sure is whatever Travis thinks he's talking about isn't good. The more Cooper and I drank the surer I became of that fact, and even more certain that I wouldn't be asking Lily about any of it today. Unfortunately, the more Cooper refilled my glass the more positive I became that this thing with Lily is getting more complicated and impossible to ignore.

And if I thought Lily was impossible to ignore before, looking at her now isn't helping matters. She's been kneeling on the ground for an eternity, mixing the paints together for us to start working on the kitchen cabinets. With any luck we'll be able to finish most of it today and then start putting them back together by the end of the week. I'm no expert on this part, but Lily knows her stuff, so I've been letting her boss me around—something I like much, much more than I should.

"I wish we could take them off the walls," Lily says. "Then we could use a sprayer instead of having to do all this brush work. Why can't we do that again?"

"Uh huh." I'm barely listening and when she turns those brown eyes up at me in confusion, I know I've mangled my end of this conversation. I shake some of the lingering fog out of my brain and try again. "Sorry, what was the question?"

"Did you get any sleep last night?" Lily laughs. "I'm guessing y'all went pretty late from the bags you've got going on under your eyes."

I can't tell her me looking like shit has less to do with alcohol and late-night discussions with my brother and more to do with staring at the ceiling thinking of every time I've made her smile. Even now that laugh has me thinking making an ass of myself is probably worth it.

"Cooper and I were up pretty late." I slide my hand to the back of my head and notice her eyes shift to my bicep before cutting back to the paint. My brother's already a few hours into his drive home and now it's just me and Lily's distracting hair here at the farm. As she leans forward to pour more paint into the big orange bucket she's using, I imagine moving toward her and sliding my palms through the curtain of shiny hair that's covering her face. I can almost feel the silkiness of those strands between my fingers, picture myself letting my hand drift lower to cup her chin, my thumb skimming her throat.

Lily keeps working, unaware of the fact that just the absence of a ponytail is affecting me more than any pornographic image ever has. I've got to get myself back on track before it becomes painfully obvious to us both that I'm thinking about more than these cabinets.

"I asked why we couldn't take the cabinets off the wall," Lily reminds me.

"Oh, yeah." I do have a good reason for this which has nothing at all to do with looking at Lily. "We can't take them down without this wood splintering. But you said we could paint them here, right?"

"It's just more work. The sprayer's faster."

I don't want anything that means less time with Lily. I secretly thank my grandfather for choosing wood that requires more time in this kitchen.

"It's more uniform, too, although I kind of like a more rustic look. It works in here, you know?"

I don't answer her, fully absorbed in the way her neck's exposed as she leans over. I've seen her neck every day for weeks now. Having her hair up has meant that's something always on display, but now, as it peeks out from between waves of dark hair, it's like I'm seeing something private, something illicit.

I cough and rub my neck again. "We should get more photos for the before part." I busy myself with my phone, snapping away in an effort to get back to thinking of Lily as a friend instead of one of those girls in the posters at the auto parts store.

"Have you been taking those all along?" Lily asks from behind me.

"Yeah, I wanted to be able to see the progress. Without the pictures I kind of forget where we started." It does look different in here, but it's more than just the house that's changing. "We should actually record some of this."

"You want to make a video of us painting? What for? You've heard about how interesting it is to watch paint dry, right?" Lily jokes and I'm relieved that things are still so easy after poker night. Of course, she has no idea what happened after she and Hadley left, has no idea that my cousin put any ideas in my head.

"We don't have to record all of it," I say. "Like, how about I just record you mixing the paint and you can talk me through the process."

"You want me to explain what I'm doing?"

"Sure. We can make one of those how-to videos and put it on the Internet." *And I can look at you without having to pretend I'm not.*

"You think people would watch that?" Lily seems unconvinced.

"You'd be surprised what people will watch on the Internet." That comes out wrong and I immediately regret the innuendo but Lily only smiles, doesn't even blush.

"Do *not* fill in the blanks, please. I don't need to know what you've been looking at on your laptop when I'm not here."

"Fine, but it's an interesting list…" I pull my phone back out and switch over to video. "Okay, so just explain what you're doing."

Lily tilts her face toward me and I'm glad for the screen between us. That way she can't see me blinking like an idiot at the way her face seems to sparkle. She's like looking at a full moon on a cloudless night and I hope she doesn't notice the sharp intake of breath that I try to pass off as technical difficulties. I jam my fingers against the phone, pretending to make adjustments as she licks her lips and gets organized.

"Ready?" she asks.

I've been recording for at least thirty seconds.

"Sure. Go ahead." I focus on her face, try to get her hands in the frame as they move back and forth between the cans of paint.

"Well, there wasn't a color that was exactly what we wanted so I'm trying to mix up a custom one. We were afraid that some of the other white paint we tried would be too yellow, right?" Lily talks to me like there's no camera there, like it's just the two of us. She's a natural and I start to relax as she tells me all about how she decides if a room needs a warm color or a cool color.

"And what about the painting process?" I ask, giving her more to talk about.

"Well, this paint is going to have to be put on with a brush or a roller since we can't take the cabinets down. But that shouldn't be a problem because this paint doesn't really show brush strokes like some other paint does."

"Tell me about that," I encourage and Lily's off and running with her explanation of different kinds of paint and how she chooses which one to use. In between her descriptions of matte and glossy finish and durability I watch her mouth on the tiny screen in front of me. Her tongue occasionally comes out to moisten her lower lip and every so often she gives me a shy little smile. I try to forget that we're recording this to supposedly share with the world, and instead pretend she's talking only to me.

"What else?" Lily asks and I snap back to reality.

"Um, we should probably get a photo of us together. For

our YouTube channel." I'm half joking, but when Lily stands up and brushes her hands off on her loose work pants, I decide not to back down.

She moves closer to me. "We need to make this quick; that paint won't wait forever."

I nod and swallow. She's close enough for me to smell the shampoo in that thick cloud of hair. It isn't the vanilla I'm used to—it's spicier—and has me taking deep breaths just to get more of that intoxicating scent. "Come here then." I extend my arm and she folds right into it like it's the most natural thing in the world. Lily fits snuggly up against my chest as I lift the phone up above us and angle it for the photo.

"You okay?" I ask, still aware that Lily's not big on touching. And this is closer than I'd ever have thought she'd let me get.

"I'm fine," she says. "Just take the picture, Chance."

I let my finger hit the red circle a few times, each time aware that if I leaned down I'd be able to put my lips on Lily's cheek. We're close enough that I've got my chin almost resting on the top of her head. I can feel her settle against me as we look at the phone. I glance down at her and find her looking back, both of us staring at each other. I keep my finger on the button, letting the shutter click away. With any other girl this would be the moment where I'd kiss her, but Lily isn't any other girl. So I don't lean down, don't press my lips to hers, don't let the phone drop to the floor so I can cradle her face in my hands. I just keep looking at her, memorizing the lines of her jaw and the angle of her nose. When the corners of her mouth tilt up I return the smile and keep her safe against me, something I know she's not going to let me do for long, no matter how much I want to keep her here.

19

Lily

You're an Internet star? How am I just now hearing about this?!

Hadley's text blinks up at me, interrupting my work flow. I'm doing my best to get this piece finished before I have to drive over to the farm to help Chance put the cabinets back together. If I power through, I can finish the painting and come back tonight to put on a coat of furniture wax. If I don't get distracted, that is. And Hadley's text is a little distracting.

I lean the brush I've been using on the edge of the can and make sure my hands aren't coated in paint. Putting a turquoise handprint on my phone wouldn't be a great addition to my day although it wouldn't be the first time it's happened. I've spent a fair amount of money on new cases since I started working on furniture.

What are you talking about? I type out and quickly hit send.

It'll be some stupid meme that reminds her of me or some inside joke that I've long forgotten. I shouldn't even respond to her if I want to get this work done, but Hadley tends to keep texting until I answer her, no matter how many times I tell her to quit. She doesn't like to be ignored and nothing short of an avalanche, or an accidental run-in with Bradley Cooper, would be a good enough excuse for me to pretend not to see her message.

This. Hadley replies and sends me a link. I let my finger hover over it for a second before I open it, giving myself time to get ready for dancing cats.

But it isn't some funny animal video or a toddler singing *The Star Spangled Banner.* It's a video of me looking at the camera like I'm crazy in love with it and talking about paint.

What the hell?

I click on the link in the video's description and it redirects me to a website I've never seen before. A website that has Chance Allen written all over it. It's still under construction—a little banner at the top tells me so—but it's clearly about our renovations on the farmhouse. Or it will be once Chance gets around to finishing it.

Which he never will, because I'm going to kill him first.

I burst through the front door ready for a fight. Chance doesn't even move from his spot in the middle of the kitchen. He's standing, hands on hips, shirt conveniently missing, with no idea I've even come in. I guess I should have slammed the door if I'd wanted immediate attention but my manners kept me from doing any slamming. That, and the fact I'd hate to damage the old door no matter how angry I might be.

I stand for a minute, watching Chance tilt his head left and then right, considering whatever the hell he's considering. He slides one hand up to his jaw and the muscles in his back flex just enough to have me forgetting for a split second why I'm annoyed. The more work we do here the better he looks, heaving around all the heavy equipment and construction supplies has him adding more muscle to what was already a dangerously muscular body. No one would ever guess he used to spend all day behind a computer.

But his stupid computer is what's got me all rankled. He can't just put things on the Internet without asking my permission. I don't want to open myself up to scrutiny from a million random strangers, not that a million people would ever look at that website, but I don't want even ten people to think they can give me advice or comment on my body or voice. I know how quickly things can get out of hand when people are anonymous—the last thing I want is more attention.

I clear my throat and Chance turns to look at me, a hint of a smile already pulling at the corners of his mouth. If I look angry he must not notice, because he looks like he's having a great day and I'm only making it better.

"You're here! I thought you were coming later." Chance motions for me to come closer. "I was planning on having all this worked out before you got here so I could surprise you."

I try to ignore his enthusiasm and keep my original goal in mind. I need to set him straight, not get sucked into whatever he's been doing this morning.

"I need to talk to you first."

The enthusiasm falls a bit from his face. "Sure. What's up?"

"Can you put on a shirt?"

"A shirt?" Chance looks down and we both end up looking at his bare chest for a few beats longer than necessary. When he straightens up, I'm distracted by the light brown trail of hair running from his belly button down to the waistband of his jeans. When I look up he's staring right at me, a mix of interest and confusion on his face.

"Yes, please." I'm talking about his shirt, but the rest of my body reacts like I've requested something else entirely.

Chance moves back to the kitchen and rummages around for his missing T-shirt. This is becoming a theme for this kitchen. Chance half-naked and me with my eyes bugging out of my head. I ease myself onto one of the kitchen chairs and wait for him to saunter back to the table.

"Why do I feel like I've been called into the principal's office?" he asks, a note of self-consciousness in his voice. I imagine Chance was used to frequent meetings with his elementary school principal, if his summer antics with his brothers are any indication. I was no stranger to the inside of the principal's office, but I've never been in the reverse position. I shift in my chair. All the anger I was counting on for this confrontation has left me, but I still need to convince Chance to take down the video and the blog before they cause me any further headache.

"Hadley sent me a link this morning to the video." I just put it out there. No need to get him to confess to anything. I've seen the video and so has Hadley, but Chance's face clouds over.

"What video?"

"The one you took of me the other day. The painting one with the cabinets."

Chance thinks for a minute, tilting his head.

"The one you said was for our YouTube channel? I thought you were joking but then I saw it online today. And I saw the website. Well, what there is of it, anyway."

Chance scratches his head and leans back in his chair.

"Hold on a second," he says before jumping up and walking down the hall. I stew while I wait. Is he actually going to pretend he has no idea what I'm talking about? My irritation starts to rise again.

When he comes back into the kitchen he's holding his laptop, the screen already tilted open. He slides it onto the weathered table and starts typing. I watch as the video of my face fills the screen and Chance's brow furrows. I can hardly stand to listen as my voice fills the room, droning on and on about paint.

"Shit," Chance whispers and then turns to me. "I'm sorry. This isn't supposed to be visible yet."

"What do you mean 'yet'?" I'm still distracted by my soliloquy going on in the background.

"I mean before I asked you for permission. This isn't supposed to be up for real." Chance seems genuinely upset as he goes to work typing furiously and cursing under his breath. "I was originally joking about the channel and stuff, but I actually think it's a great idea. And then when I was here last night with nothing else to do, I started fooling around with it. I would never have put this up without asking you first."

"It's okay," I hear myself say even though that's the exact opposite of how I was feeling two minutes ago.

"It does have two thousand views," Chance says. "And fifty comments."

"Already? How did people even find it?" My heart starts to beat faster. I'm not hiding out or anything here in Mint Springs, but it's a small town where almost everyone already knows my business, well, most of it. Fifty comments? From strangers? I'm definitely not ready for that.

"They're probably searching for painting tips and stuff like that. I'm pretty good at optimizing the number of hits I can get from a regular search." Chance looks up from the screen and notices my horror-struck face. "Sorry. The comments are all great, though. People want to know more about the paint you're using. This one's Hadley, and this guy wants to know if you'll marry him." Chance's nostrils flare as he points at that last comment.

"Let me see." I stretch my fingers out to grasp the edge of the screen and turn it toward me, relaxing a little as I scroll. He's right, there's not a mean comment in the bunch. Still, I'm not sure how comfortable I am with having strangers looking at me. Or people I know but would rather avoid.

"I'll take it down." Chance reaches to take the computer back. I keep my hands on the computer, preventing him from moving it.

"Wait," I hesitate. "Is this the kind of stuff you used to do for your old job?"

Chance sighs. "Not really, or I'd be better at not having things go live when I don't mean for them to." He gives me a little shrug. "I've done some work with search engines and I can put things like this together, but mainly I did programing. Things like that."

I have no idea what the difference is between putting together a website and programing. I prefer other kinds of work, more tangible things. Although this website feels pretty tangible to me right now.

"Would you like to have a website? About fixing up the house?" I ask, almost hoping Chance says no.

"Maybe. There are lots of other websites out there so I'm not thinking it would be some big money-making thing. But it would be interesting to document the work we're doing. Fun to look back on, maybe?" Chance gives me a questioning look. "And we could put in a few plugs for your store, maybe drum up some additional business for Southern Comforts and your furniture…"

This last part has me thinking. If I put Chance in charge of the technology part, but I have final say on what parts of me I'm willing to share, would it be worth the publicity to make a bit more money? Would it put me back on track to leave Mint Springs faster? I picture my Chicago apartment with its bare walls and three flights of stairs, and realize I don't feel the usual urgency to get back there. Would having this extra project mean more time with Chance? And why is that suddenly not a drawback but an overwhelming plus?

"If we did this, could I have control over the things you put online about me?"

"Of course, Lily. I would never put anything up without asking you first. I'm so sorry this came out like this. You're a private person, I know that. You'd have the final say on anything about you. Photos, videos, you name it."

Chance's apologetic face is what actually convinces me. He's genuinely sorry—something I haven't seen on a man's face in years. I'd almost forgotten what that looked like.

"But if I change my mind at any time…"

"I'll take it down. Promise."

And, to my surprise, I believe him.

"Do you want to shake on it?" he asks.

"No, you've told me. I'm going to take you at your word."

We stare at each other for two beats and I swear I can feel his eyes boring a hole into mine. I get that little flutter in my belly and know I have to change the subject before those butterflies take over.

"What were you so excited about when I came in?"

Chance's smile lights up his face. "Come see." He stretches out his hand to me as he slides his chair back from the table. I surprise us both by letting my own hand come forward and settle into his. His palm is warm and callused and when his fingers close around mine I let the contented feeling wash over me instead of fighting it.

Chance gives my hand the slightest tug and I'm on my feet following him into the kitchen. "Wait until you see this." We round the edge of the new island we still have to paint and position. Behind it sits a large square shipping container.

"I was going to leave it on the porch and unpack it out there." Chance runs his free hand around the edge of the box. His other hand stays firmly attached to mine. "But I was afraid it would rain or something."

"What is it?" He's way too excited for this to be anything I'm going to enjoy. "There's not a stripper in this box, is there? An alligator?"

"Better," Chance tells me. "And now you're here to help me open it up." He lets go of my hand to pull his multitool from his back pocket and gets to work, prying the top off the box. There's layer upon layer of cardboard and bubble wrap that Chance has to keep pulling from the inside.

"Look." He pulls me toward the crate.

When I peer over the edge, I'm surprised to find a stove top. I take in the burners and grill surface.

"Is this what I think it is?" I'm a terrible cook but I know a thing or two about vintage stoves. The gleaming surface of this one has me swooning and we don't even have it completely unpacked.

"It's the Chambers. The one from the flea market." We're standing close enough that our hands keep brushing against each other. Tiny zings of pleasure race up my arm, and I'm not sure if it's from the surprise of the stove or the contact with Chance's skin. When he shifts to start disassembling the front of the crate, I notice the new space between us and consider sliding the two inches back over toward his arm.

"I had it restored."

It was on my wish list for the kitchen but we both agreed it was a terrible idea, especially if Chance's father decides to sell the house. We decided on a more practical stainless steel chef's range to match the rest of the appliances. And yet, here we are unpacking my dream stove from its protective packaging like it's Christmas morning.

"I thought we agreed the other stove was a better choice," I venture, almost hating to remind Chance this wasn't the decision we made weeks ago.

"I know, but you love this one," Chance says without looking up. "And if you love it, then it should be here." He pauses, still not looking at me. "I know what you're thinking."

Chance has no idea what I'm thinking. He's just bought something based solely on my wants, even though it might make things harder for him in the long run. I should be thinking about how impractical he is, about how he needs to think things through, about how we both know all this is temporary. But I'm not thinking any of those things. What I'm doing has absolutely nothing to do with thinking.

"I can swap it out if we have to sell the house. I can take it with me. Or you could take it. You could use it in your kitchen when you get settled," Chance keeps talking while my brain whirs inside my head. His hands work to free the shiny stove from its wrappings and I remind myself to breathe in and out.

"Ta da!" he announces and finally turns, the stove sparkling behind him.

I move toward him, my legs shaking. I almost feel drunk —lightheaded and dizzy—but I can't stop my feet from taking one step and then another until I'm close enough to see the stubble on Chance's chin, the faint drumming of his pulse on his throat. He looks down at me and I raise myself up on my toes, plant my palms on his chest, and press my lips to his.

20

Chance

I don't think I've ever been more surprised in my life. Not when I found out that brown cows don't make chocolate milk; not when Cooper told me babies don't really come from the stork; not even when I realized for the first time that my grandfather could make a mistake.

None of those things surprised me as much as finding myself pressed lip to lip with Lily Gentry.

One second I'm pulling plastic off the stove, trying my best to convince Lily that it wasn't a stupid decision, and the next she's got her hands on my chest and her warm mouth on mine. I'd like to think that if a woman kissed me out of the blue I'd be ready, that I'd pull her closer to me and enjoy myself. That's not even close to what I do when met with the softness of Lily's mouth and the heat of her palms burning holes through my T-shirt.

Lily's never given me even the slightest hint that she's got any interest in me. We're friends now, but nothing thus far has made me think she *want*s me to kiss her. I tease her, sure, but if she wanted to take me up on any of my innuendo she could have said so. I've given her plenty of openings. But she's done little more than blush, never even given me a sideways glance. So instead of responding to the closeness of her chest and the slight cherry taste of her lip gloss, I just stand there like an idiot, hands fisted at my sides.

It takes Lily two beats for her eyes to fly open, her feet to propel her backward, and her hands to come up to her face. She covers her mouth and we stare at each other for what feels like an eternity.

"Oh my God," she blurts out before I can say anything. "I'm so sorry. I shouldn't have..." Her face flames and she starts that stuttering that renders me even more stupid. Flustered Lily does something to me, but right now I'm just as flustered as she is.

"It's okay," I start just as she tries to apologize again.

"I'm—"

"No, I should —"

We babble over each other's words until an uneasy silence settles over the kitchen.

"I never should have done that. I don't know what possessed me to do that." Lily's eyes are wide, her voice shaky. "I..."

"You don't need to apologize. I had the same reaction to the stove when I saw it. I probably would've kissed the delivery guy if I'd known what a good job they did on the refinishing." I try to joke but Lily doesn't crack a smile. Instead of convincing her that I'm glad she kissed me, I'm acting like that's the furthest thing from my mind.

"We should get to work." Lily moves past me to the spot where she's been reattaching all the pulls on the cabinet doors. I stand where she left me, not sure if I'm going to be able to concentrate on work now that I know what she feels like up against my body.

"If that's what you want," I say, knowing full well that I may have just blown my one and only opportunity to move from the sort-of friendship we have now to something more. I'm kicking myself for not seizing the moment, for not kissing her back.

Lily eyes me suspiciously. "Isn't that what you want?"

"I think I want the chance to try that again."

"To try what again?" Lily asks and I can see the way she's getting ready to run.

"Kissing you."

"You don't have to do that. It's obvious that you didn't want to the first time." Lily's eyes rake the floor.

My head snaps back and I give it an incredulous shake. Didn't want to? Nothing could be further from the truth. Time to put that notion to rest once and for all. *Now or never, Chance.*

"Believe me, I want to. I've wanted to since I was sixteen years old so you have to at least give me a shot at doing it right."

Lily's brow furrows and her lips purse, but she doesn't tell me no, doesn't try to stop me when I close the distance between us. When I'm close enough to touch her again, I can see her pupils dilating, her hands shaking just enough to remind me to take it slower for her.

"Unless you tell me otherwise, Lily, I fully intend to kiss you now." I give her time to warn me off, time to make her decision.

Lily's nod is so slight I almost miss it, but it's not enough.

"I'm going to need more than that to let me know you're on board with this." Either it's a hell yes or it's a no. Especially when it comes to Lily.

"Yes," she finally says, taking a deep breath and squaring her shoulders in a way that makes my heart ache a little. If I didn't want to kiss her before, I definitely do now. "Yes, I want you to kiss me."

I bring my face close to hers and fasten my palms on either side of her face. Her breathing's ragged and I can feel her pulse thrumming in a beat that matches mine. Her eyes flutter shut, leaving her dark lashes resting against the pale skin of her cheeks. I let my thumbs glide over her jawline before I tilt her face up toward me and slowly lower my lips to hers.

From the first brush of my mouth on hers, I feel the contact down to my toes. I hold her like she's made of glass because even with the electricity that runs through every inch of me, I know Lily Gentry's breakable. I know without her telling me that someone's broken her before and it's up to me to be careful of those cracks, to be mindful of her scars. I take it slow, savoring her like this is the only time I'll be able to wrap her in my arms. I let her tell me when she wants more, test my patience by not mauling her the way my body's begging me to. When she parts her lips and relaxes into my touch, I slide one hand to the nape of her neck and let my tongue get tangled up with hers. My other hand aches to slide south, to make its way down Lily's back and haul her up against me, but I fight the urge and keep it where it is, cupping her cheek. I kiss her until I can barely breathe, knowing if Lily'd let me, I'd spend the rest of the day right here memorizing the way she tastes and the little sounds she makes.

When I reluctantly break contact, Lily's blinking and breathless.

"Now we can get back to work." I put one last kiss on the tip of her nose before I start pulling the stove against the wall.

21

Lily

I'm shaking as I stand in front of the mirror. I smooth the front of my dress just to give my hands something to do. If I'm this nervous now, how in the hell am I going to manage once I get over to the farmhouse and have to try to make conversation? I've gone around and around in my head trying to imagine what tonight will be like, but I always come up with nothing but blank space where my imagination should kick in.

Who am I kidding? There's not so much blank space as a replay of Chance kissing me. I have that on repeat. Over and over I feel his hands on my cheeks and the soft way he explored my mouth. I hadn't expected him to be so gentle and even that had made my knees buckle. And then we'd gone back to work like nothing had happened. Well, not exactly like nothing had happened, because my lips continued to tingle all the way to lunchtime and I couldn't keep from looking over at Chance any time I thought he wasn't looking at me. More often than not, though, when I turned my eyes toward him he was staring right back. It made putting the cabinet fronts back on more difficult than necessary. That kind of work is a team effort and as Chance held the doors upright and I screwed the hinges back in place neither one of us could seem to stay focused.

Which should have made me automatically say no when Chance invited me to dinner to break in the new kitchen.

"We have to test it out, right?" he asked while I stood there trying to remember to put air in my lungs.

"You want to use it?" I asked like an idiot. Of course he did. That was what he had just said.

"I'm not much of a cook, but we should make sure everything's hooked up correctly." Chance's face told me there was more to the invitation than just a need to check our work. The kitchen looked fabulous, the new appliances gleaming against the creamy white of the cabinets. With the new farmhouse sink and the dark countertop it was a chef's dream. Not that I'm a chef by any means. Apparently, Chance isn't gifted in the kitchen either, so his decision to use the kitchen instead of leaving it pristine probably wasn't the smartest one.

"Do you really want to get it dirty, though?" I asked not even thinking about how suggestive the question might sound.

Chance hadn't even tried to hide his smirk. "I'd love to get this kitchen dirty with you, Lily."

And so now I'm obsessing over what to wear and how to act. We didn't talk about the kiss at all and now I'm left asking my reflection if I'm reading too much into this dinner invitation. Is it a date? Just two friends hanging out together? What do I even want it to be?

"Whoa, hot mama!" Hadley rounds the corner and flops down on my bed. "Are you wearing a dress?"

The dress may be long, but the material is clingy. He'll

be able to see the curves that I've spent so much time hiding. "Is it too much? You'd tell me if it was too much, right?" My wild eyes meet hers in the mirror.

"Calm down. It isn't too much; it's just right, Lily." Hadley's smile is genuine.

"But what if he isn't thinking of this dinner the same way I am? If I show up in this and he's expecting one of my sweatpant ensembles..."

"Then he'll be surprised. In a good way. Don't overthink it. He's a man. He probably won't even notice that you've done anything different."

I'm pretty sure Chance is going to notice that I'm not in my usual camouflage. I've even shaved my legs in case he brushes up against me. I take in a deep breath; I'm not even in the car and I'm hyperventilating.

"Here, let me help you with your hair. You're going to wear it down, right? He seems to like it down." Hadley's referring to the first YouTube video. It's one of her favorite subjects to tease me about. She's convinced it's basically soft porn that Chance watches every night before he goes to sleep.

I follow Hadley into the bathroom and watch her get out the million beauty tools she likes to use. Once she's twirling sections of hair over the hot curling iron, I close my eyes and try some of the breathing techniques I learned in therapy. I count out the seconds of inhale, hold the breath, and count out the exhale. It makes me feel marginally more relaxed as Hadley's fingers move through the waves she's creating on my head.

"There! Perfect. He doesn't stand a chance." Hadley's lips quirk up. "Stand a chance. Get it?" When I ignore her she keeps on explaining, "Because his name is Chance. You get it, right?"

"I get it. I'm just not sure I'm able to joke right now. I think I might be close to throwing up."

Hadley looks at me with a mix of pity and amusement. "You most certainly are not. Let's get some lipstick on you and then you need to get your butt in the car. If Chance Allen's making you dinner then you're going to get your ass over there and enjoy it."

I walk to the front door like my feet are made of concrete. I'm excited to see Chance again—the flutters in my belly keep reminding me that the emotions I'm feeling aren't all fear. Still, I don't normally put myself in situations like this and my brain still tends to get some of the signals mixed up.

Excitement feels like panic.

Instead of appreciating the butterflies I go straight to wanting to run.

I ring the bell and hear Chance cursing on the other side of the door. "Just a second!" he shouts before he yanks it open, and then he's standing in the doorway, smiling at me like he's never been happier to see me. Immediately some of the tension melts away and I smile right back at him.

"Come in." His hair's still slightly wet like he's just gotten out of the shower, and I can smell the woodsy soap he uses as I brush past him into the house. I breathe deeper than necessary and let my body relax.

"It smells fabulous in here." I'm actually surprised at how good it smells, like an Italian restaurant with a particularly delicious smelling waiter.

"I made lasagna. I hope you're okay with that. I had to call my mom to ask for some helpful hints, so don't be surprised if she's called her sisters already." I'd forgotten that Chance's mother grew up here. She's the reason he's got so many cousins. By tomorrow everyone in town will know about our dinner.

They'll probably have started a betting pool on when we'll have the wedding.

"Lasagna? Isn't that kind of advanced?" I can barely make toast so I'm more than impressed Chance has made something that legitimately counts as cooking.

"Don't be too impressed. The salad's from a bag and I bought the bread. And lasagna's not that hard. I can show you how to make it." Chance shifts his weight from foot to foot and puts his hands in his back pockets like he's not sure what to do next. I look up at him and realize he's just as nervous as I am.

"You look really pretty," he says and I know it isn't some throwaway line. Chance doesn't bother with flattery just to have something to say.

"Thank you. I figured no work clothes for dinner." As if I've been wearing my sweatpants in the middle of July because I'm afraid of ruining my regular clothes. "You look nice." I take in the button down with the sleeves rolled up to his muscular forearms, the dark jeans that he never wears on a regular day.

"Can I take that from you?"

I remember that I'm holding a pie fresh from the oven over at Patty Cakes. When she found out it was for Chance, Patty insisted that I buy the peach. Apparently, he's a big fan.

"Sure. And Patty says hello. If your mother doesn't start tongues wagging, I'm sure Patty will have that under control."

Chance laughs as he takes the pie from me and puts it on one of the brand new counters. "Do you want a drink?" Chance moves away from me toward the refrigerator. I watch his backside as he goes, anticipating the first hurdle of the evening. But I should have known he'd be prepared. "I have lemonade. You can even drink it out of the carton if you want."

"I'll take it in a glass, thank you."

He leans into the fridge to grab the carton and I realize I don't have anything to worry about. "Do you need help with anything?"

"I don't think so." Chance looks at home in this kitchen, opening cabinet doors and checking the oven. "Just have a seat and dinner'll be ready in five."

I settle myself in one of the chairs we refinished together, realizing that I feel at home here as well. Chance brings the bubbling pan of pasta to the table and I make sure it's positioned over the trivet. Neither one of us wants to ruin all the work we've put into making this room perfect.

Before he comes around to his side of the table Chance leans over and kisses the top of my head. "I'm really glad you're here," he says before he slides into his chair. And I'm really glad I'm here, too. So glad all I can do is smile back at him.

22

Chance

"Is this too much?"

"That little sliver? You can do better than that, Lily." I'm teasing, but I am a fan of Patty's pie.

"I have heard this is your favorite." She gives me a look and a shy smile—one I'm not used to seeing. With Lily it's all or nothing. I either get a scowl or that smile that lights up her whole face. Until she realizes she's doing it. Then that smile can vanish so fast you swear you imagined it.

"Patty knows me, I guess." I don't confess that it's because when I was younger my brothers and I would beg my grandpa to take us to the bakery. Patty's a saint for putting up with all of the fingerprints we left all over that display case. But there are few people—Mae and Sadie excepted, of course—who really recognize the allure of baked goods. It still surprises me that no one snatched my aunts up when they were younger. I would have thought a steady stream of cakes and cornbread would have been enough to tempt any of the eligible bachelors in Mint Springs. Of course, that kind of cooking does come with a price, and Patty's husband is living proof. He easily tips the scales at three hundred pounds.

Dinner is going so much better than I expected.

I had had nightmares about burning the food—or burning the whole house down—but none of that even came close to happening. Instead, I watched Lily devour her lasagna like it was the best thing she'd ever eaten. I'm pretty terrible in the kitchen, so I'm basking in this little victory more than I should. That, and I'm still celebrating the fact Lily showed up here looking like something out of a magazine. Her hair's down, soft and wavy over her shoulders. More than once I've had to stop myself from burying my nose in it when she comes close. And there's no baggy jeans or giant T-shirt. I could almost pretend that those outfits were just a blip, but I know better.

I had debated acting like tonight was nothing special, but once Lily walked in I knew I'd made the right call treating this like more than friends. We hadn't discussed it; we haven't even talked about the kiss. But I haven't stopped thinking about Lily's lips for a second, reliving the way she trusted me enough to let me touch her. And now she's in my kitchen, worrying her bottom lip as she tries to cut even slices of pie and slide them onto plates. Her brows furrow and she gets the little wrinkle in the middle of her forehead that tells me she's concentrating. It's one thing I know so well about her now, even if the rest of her is still mostly a mystery.

"You sure you don't want my help over there?" I ask, wishing she'd let me come and stand close to her so I could breathe her in again without looking like a stalker.

"No, I've got it. You made dinner. The least I can do is serve dessert."

Lily comes to the table balancing a plate in each hand.

"So, peach," she says as she slides one in front of me. I nod, my mouth already watering, probably from the smell of the pie, but maybe from the sight of Lily's mouth already priming itself for what she's loading up on her fork.

"Mmmm." When she groans, I swear I feel the vibrations through my entire body. Lily should really warn a man before she starts doing things like that. "This is pretty good, but I'm going to have to side with Cooper and say that blueberry might still be my favorite."

"Blueberry?" I pretend to be wounded. "There is no way blueberry beats peach. Never ever."

"What about strawberry?" Lily puts another bite in her mouth and chews while she waits.

"That's Cade's favorite. Mae makes this fresh strawberry pie that will literally kill you." I smile just thinking of all the times we'd clamored up my aunts' front steps to see what they were making. Strawberry, then blueberry, then peach because that's how the fruit would ripen.

"And Charlie?" Lily's looking at me with those big brown eyes and I can barely remember anything at all about my brother Charlie. What does he even look like? My brain sputters. Lily's got the tiniest little crumb right on the bow of her upper lip. I wonder what she'd do if I reached out to touch her. I have the perfect excuse to lean forward and run my thumb over the curve there, but then her tongue darts out and snags the little speck of pastry. I watch, fascinated, as she puts another bite of pie on her fork.

"Doesn't Charlie have a favorite?" Lily prompts again and I bring myself back to polite conversation.

"Charlie likes apple. He didn't really think that through."

"Why do you say that?" Lily asks, unaware of the hold her mouth has on my thoughts.

"Because apples aren't ripe until the end of August so Charlie hardly ever got a pie." I laugh and Lily laughs with me.

"I guess when you're only here for the summer you have to make informed decisions." She smiles and I'm wishing I'd made some better decisions during my own summers here a few years ago. Wishing I'd been brave enough to make a move on Lily back when she was invincible, before whatever made her decide to make herself small put its mark on her.

"Do you want to go for a ride?"

"Shouldn't we do the dishes?" Lily eyes me with suspicion.

"Dishes'll wait. And the longer they sit the better test they'll be for the new dishwasher." I tap the side of my head with my index finger. "Always thinking."

"It isn't laziness if it's science?" Lily doesn't look convinced.

"Exactly." And a way to make sure I get to spend as much time with Lily as possible. Washing the dishes means the night might be over, and I'm not ready for that. Not by a long shot.

"Where would we go?" She's thinking about it, considering it.

"You'll see. Let me surprise you." I regret this as soon as it's out of my mouth. Lily doesn't like surprises. Not anymore.

But she surprises *me* with a nod of her head. "Okay, let's go."

"Really?" I squeak before I come to my senses and jump up out of my chair. Lily's laughing and all that touchable hair's tumbling all over the place.

"Sure."

She slips her hand into mine when I offer it to her and lets me lead her to the truck. The Chevy starts on the first try so I send up a little thank you to my grandpa. I'm pretty sure he's looking out for me on that one. The sun hasn't been down long, but out on the farm road there's hardly any light. Only my headlights cut through the darkness as I drive us toward the middle of our property. Lily sits next to me, her window rolled down. She lets one arm dangle outside in the breeze, every now and then letting the force of the wind move her hand like an ocean wave. I sneak looks at her as I drive, watching for any sign that she's getting wary or feeling uncomfortable, but her face stays relaxed, her eyes even close every now and again as the night whips strands of her hair around her cheeks.

"We're goin' off road up here, okay?" I ease the truck off the dirt road and onto the bumpy edge of the old cow pasture.

"That's the most Southern I've heard you sound since you've been back."

I shrug. Mint Springs is bringing that out in me, I guess. "You might want to hold on here for a minute." The truck bounces along as I steer us farther and farther from the road. Finally, I come to the spot I was aiming for and put the truck in park.

"Where are we?" Lily asks, tilting her neck so she can better see out the windshield.

"This is the exact middle of the property."

Lily twists to look at me in the darkness of the truck cab. "What's so special about the middle of the farm?"

"Look," I tell her and point my finger toward the night sky. "Here there's hardly any light pollution so you can see the stars better than anywhere else."

Lily's eyes glide along the constellations perched above us.

"It's better from the bed of the truck, but we don't have to get out if you don't want to. I have blankets." Hopefully that doesn't sound too crazy—that I've got a stash of blankets in the truck. It isn't every day that I end up with a girl in my truck and even less likely to happen in this Chevy, but I did have this moment in the back of my mind when I decided to keep a few old quilts wedged behind the seat.

"Let's see it from the back then," Lily says and goes to open her door and step out into the darkness. "I'm game if you are."

I scramble around, pulling the blankets free from their hiding place and following Lily into the night. For a summer night it's cooled off more than usual. The humidity's gone, too, and if it turns out we aren't swarmed by mosquitos, I'll know there's a higher power controlling the weather for tonight. Nothing buzzes around my head as I arrange the quilts in the truck bed. A nearly perfect summer night feels like a possibility.

Lily waits while I try to make the back of the truck less uncomfortable. No matter what anyone tells you, trucks were not made for romantic picnics or tailgate snuggles. Every time I've tried to put the moves on a woman in the bed of a truck, I've been met with metal biting into my back and the inevitable dust and dirt that comes with sitting in a place you recently used to haul hay. I hosed out the back of the Chevy this afternoon, again because there was always this sliver of hope that Lily might eventually let me show her my favorite spot, but it was never something I thought she'd really agree to tonight.

"You want a hand getting up here?" I ask once I've got things situated. She's wearing a dress, and climbing into the bed of a truck isn't the easiest thing to do even in pants. Not that I want Lily to ever go back to her old outfits. When she shows up in her sweatpants again, I'm going to have to work hard to keep my disappointment to myself.

For the third time tonight, when I offer Lily my hand, she takes it with no hesitation. I may never get over the feeling of having Lily casually slide her hand into mine. I swear just that two seconds of contact has me feeling like I could conquer the world—because Lily Gentry trusts me. She hops up and scoots toward the cab more gracefully than I would have ever imagined. She sits up on her knees, tucking her legs underneath, and the fabric of her dress ruffles around her. I stay stuck on my knees on the tailgate, my brain stalling out now that I've got Lily here.

"Are you coming back here?" She has to notice I'm suddenly an inexperienced teenager. I can barely figure out how to get my body from one end of the truck to the other. I manage it somehow and finally end up next to Lily, my heart beating like I've run a marathon and my head suddenly realizing that I haven't thought past this part. I mean, I've imagined being alone with Lily more times than I'd like to admit, but most of those fantasies are pretty explicit—even the ones I was having when I was an actual sixteen-year-old. With Lily now I have to put those ideas aside and let her tell me what's comfortable, even if I'd love to pull her up against me and start by kissing the hell out of her.

"Is this too close?" I ask her and she shifts self-consciously. If it weren't dark I imagine I'd be able to see the start of a blush creeping up her neck and onto her cheeks.

"No, you're fine." Lily actually scoots the tiniest bit closer. My heart thumps louder in my chest and I hope she can't hear it. If she can, she's likely to think I'm having a heart attack.

"Can I lean up against you?" Lily's voice is shy and quiet. I put my arm out and her face comes up against my chest. She snuggles up, the side of her body melding against mine and her cheek resting on my pec. Now she can hear the riot of drumbeats my heart's putting out. No doubt about it. She sighs a little and I feel her relax, tilting her head up a bit to look at the stars. I relax too because there's nothing to do now but let Lily tell me what's next.

"Do you know much about the constellations?" Lily asks. "I used to be able to find some of them, but now it just looks like a bunch of little pinpricks."

"I can find a few things if I look hard enough," I tell her, keeping my voice low. Right now, in the middle of this pasture, we're the only two people in the universe and there's no need to shout. "Fall and winter are better for stars out here, I think. Less humidity or something. But I was only here in the summer, so this is the only time I could come out."

The sweet scent of Lily's hair drifts up as the warmth of her body spreads through mine. "Look right there." I point my finger at the night sky and Lily's head turns to follow it. "That's the North Star. Polaris. It's the end of the little dipper. That's harder to see, but you can see Polaris from anywhere in the Northern Hemisphere."

"You could go outside in California and I could go outside in Chicago and we could both see it," Lily whispers.

"Yeah," I whisper back. There's probably a catch to that. Light pollution and all that, but I don't think now's the time to debate the reality of seeing Polaris when Lily and I are back in our own worlds. "Lily?"

"Uh huh?" she mumbles, still looking up at the night sky

and the twinkling dots light years away from this moment in the back of my grandfather's truck.

"I'd really like to kiss you again."

She stiffens, the muscles tightening where they're pressed up against me. But then Lily relaxes again and turns her head to look at me. "I'd like that, too."

23

Lily

There was a split second of panic. That moment when my body refuses to listen. Everything was going so well and you'd think my brain could run the show for once, but when Chance's voice got low and husky my body didn't react like it should. *You want to kiss him, damn it! You don't need to keep being afraid!* Still, he felt me tense up before I could manage to stop myself.

If anything can be sure to throw a bucket of cold water on a man's libido, it's having someone act like the worst thing they can think of is letting you kiss them. Chance has never stepped over the line. His flirting's been harmless, his invitations always polite, and the one kiss he's given me was the most reverent thing I've ever experienced. He's patient where other men have been hurried, understanding where other men have thrown their hands up in exasperation. He's a keeper, Chance Allen. Only I insist on doing things that make him think otherwise.

He asks to kiss me. Doesn't demand it. Doesn't expect me to say yes. Gives me more than a second to think before just smashing his mouth on mine. I've come to think of this as the difference between a boy and a man. My mama has always said she never found a man—only boys. And what I've known before hasn't been too far from that. But Chance does all the things I'm not used to, all the things that have me thinking I can try this.

"I'd like that, too," my mouth finally manages. *Thank you, brain.* There's no hesitation, but he takes his time lowering his face to mine.

Chance slides his nose along mine, our foreheads meeting for a brief second. He tilts his head and then his lips brush mine, softly, like he's almost done it accidentally. I whimper a little bit and fight back a wave of mortification. One minute I'm hot and the next I'm cold, but in this moment all systems are suddenly go. Chance chuckles and then puts one of his big hands at the base of my skull. When he kisses me again I have nowhere to go, nothing to think about but the firm pressure of that hand matched with the firmness of his mouth. He tastes like peaches and lemonade, brown sugar and summertime, and when he shifts up onto his knees, I turn my body to get closer to him. I run my fingers through the short hair at the back of his neck and he groans, the sound only making me want more contact. My hands find his shoulders and run down his biceps, sneak over to his chest and glide along there. My kisses get more and more frantic and when Chance pulls me onto his lap, I feel his erection through his jeans. I settle myself against him, trying to get even closer, surprised by my own desire. He moves to plant kisses along the side of my neck, along the exposed skin of my collarbone. I tilt my head back and see nothing above us but stars. I find the star Chance showed me earlier. Polaris. It glitters and winks at me, as Chance Allen kisses me in the back of this truck.

I pull at the hem of Chance's shirt, too uncoordinated to worry with the buttons. The skin there is warm and smooth; the muscles underneath ripple a little when my fingertips make contact. Chance's hands skim along my back, find my ass and settle there as his tongue explores the shell of my ear.

Then one hand moves forward, gives my thigh a squeeze, and I jump back like he's slapped me.

We're both panting as I scuttle like a crab to the side of the truck bed. Chance's hair is sticking out all over the place and I realize I've done that; I've had my hands all over him. In the dark I watch his face register confusion, his features twisting as he tries to figure out how we went from hot and heavy to two feet apart in the span of two seconds.

"What did I do? What just happened there?" Chance's hands reach for me. I startle and move further back, the tears already threatening to fall.

"Lily, talk to me, please. Tell me what's going on." His voice is gentle but insistent. I wait for him to get angry, but the yelling never comes. "Just let me know you're alright."

I'm still trying to get my heart to stop beating so wildly, both from the kissing and the sudden spike of adrenaline, but it flutters in my chest, banging around inside my ribs. Chance is breathing hard, sitting back on his heels, hands splayed over the expanse of his thighs. He doesn't try to move closer—doesn't move at all—just watches me like I might jump over the tailgate and bolt any second now. Which isn't entirely unlike me, if we're being honest.

"God, I'm sorry," I blurt, the tears coming hot and fast now. There's no way to stop them.

"No, no. I'm sorry. Whatever I did..." Chance's voice tapers off and then there's nothing but the sound of the peeper frogs and the crickets. Of course he thinks he's done something wrong. He still doesn't realize that the problem is *me*.

"It's not your fault," I try to explain. It's someone else's fault entirely. Someone who hurt me and probably didn't give it two seconds' worth of consideration.

"If you don't want to—"

"I *want* to!" I nearly shout and Chance's face wrinkles in confusion again as he flinches back. "God, I want to." I choke on the tears that refuse to stop coursing down my cheeks. "It isn't anything you did, Chance. It's all about what's wrong with me." I wipe away some of the tears, wishing for a tissue or the opportunity to hide my face more effectively.

"Lily, don't cry," Chance begs. "What can I do? How can I make this better?"

The kindness in his voice has me calming down a bit. *It's Chance*, I remind myself, but my breathing stays ragged and my face stays wet.

"I have to tell you something." I should have told him from the beginning although finding a way to tell someone you've just met that you're ruined is next to impossible. There's never a good time for this discussion. Should I have brought it up when I realized I felt more than friendship? After that first kiss? Maybe I should wear something like a caution sign to warn people away. Then Chance would have known to run.

"You can tell me anything. You know that, right?"

I'd love to believe this, that letting Chance hear the details of my secret won't make a difference when it comes to how he feels about me, that it won't put a swift end to whatever was happening here.

But I've seen the way people's faces change once they

know what happened, the subtle ways they treat me differently, if they stick around at all.

People who allegedly cared, who claimed to love me.

"Can you turn around?" I ask. I don't think I can bear to look at him while I make this confession.

"If you promise you won't jump out of the truck." He isn't kidding, because he knows me too well. Even this burns a little. "Seriously, Lily. Promise me."

"I promise," I whisper and he slowly turns himself around. His shoulders rise and fall as he waits for me to start. I open my mouth and quickly shut it.

These are my last few moments with Chance.

I try to memorize the back of his head, the tilt of his shoulders, the way his hair curls just enough to touch his neck. I file all these things away because once I start talking, any hint of easy will be gone from whatever this is Chance and I have together. He isn't the first, and he probably won't be the last, to run.

I take a deep breath. "You know how I started college here?" I begin like I'm telling a bedtime story, not the tale of the end of everything.

Chance nods his head. "Um hum."

"Junior year I had a bad experience." That is the understatement of the year, and not the best beginning to this story. "A very bad experience with some guys from Riley's fraternity."

At the mention of his cousin, Chance's shoulders hunch. Maybe he's heard something about that night from Riley or from one of his other family members. Thinking about Chance sitting around with his brothers discussing the night my life turned upside down makes me shudder, but I know Chance isn't like that, so I ignore the fear and try to be brave.

"There was a party and, back then, I was always down for a party," I continue bitterly. Those days seem far away now, back when I worried about my hair and make-up more than the possibility that something horrible might go wrong. The start of a Saturday night meant the possibility of a good time. Not anymore.

"At Riley's fraternity house?" Chance prompts. He's pushing the story along, making sure I keep talking, all but ensuring I get to the horrible point.

"No, it was someone's house. One of the guys in the frat, I guess." That night is at some points crystal clear and at others a complete blur. I remember the excitement of getting ready, pulling on a pair of boots and a sweater because it wasn't quite spring. I'd spent half my life with Chance's cousin Riley; he was my go-to date in high school, not because there was anything romantic going on, but because we had such a great time getting in trouble together that it seemed the natural thing to do. For him to take me to a party was second nature by the time we made it to college.

I remember the house—one of those slightly shabby rentals that lined the side streets of campus. It was already crowded when we got there, people spilling out onto the porch and into the muddy little front yard.

"I was drinking. There was a keg and some of the guys were mixing crazy drinks. Typical Saturday night stuff." Although it wasn't and it was the last Saturday night I'd ever feel was normal for a long, long time. "I remember feeling pretty drunk and somebody helping me into one of the bedrooms."

Chance's back stiffens. This is a story that's as old as time in some ways, and I can already see him reacting to it. Drunk girl gets herself in a bad situation, there's nothing new about that.

"The next morning, I woke up, still at the house. It wasn't obvious that anything had happened, exactly, but someone had messed with my clothes. And I was pretty... sore." Chance flinches at this, but I keep going.

"I got myself together and managed to get back to my dorm. I couldn't get ahold of Riley for most of the morning; I was just trying to make my head stop pounding." I don't tell Chance about the churning in my gut or the little voice in my head that kept telling me something was very wrong. I don't tell him that I brushed off the concern of my room-mates, refusing to talk to anyone about what might have happened even after I found all the bruises up and down my body as I showered. "When I finally did talk to him, he told me that I'd been with one of his fraternity brothers and insisted on staying at the party, even though he had tried to get me to leave with him. I couldn't even remember who that guy was, honestly. He hadn't been there when I woke up so I kept thinking maybe I hadn't slept with him, though it was pretty obvious that I had. I kind of chalked it up to all my partying catching up with me. Sleeping with some guy and not even remembering it felt pretty shitty, but it wasn't like I could argue that I'd said no—I didn't remember anything."

I look at the broad expanse of Chance's back as I get ready to explain the next part. I wish 'party girl goes a little too far' was the end of what I need to say. Chance's hands are already bunched into fists, clenched on the top of his thighs. If he's upset at the beginning of this story then he's about to be furious. The only question will be who he decides that fury is meant for.

"Riley left you on your own? Knowing you'd had too much to drink?" Chance asks, his voice angry but controlled. "Did Riley not talk to that guy?"

"He did," I say. "It isn't Riley's fault, Chance. He didn't realize what was happening." And once he figured out the whole story, he felt guilty enough to leave school right along with me.

Chance lets out a puff of air. "He should have done more than talk to that son of a bitch." He's angry and he hasn't even heard the worst part.

"That's not the bad part," I whisper and Chance's head snaps toward me, the confusion on his face still visible in the moonlight.

"What do you mean?" he asks and the edge in his voice is unmistakable.

"It wasn't just one."

24

Chance

The anger that starts to come over me is no surprise. From the moment Lily made me turn around I knew whatever she had to tell me was going to be hard to hear. Listening to her voice get smaller and smaller behind me makes it impossible for me to keep my body loose. She has to be able to see me reacting every time she gives me a new detail, every time this story takes a turn for the worse. I'd thought we were over the bad part. She got drunk and some guy took advantage of her. That has me wanting to hunt that asshole down and beat the living daylights out of him, but I know that won't fix the problem. And to have my cousin be the one who left her on her own when she obviously couldn't defend herself? Riley's lucky he's a few states away right now. He deserves more than just a talking to. I'm thinking of the best way to convince Lily to let me turn around when she tells me that there's *more* for me to hear. I look at her without waiting for permission, my body no longer taking orders from my brain.

"What do you mean there was more than one?" I'm already shaking with rage.

"I would never have found out if Riley hadn't been raising hell about it," Lily says, barely able to make eye contact with me. "But it was something they'd done more than once. To other girls."

I turn my body toward her and see her push back an inch or two. This isn't the time to reach out for her and I make my arms stay at my sides, digging my fingers into the fabric of my jeans. Lily's face is wet, the light from the stars highlighting the tears I can see streaming down her cheeks.

"They put something in my drink so I wouldn't be able to fight them off. So I wouldn't remember."

The urge to punch a hole on the bed of my grandfather's truck is almost overwhelming. That someone hurt Lily has had me seeing red for a while now, the fact that it was something planned, something organized, makes me want to wipe out every last one of Riley's fraternity brothers.

"There were pictures." Lily's voice cracks as she tells me this and I can tell that she'd have kept this to herself if she could have. I close my eyes and count to three, trying to stay in control until Lily's finished. "But you can't tell how out of it I am. It isn't proof of anything. At least that's what the school said."

"You reported it?"

"Once we figured out what had happened and Riley heard about it, he convinced me to go to the administration. But it didn't do anything except stir things up. There was no rape kit, no evidence. It was my word against theirs and they made sure my word didn't count for much."

"Lily..."

"I wasn't exactly known for being a good girl, Chance, and they used my reputation against me." Her words break my heart. That's what happened to the fearless girl I knew before. She got snubbed out, ground down to nothing. I don't need to know all the details, don't need to hear more of what they did to hurt the girl who used to light up a room just by walking in.

"You know that none of this was your fault, right?" I wait for some sign of confirmation from Lily, some hint of agreement but she only bites her lip through the tears. "Even if you'd slept your way through the entire campus, that doesn't give anyone the right to decide to take advantage of you. They drugged you, Lily. You didn't do anything wrong."

"My brain knows that, Chance, and God knows I've had enough therapy by now that the rest of me should know it too, but that doesn't change the feelings. It doesn't change the fear. How can I trust that something like that won't happen again? Sometimes bits of that night come back to me. Just little flashes, but it's enough. It's been better just to stay cautious. Those boys weren't monsters; they were regular guys. But they ruined my life. They ruined me, Chance."

"You're not ruined." It comes out fierce and Lily jumps. "Don't you ever think that." I reach for her and she lets me wrap my arms around her and presses her wet face to my chest. "Not ever," I whisper into her hair. Lily sobs against me, her tears soaking through the cotton of my shirt. She's anything but ruined. She's walked through fire. In my mind she's even more of a warrior than when we were sixteen— even more ferocious.

Lily's crying settles down a bit and I loosen my grip on her. When she tilts her head to peer up at my face, I use my thumb to wipe away one of the remaining tears. "Are you ready to go back?"

She shakes her head no. "Can we stay out here a little bit longer?"

"Sure. You want to look at the stars some more?" I let my arm hang loose around her shoulder.

"Yeah, just for a few more minutes." Lily eases away from me and stretches out on her back in the truck bed. I slide down next to her and startle when she snuggles closer. "Is this okay?"

I slide one arm under her until she's resting up against my chest. Her head settles over my heart and I wrap my arm back up around her. There are plenty of things that feel great in this world: the pull of a fish on the line, sunshine on my face, the way my muscles ache after a hard day's work. None of those compare to the feeling of Lily in my arms. Not even close.

"More than okay." I listen to her breathing start to even out. I grab the edge of the blanket with my free hand and cocoon us in it, wrapping Lily's sleeping body up safe and sound against me. The stars twinkle above us, the only ones that can see what's happening here in the bed of this truck. The only ones that hear me whisper to her before I let myself drift off to sleep. The only ones to witness my vow that no one will ever hurt Lily again, not as long as I'm around.

However long that might be.

25

Lily

The hot sun on my face forces me to open my eyes. Well, more like one eye because after all that crying, I'm a little swollen. I'm sure I look a little worse for wear after last night. Chance's chest rises and falls under my cheek, the cotton of his shirt wrinkling around my face. I wrap my arms around him a little tighter, both because he's still here and because I'm not sure for how long. We've slept all night in the back of his truck and now that the sun's coming up over the mountain, I'm not sure what comes next. Chance listened last night without pulling away, without seeming repulsed by what happened to me. But in the harsh light of day I won't blame him for changing his mind. I won't blame him if it turns out he can't stick—if all this is too much.

Chance groans a bit and stretches out underneath me. He's been taking the brunt of the metal truck bed along his back and I'm sure it hasn't been the most comfortable way to spend the night. His arm rests beneath my shoulder and I can feel him flex as he tries not to jostle me too much.

"I'm awake. You can move around if you need to." I'm

fully aware that I'm breaking the spell. I've still got one bare leg thrown over him, my dress riding high up on my hips. With the blanket over us, there's nothing on display, but we both know exactly where our bodies are touching. Once we untangle we'll have to make some decisions that I'm already dreading.

"I was trying to let you sleep," he says, his voice rough. He doesn't roll away or put any distance between us, and I'm grateful to have these last few seconds with him.

"I should let you get back to the house," I say, giving him the chance to be free of me.

"I'm fine right here." And when I look up at him there's not a trace of regret in his eyes, not an ounce of pity on his face. "I like holding you when you let me."

I settle back down against his chest and decide to take him at his word. He may change his mind later, but for now I'll stay here pressed against him. One big hand starts to move against my back and for once I don't flinch. Chance's fingers glide across the exposed skin between my shoulder blades, tentatively at first and then more confidently, where my sundress leaves me uncovered. I tilt my head up until my lips find his throat and give him a kiss so whisper-soft I'm not sure if he can even feel it. His skin is warm, and the scruff on his chin scratches my forehead as I settle in closer. I breathe in the sunshine smell of him, and before I can stop myself, I give him just the tiniest little lick there, letting my tongue dart out for a quick taste. Chance stiffens and I wait for him to skitter away, but instead he pushes closer and lets me put another kiss there, this one open-mouthed and wet.

Chance clears his throat. "Lily," he warns. I keep my mouth attached to his neck, tasting the slight saltiness of his skin. He rolls toward me, wrapping me up in his arms and tangling us up even more in the quilt. His eyes lock with mine. "This okay?"

"Yes." I wiggle closer, pressing myself up against him. My breasts flatten against the muscles of his chest, my bare legs rub against the fabric of his jeans.

"Are you sure about this?" Chance slides his hand down my back.

"Yes." I tilt my face up, aiming my lips toward his.

"We can stop any time, no matter what. I'm not expecting anything." Chance looks at me the same way he always has. There's concern there, but it's overridden by desire. Unexpected heat licks up my belly, and more than anything I want to be able to let this happen—to *make* this happen.

"Let's just go slow," I whisper before I press my lips to his. Chance grunts in surprise but lets his mouth meld to mine. His hands move slowly, one caressing my back and the other coming to cup my cheek. He's wrapped around me, his big body protective and solid. Despite the drawbacks of the truck bed, I find myself relaxing. I let my hands wander to Chance's chest, sliding over the row of buttons down the middle of his shirt. When I sneak my fingers underneath he breaks the kiss to look at me.

"Go slow, Lily. This doesn't have to lead anywhere. You tell me what you want."

I bite my lip but don't remove my hand. I like the feel of his stomach underneath my palm. I leave it where it is and lean in for another kiss. Chance is cautious, letting me lead the way. He's already seen what can happen when I get ahead of myself. Still, I want more. I guide his hand from my cheek down the front of my body, his fingertips barely grazing me as they travel. I keep my mouth fused with his as I position his palm over my breast. His eyes fly open, but he doesn't stop kissing me. I can feel the heat of his hand, but he doesn't make contact the way I want him to. I furrow my brow and pull my lips from his.

"So now you don't want to touch me?" I sound angry, but that emotion is only to cover the hurt of the rejection I'm sure is about to happen.

"Lily," Chance whispers, moving his hand back up to my face to smooth some of the hair away from my forehead. "There's no way I'd ever not want to touch you. I just think we shouldn't rush this."

I let out a frustrated breath. I'm not even sure I'd really be able to go through with letting Chance's hands roam all over me, despite my bravado. As much as I want to be able to be completely healed, I know my reactions are unpredictable and now Chance knows exactly why. I can't blame him for hesitating.

"Let me take you back up to the house and feed you. I'm nowhere near giving up on this, but we can baby step. I don't want you to feel any pressure. I want you to be comfortable."

I'm not sure how likely it is that I'll ever be comfortable. This morning I'm more inclined to just rip the Band-Aid off and hope for the best. Even after years of distance and therapy I've never gotten as close to a physical relationship as I have with Chance in these past few weeks.

But freaking out on him last night has made him gun shy, and there's no way I'll be able to convince him just to power through, especially if I act like the world is ending. And I can't guarantee that's not going to be what happens. That's not exactly a ringing endorsement for sleeping with me.

He's already easing up, sitting in the truck bed and stretching those strong arms up over his head. I try to school my face to hide my disappointment. He's not running, but he's not jumping in head first either.

Chance helps me down and we fold up the quilts that have been barely padding the back of the truck all night. They're obviously homemade and I run my fingers over the stitching absentmindedly. I imagine that whoever made these probably didn't envision them being used the way Chance and I almost used them last night. *Almost.* Because I couldn't keep the broken part of me a secret anymore.

The drive back to the house drags on forever. Even having Chance's hand resting on my thigh doesn't make me feel much better. I should be relieved that he's calm, that his anger from before seems to have been forgotten for now. I should appreciate the way he's not pushing me out the door and I should be looking forward to spending some more time with him this morning, but that lingering shame keeps tugging at me. The reminder that I'm work weighs me down and I'm sure eventually it will feel the same way to him.

When we come to the top of the hill, it looks like a party's going on. The driveway's full of cars, packed bumper to bumper all along the gravel loop in front of the house.

Chance curses under his breath. "I'm guessing you didn't let Hadley know you were staying over last night." He jerks his chin toward her car.

"I didn't exactly plan to fall asleep," I say, knowing that won't be an acceptable excuse for Hadley. But that only explains one of the cars. There's a lot going on here for a Saturday morning, especially one where Chance and I get to rock up looking like we've been up to more than we actually have.

The contingent of people on the front porch has my cheeks already burning. Hadley's parked in one of the camp chairs with Cooper standing next to her, his arms folded across his chest as he glares at us. An angry Hadley isn't something he probably planned to deal with this morning. Chance's aunts are on the porch too, adding to my humiliation. I'm hoping they aren't the ones who made those quilts everyone is going to think we defiled in the back of this truck. Two other sandy blond heads turn to watch us creep up the gravel road and onto the edge of the driveway. Grown up versions of Charlie and Cade Allen give us both curious stares.

"Are those your brothers?" I ask as Chance scans the group.

"Looks like it." Chance lets out a breath. "I wasn't expecting to have to bring you back to this, obviously."

"I'll be fine." If anything, it might be nice for people to assume that Chance and I have been fooling around all night instead of me spilling my guts and letting him comfort me. There's nothing sexy about that.

"Time to face the music, I guess." Chance puts the truck in park. "Stay right there." He jogs around to open the passenger door and offers me his hand. I take it and don't let it go. "Look at me." His voice is low and strong. "You have nothing to be nervous about. I'm right here and I'm not going anywhere."

I nod even though I know that's a lie. Before too long Chance will be back in California and I'll be back in Chicago just like we planned. This farm will belong to someone else, maybe, and all the secrets I spilled last night won't be anything other than a rumor again. People will fill in the blanks, or they won't, but Chance won't be holding my hand. He won't be smiling down at me like I'm the most amazing thing he's ever seen, even after a night of crying. But for now, I'm going to pretend I don't know any of that. Right now, there's only me and Chance and this awkward

Saturday morning with more witnesses than I'd counted on. I give him a smile when I tilt my head up toward him and he smiles back before he gives me the softest, sweetest kiss in the history of the universe and I wish I could stay just like this forever.

Hadley's gasp has me pulling back, remembering that we have an audience. One of Chance's aunts lets out an *oh my* and Chance leads me toward the porch. Hadley's mouth hangs slightly open, only closing when Cooper starts a slow clap that has the rest of the Allen brothers joining in. Her sharp elbow to his hip has him stopping, rubbing the spot where she jabbed him.

"What the hell was that for?" he asks as Hadley growls up at him from her camp chair.

"Well," Mae starts, more flustered than I've ever seen her. "Since we're all here so bright and early, why don't Sadie and I whip up some breakfast? I'm sure everyone's hungry."

Sadie agrees and the two of them start off toward their house, heads bent together. The boys all follow, some good-natured shoving happening as they weave down the path. Hadley's next to me in an instant, walking beside me as Chance keeps my hand firmly in his.

"You have some explaining to do!" she stage whispers into my ear. "I was worried sick."

"Sorry, Hadley." Chance leans forward to make eye contact with her. "We weren't planning on staying out all night."

Hadley gives him a harrumph that sounds more like my mother than anything I've ever heard. "Well, it looks like it worked out fine," she says before whispering in my ear again. "Details later."

Then Hadley's running up ahead to catch Cooper and

the rest of his brothers. Chance brings the hand he's holding to his lips and gives my wrist a kiss. I'll survive this morning, but I'm not so sure I can say the same for my feelings for Chance Allen. They're bubbling up and refusing to cooperate with the plan my brain has so cleverly concocted. I look at Chance's profile, the morning sun hitting the stubble along his chin, bouncing off the tips of his eyelashes. Nope. I won't be able to come back from this. Not in a million years.

26

Lily

"If another person walks in here asking about that tube thing, I'm gonna throw something."

"What tube thing?" It's been a while since I've spent the morning in the shop with Bunny and something's obviously gotten her panties in a wad. She moves to straighten the ceramic dog statues she keeps on the counter and rolls her eyes at me.

"You know what I'm talking about. That tube thing you and your boyfriend are always messing with."

I let the boyfriend crack go without comment. Ever since Hadley told them I stayed out all night with Chance, my mother and Bunny have been relentless in their hunt for more information. But even I'm not sure what to call my relationship with Chance right now and I'm afraid of jinxing things by demanding a definition. We've continued working and spending as much time as possible together, much of that with me slowly testing out my boundaries. I've gotten better at relaxing and enjoying the way Chance touches me, gotten hungrier in my need to touch him. Still, it isn't anyone's business how I spend my free time. Not even Bunny.

"I still don't know what you're talking about."

"The thing on the computer. People come in here asking if you're the girl from the videos." Bunny turns on her stool. "Exactly what kind of videos are the two of you making?" She raises an eyebrow and her real question is clear.

"Bunny! I'm scandalized!" I fake outrage and bring my hand to my chest. "Like I'd willingly participate in something like that."

Bunny's face clouds. "I know, honey. That wasn't a very considerate joke."

I smile. Maybe a while ago that would have wounded me more, but I know Bunny wasn't being malicious. She wasn't out to hurt me or to dredge up any old memories. And now that I feel like I'm moving forward, those kinds of barbs don't sting like they used to.

"Are you talking about YouTube?" Chance has been filming everything we do to the old farmhouse and posting almost daily about the project. I have to admit that the website looks good and even if I'm uncomfortable in front of the camera the videos are getting some views.

"Whatever it's called. All I know is that people have been coming in here wanting to buy the paint you use, looking around."

"Well, that's good, isn't it? Are they buying things?" There's a mention of Southern Comforts on the website, but I hadn't really expected it to generate too much interest in the store.

"They spend a little money," Bunny concedes. "But they're awful chatty. They interrupt my reading." She pats the stack of tabloid magazines she keeps next to her.

"I'm not going to apologize for that. If there's a way to

make more money around here you might have to give up a little of your reading time."

Bunny sniffs. "I guess I can make the sacrifice. Now, why don't you show me those videos everyone's talking about."

The entire drive to the farm I plot and plan. I've been hands-off with the Internet stuff, letting Chance post almost everything he shoots. He's the savvy one with the good ideas, but I'm starting to have a few ideas of my own now that I've gotten more information from Bunny. People are coming by the shop looking for specific things, inventory I'm not selling but maybe I could with a little assistance. I just need to convince Chance to help me figure out the details.

My happy brimming-with-plans walk up the front steps comes to a sudden stop when I get to the door. Through the screen I can see Chance working—shirtless, of course—on an area of the living room ceiling. Now that we're in full swing we're tackling projects that originally had seemed too involved. The entire house has that old popcorn ceiling that Chance and I both agreed would be a drawback for selling the place. It had seemed too overwhelming at first, but it turns out Chance is a regular handyman when it comes to jobs like these. He's even started building things we decide the house needs—built in shelves and new cabinet doors in the master bath, a new railing for the steep staircase to the second floor. And now the popcorn ceiling has got to go, which means Chance on the ladder and plenty of time with his abs out.

He turns when he hears the door open, and climbs down, wiping his hands. He's gotten tan from weekends out at the barn with his brothers, and his hair's a shade lighter than when he first stormed into Southern Comforts months ago. He gives me the smile that always makes my knees a little weak and I all but forget about the things I was ready to discuss with him. Right now there's nothing more pressing than letting him wrap those strong arms around me and bury his nose in my hair.

"I'm probably a little sweaty." He apologizes but doesn't loosen his grip. "This ceiling's a bitch to scrape. I'm not getting that dust all over you, am I?"

I snuggle my nose against the muscles of his chest. I could be covered in toxic powder right now and I wouldn't care one bit. "How long have you been working?" My question is muffled against his skin.

"A little while. I can take a break." He lets me pull back just enough to look up at him. The stubble on his jaw taunts me and I want to run my tongue over the edge of his chin. Since there's nothing stopping me, that's exactly what I do. I slide across his skin, tentative at first, but then more confident as Chance groans a little. That's all the encouragement I need to let my mouth wander down his neck and along his collarbone.

"We're taking that kind of break, huh?" he teases as he lets me explore his chest with my mouth, run my hands down the muscles of his back. I've gotten bolder since our night in the truck and he's let me. Slowly but surely, I'm opening back up, able to trust him and myself.

"I should probably shower if this is what we're doing this morning." Chance tries to pull back but I keep my grip on him firm. I'm not bothered by the slight sheen of sweat that covers him, I'm more interested in the goosebumps that have started to break out wherever my mouth touches him.

"Lily," he warns because he knows that slowing down is hard to do once we get going.

"Chance," I taunt back even though I appreciate the way he likes to check in, the way he makes sure each and every step is one I'm comfortable with.

His hands move lower down my back, his fingers trailing along the waistband of my shorts. I've finally started dressing for the weather, wearing short sleeves and shorts when the temperature threatens to hit triple digits. Which, in Georgia at the end of July, is always. Chance hasn't said a word about it, but I notice how his eyes track along the exposed skin of my legs, the way he finds excuses to touch my bare arms now that he has the opportunity. Those little touches have me nearly bursting out of my skin every single day. It doesn't help that he's usually shirtless and sweaty for half of the jobs we do. I don't need any more images running through my mind as I try to fall asleep every night, but Chance has been providing them whether I want them or not. Now, as my fingers trace along his stomach muscles I find myself thinking about how much more I want.

I bring my face back to Chance's and give him a slow, lingering kiss. He opens immediately, his lips willing, his hands still circling my mid-back. I push myself closer, hoping he'll recognize that as a signal, but Chance doesn't ever try to guess with me. If I don't come out and ask for what I want he seems content to continue with what we're already doing. He doesn't want any miscommunication, no misunderstandings that might upset me.

I let my hands move lower, down over the back of his jeans until I can feel the stitching of the pockets and the firm ass underneath. There's a grunt of surprise when I tug him closer to me, lining us up the way I want. Chance is tall, but even if we aren't perfectly aligned, he gets the picture. I guide his hands further down my back until he's cupping my backside. His hands tense, then relax. We've gone further than this before, but he always seems surprised when I push for more, when I let him touch me in ways that I've started to think of as normal. What I used to think of as normal for other people but not for me.

"Are we not working on the house today?" Chance asks as he moves his lips from mine. The whisper of his breath on the shell of my ear makes me shiver.

"Could we work on this instead for a little bit?" I ask, my voice more hopeful than I intend.

"I'm always happy to help you work on this." He leaves a few kisses along my hairline. "Are we good so far?"

"Yes, but I was hoping..." The talking part ends up being harder than I thought, but just letting my body do the communicating isn't how this works anymore. Still, sometimes I want to be able to have less talk and more action, so instead of telling him what I want, I pull away from Chance. His face clouds when I reach for the hem of my shirt to pull it over my head. I kick off my sneakers. When I pop the button on my cutoffs and ease them down my legs there's less confusion.

Even though I can plainly see his desire, Chance doesn't make a move.

"Now you," I whisper. I'm standing in nothing but my bra and panties in the middle of his grandpa's house but for the first time in a long time I don't feel exposed.

Chance hesitates while reaching for the button on his jeans. "What's the plan here, Lily? I'm fine with whatever you want; I just want to manage my expectations."

I want to be able to promise him everything in this moment, but I know there's the possibility that I won't be able to go through with it. My body might betray me no matter what my head and my heart want. And right now they want to be able to give Chance what any other woman could give him—would want to give him—after he's given so much to me.

"I want to try," I say, which I know doesn't answer his question. Try is a loaded word that doesn't set the parameters we need.

"Try what?" His hand's still frozen over the waistband of his pants, his thumb nearly touching the abs I'd like to be closer to right now.

Before, I would have known exactly what to do to seduce a man. I'd close the distance between us and make short work of Chance's jeans all by myself. There'd be none of this back and forth. My hands would take care of this hesitation, my mouth would seal the deal. We'd have been sleeping together months ago and there'd be nothing to stop me from enjoying every second. Now, we're both in uncharted waters, trying not to drown. Chance just wants to be sure, wants *me* to be sure.

"I want to try..." It sounds ridiculous when I think about saying it out loud. It's too clinical to call it sex, too vulgar to ask him to fuck me. I know that asking him to make love to me makes assumptions. There isn't any word that does what I'm about to ask him to do any justice. "I need you to try to make me whole again."

Once it's out of my mouth I wait for Chance to bolt. I've put too much pressure on him and he's well within his rights to refuse. I brace myself for the rejection, can already see myself pulling my clothes back on and driving home with my cheeks on fire.

But Chance doesn't blink, instead he keeps his eyes locked on mine as he toes off his boots and loses his socks. He unfastens his jeans and lets them fall to the floor. He kicks them to the side and then we're both nearly naked.

"Come here," he says, his voice tight. I come willingly,

bringing my body back against his. "You were already whole, Lily, and you did that all by yourself. That's got nothing to do with me."

The weight of that realization hits me right in the gut. *I did it by myself.* Chance is a want, not a need. And I can let myself want him.

He kisses me softly. "We can stop at any time. No matter what."

I nod. I have no intention of stopping this time.

"We should go upstairs."

I shake my head. I don't want to go to Chance's bedroom. I want this to happen here in this place we've made together. In the place where things between us were made at the same time.

"We can't do this here, Lily. I should take you to bed. I should do this right."

"Here is right," I whisper, guiding him back toward the kitchen.

"But this isn't..." Chance tilts my chin up, looking into my eyes. He's so earnest, so serious that it makes me want this even more. Makes me want him more, if that's possible. Because right now, even though there are parts of me lighting up with fear, that fear is being overcome by my feelings for Chance. "This first time, it should be softer. Gentle."

"You'll be gentle." He will be because he knows me and I trust him to be because I know him.

"It should match," he says, even as his hands start to move over my exposed skin.

"Match?" I ask, confused.

"It should match us." His forehead wrinkles a bit as he struggles to explain. "It's supposed to match how we feel. That won't happen in here."

"It has to happen here," I tell him. "This is what I want."

Chance's still struggling to understand my stubborn decision to stay put.

I'm tired of explaining.

I need to show him how right this will be if he'll only let it. I rise up on my toes and kiss the dimple in his chin, letting my mouth slide higher until our lips meet. Pressed against him I can feel the willingness of his body even if his brain is having trouble with my choices. I know why he wants this to be all hearts and flowers, why he thinks he should be treating me like I'm breakable. Because a few months ago I was, but now I'm standing in the middle of a room he and I made with our own hands. I can see Chance's fingerprints on every surface in here the same way those fingerprints will be on my body.

"Lift me up," I tell him. "Put me on the counter."

Chance picks me up like I'm nothing, setting me down more gently than I would have thought possible. I open my legs and pull him closer, nothing between us but two layers of thin cotton and this one giant shadow of expectation. I kiss him again and slide my hands over the muscles of his shoulders. I can feel his heart beating when he wraps his arms around me and holds me against him.

"You're sure you want to do this here?" His voice is still laced with trepidation. He doesn't want me to have regrets. He doesn't want me to regret him.

"We took something that needed work and we made it beautiful," I tell him, whispering it into his ear like a secret. "I want to be here when we do that to me."

Chance blinks, understanding finally dawning on his face. He exhales and pulls me close again. "Same rules as always. Never too late to stop."

I relax into his embrace. "I know." I take a deep breath and fill my lungs with the smell of Chance's skin. I let my hands slide lower until they rest on the globes of his ass. Chance grunts but moves closer, lining himself up perfectly with me. He lets me lead, lowering his head for a kiss but keeping things slow. Chance's hands cup my cheeks as we continue our unhurried kisses, like making out in the kitchen is something we do every day and we have all day to do it.

I pull one hand away from Chance's body and reach around to unclasp my bra. We're still pressed together, the fabric staying put between us. I pull back from him with swollen lips, my face heated. That tiny bit of space has the straps sliding down, the tops of my breasts peeking out just enough to have Chance's eyes flicking between my face and my chest. I lean back on the counter and let the thing slide the rest of the way down, dropping it onto the kitchen floor. Chance keeps his eyes locked on mine, his breathing shallow.

"Lily?" I know exactly what he's asking.

"Please," I say and his head dips, planting kisses along the skin of my collarbone before sliding lower. When he captures a nipple between his lips I whimper. Chance's eyes dart up to mine but he keeps his mouth where it is. I lean my head back and fill my lungs with desperately needed air. I'm already drowning and he's barely touched me. Instead of fighting to get to the surface I let myself sink lower, remembering how it felt to *want* this rather than fear it.

My skin heats as Chance moves to my other breast. He's gentle, the warmth of his tongue steady. One callused hand slides lower, circling the elastic of my cotton panties. Again, he waits, never making the choice for me. The patience of this man is something that I try to remember never to take for granted. I guide him lower, encouraging his hand to move where I want it. Chance grunts in surprise when he finally lets his fingers move underneath that cotton barrier. His eyes fly back to mine as his mouth makes its way back up to the skin of my neck.

"How're we doing here?" he asks. It would be funny if it wasn't a question laced with years of mistrust and panic.

"You tell me," I whisper as his hand dips lower.

I'm wet. Very. Chance's eyes widen before he lets his fingers start to move. I surrender to his touch, moving my mouth back along the warm skin of his neck and up until I find his mouth. I kiss him until I see stars, until I can't keep my hands from running down his stomach and into the waistband of his useless boxer briefs. Chance jerks, but doesn't stop me from wrapping my fingers around him. He's perfect and suddenly I can't get close enough. We're skin to skin and I'm dying for more of him.

"Do you want to finish like this?" Chance asks, panting. He presses his forehead against mine, grunting as I give him another squeeze.

"More," I manage. "I want more." Because now that I'm tipping over the edge there's no way I'm stopping.

"You sure?" he asks, but the way his hips keep moving in time with the motion of my hand tells me he's going to have trouble slowing down, too. But he would, if I asked, which makes me even more certain of my answer.

"Yes." I use my free hand to slide his boxers over his backside and down to his ankles.

Chance groans. "Condom. We need a condom." His eyes scan the room, looking for his discarded jeans, I'd bet. But after all this time I suddenly can't wait even the sixty seconds it'd take for him to run into the living room to grab them.

"I have an IUD." I've had it ever since I realized it didn't always matter what I had planned for my body. Constant birth control had given me back a sliver of my sanity. "I got tested after and there hasn't been anyone since so... If you're okay with not using one."

Chance's brow wrinkles. "I'm clean," he says. "But that's a lot of... trust right there, Lily. It'll take me two seconds to get one if you want me to. Don't feel any pressure to—"

I ease my hips up and wiggle out of my panties. Chance's eyes move down my body before returning to look at my face.

"I don't need a condom if you don't need one." I return my hand to his cock and Chance's eyes flutter closed. He positions himself between my legs and our chests meet. When he tilts his head down for a kiss I open for him, gasping as I feel him pushing at my entrance and then finally sliding into me. The noise he makes has me grabbing for the hair on the back of his head, trying to steady myself.

I was far from a virgin the night of that party, but here with Chance it's like none of that even matters. It's like I'm doing this for the first time all over again as he pulls his hips back and thrusts again. I wrap my arms around his neck and keep my mouth pressed to his. Never have I felt cared for like this, never have I felt as worshipped as I do in Chance's arms. He presses his forehead to mine.

"Tell me what you need," he says, panting just enough to have me coming back into my body.

"Just this." I wrap my legs around his hips. "Just this." I grind myself against him and feel my body beginning to go tight. Our eyes are locked together when I finally feel myself tipping over the edge. Chance isn't far behind, coming with a groan that will probably have his aunts running over to see what's going on. He keeps his arms wrapped tight around me as I shake and shudder against him. He pulls back, startled, and I flinch at the sudden loss of his chest against mine.

"Are you crying?" The horror in his eyes is impossible to hide.

"No," I protest just as a huge tear drop makes its way down my cheek to land on his forearm. I am crying. Because I've come through to the other side. I'm crying tears of joy.

27

Chance

Happy tears.

That's what Lily told me after she started sobbing, seconds after we finished. I've never had a woman cry during sex before, but Lily insisted that her reaction wasn't something for me to be upset about. I hope she's telling the truth, because if she's lying then I have seriously fucked up. I was already worried, especially when she insisted on staying in the kitchen, but she seems fine, better than fine even.

I tuck a strand of her hair back behind her ear and she wiggles closer to the pillow. We're upstairs in my bedroom— my temporary bedroom—and Lily's snoozing away. I managed to convince her to come up here for round two and the completely unexpected round three once we both realized this was all we were going to be able to concentrate on today. There's been no more crying but there's also been zero work done on the house.

I couldn't be happier about it.

Wiping this smile off my big, stupid face is going to take

some effort. But my brothers will start trickling in here soon and I don't want any of those nosy assholes intruding on this moment with Lily. I certainly don't want them to find us up here after walking through a sea of discarded clothes in the living room. Lily doesn't need to hear any of my brothers' comments. Neither do I.

I know I've waded in deep here but there was no way I could stop myself. I've been gone for Lily since before I knew what that even meant and watching her fall apart in my arms has made my heart even more stubborn. It seems like fate that we're up here together, her dark hair fanned out over my pillow. I never want to leave.

But I know none of this is forever. Sure, I've moved from the room with the twin beds to this one with a queen. I've even replaced this mattress so Lily's resting on something less than two hundred years old. My things are scattered all over the place like I'm planning on being here for a while. Which isn't true for me or for Lily, either. Sleeping with her is only going to make it that much harder when this all comes to its inevitable end. And sleeping with her when the stakes were so high kicks everything up a notch.

Lily rolls over and opens her eyes, stretching her arms up over her head. I get a hint of a nipple as the sheet slips lower. If Lily notices she doesn't seem to care. That's a win from where I'm sitting—for both of us.

"What time is it?" she asks, still groggy.

"Close to four." I let my hand run down the length of her arm. She shivers but doesn't pull away. "We should probably get up before we get overrun with Allen brothers."

"Are they all coming this weekend?" she asks and I wish like hell they weren't.

"Every weekend from now until this place is perfect, apparently." Once Charlie and Cade found out about the barn they wouldn't hear of missing a work weekend here at the farm. My grandpa would've been proud... right now I'm annoyed their help is keeping me from snuggling back down under these quilts with Lily.

"We don't have time to go again?" Lily asks from underneath her lashes. That shy routine isn't fooling me, but her eagerness does have the tiniest bit of worry rattling around in my brain.

"Again?' I lean down to kiss the spot under her ear that it turns out she loves. "Woman, you're going to kill me. You've gone from zero to sixty pretty quick here."

Lily's face clouds. "We've been working up to it," she protests.

I frown against her shoulder. That's technically true, but her sudden interest in fucking my brains out is something I hadn't expected.

"I'd forgotten how it could be," she says and that makes my chest puff up even though I know it shouldn't. Truth be told it's never been like it is with Lily for me. Maybe I'd never really been needed the way Lily's needed me, never had to put so much of myself into something. She's ruined me for anyone else. Not that I can tell her that.

"But we don't have to act like going slow is terrible. I'm happy this is working out, that you're still feeling good about everything, but that doesn't change the fact that you could still have some hesitation. I'd understand."

Lily turns her face away from me.

"You're still feeling okay about all of this, right?"

Lily lets out a breath. "Yes."

"Then we're good. But I don't want you to have to deal with my brothers naked."

"Can I shower here?" That nipple's still in full view of my wandering eyes.

"Sure. You want to use the master? You can give me suggestions for what we should do in there. Jets or one of those rainfall things."

"I can't make suggestions unless I have you in there with me."

My dick twitches. Lily in the shower is one of my go-to fantasies. Even the idea of my grandpa's shower isn't making me any less eager.

"We'd have to test out how people would really use the space," Lily says and I don't miss the fact that she lets the entire sheet fall to her waist as she sits up to argue her point. "We'd need to try things out."

That's all I need to scoop her out of bed and carry her out into the hallway. I'm swayed by the research, I tell myself, not by the sight of Lily's naked body and the possibility of soaping it up. But this is a fact-finding mission in more ways than one.

I'm so dead.

"Explain to me again why we're doing *this* instead of fixing the fence like we talked about last weekend." Cade gestures to the array of bottles and paint that I've got spread out over tarps on the front porch.

"Because Chance got laid." Cooper doesn't even bother to look up when I slap the back of his head.

"Is that seriously why we're pouring paint into Mason jars?" Charlie asks. "Because I'm not here to make sure you can keep getting naked with Lily."

"Like you have anything better to do at home."

Charlie just shrugs, ignoring my challenge, but Cade's eye roll is hard to miss.

"Wait," Cooper says. "Did you seriously get laid? I was kind of joking."

All eyes fixate on me. I'd managed to get Lily out of the house yesterday without arousing any suspicion but now it looks like I've gone ahead and blabbed everything to the biggest group of church ladies ever assembled.

"That's none of your business," I answer.

"That's a yes," Charlie responds and my other brothers all shake their heads. "No wonder you haven't yelled at us today."

"So now we're slave labor for Lily until she kicks you to the curb?" Cade asks.

I hope that's not going to fucking happen. Being here without the possibility of Lily? No, thank you. "No one's slave labor. Mixing this paint up helps us too. We're going to sell it at Southern Comforts and promote it on the website and our YouTube channel."

When Lily told me people had been coming into the shop to buy the paint she's been using on the furniture, I'd come up with a plan to get it on the shelves in the short term. It isn't perfect, but she's given me the ratios for mixing the stuff up and we're pouring it into jars until I can come up with a better solution. Lily can make the packaging look presentable and she's at the store right now setting up the furniture so that corresponding paint colors can be featured next to a piece that actually uses the paint.

Which leaves me with my less than enthusiastic brothers.

"This doesn't have to be exact, does it?" Cooper asks and I give him a death glare.

"Of course it has to be exact. That's what the chart's for. Follow the instructions and we should be able to move on to the fence before ten." I shake my head and, uncharacteristically, all three of my brothers get right back to work, pouring paint through the collection of funnels I've dug up from the basement. I reach for a jar of my own and start mixing the color on the chart in front of me. Lily's going to give all of the paint colors cutesy names that she thinks will sound farmhouse, but right now I've got the chart that reads "dark blue."

I'm so busy concentrating on getting the color just right that I don't notice Cooper sliding up next to me. He's supposed to be mixing the red, and I get set to tell him to go back to work, but his section of the tarp already has fifteen full jars of paint. He gives me a look that lets me know he's about to start talking, and I brace myself for whatever bit of terrible advice he's about to give me.

"So you and Lily," he says. It isn't a question so I don't bother answering. He clears his throat and I look up from my paint. "Are you sure that's a good idea?"

Now I can either answer him or continue to ignore him. I split the difference and shrug.

"She on the same page as you?" He leans back against the side of the house. "Because this could get messy."

"I can work out my relationship with Lily all by myself, thanks."

Cooper raises an eyebrow and I can see Cade and Charlie's backs stiffen. "You're calling it a relationship?" he asks, the disbelief in his voice stronger than I'd like.

"I can call it whatever I want."

"What's she calling it?"

I put down the jar I've been filling and look Cooper in the eye. "I'll let you know once I find out."

"I'm only trying to look out for you. And for her. You'll be heading back to California before too long."

"Probably." I don't know what my next move will be, but it's not worth saying that to Cade and Charlie.

"I thought you were going to let them buy you out," Cade says without turning around to look at me. "Did you decide to keep working with those guys?"

I scowl. Those guys used to be my closest friends. Now we're business partners and barely even that. I've been ignoring my emails and calls from them—out of spite more than anything else—but now I'm feeling the need to untangle myself from everything. A fresh start doesn't sound as bad as it did a few months ago.

"You should just take the money. Fuck those guys," Charlie says. "You could start something else on your own."

That's another possibility appealing less and less to me by the day. These days I look forward to waking up and working on the house, to being exhausted both mentally and physically at the end of the day.

And to seeing Lily's face light up when she comes into a room and sees me standing there.

As if he can hear me thinking about Lily, Cooper chimes in again. "You'll be back in sunny California soon and Lily'll be in Chicago, right? There's no need to start something that can't go anywhere."

"I thought you liked Lily."

"I do. I like her a lot. But she's like a barn cat. You don't pick one of those up without getting bit. And I know what it's like to not be able to live up to expectations." Cooper's face clouds.

"What's that supposed to mean?"

"And after what Travis said..." Cooper has the good sense not to finish that thought.

I straighten up and square my shoulders. "We're not going to talk about what Travis said."

Cooper puts his hands up. "You know I don't mean anything by bringing it up."

"Then how about you don't mention it again." Charlie and Cade don't have any idea that Lily's been through hell and I'm not about to tell them. I'm not even going to fill in the blanks for Cooper. That's not my story to tell and I won't break Lily's confidence even to make my brothers better understand why I'm so protective of her.

"I just want you to be careful. Don't get carried away and break her heart."

Cooper has no idea that it isn't Lily's heart I'm worried about right now.

"How about we let Chance figure his own shit out and stick to getting this paint bullshit over with?" Cade calls from his corner of the porch. "I'd like to finish the fence this weekend before my classes start up again." He's taking valuable study time to help out and never lets us forget it.

Charlie grunts in agreement, keeping his head bent over the jars in front of him. He's mixing yellow and has gotten more of it on the tarp than in his containers.

"That's fine by me," I say and Cooper starts to move back to his section of the porch, still giving me that wary look.

"Don't say I didn't warn you," he says before picking up another jar. "Summer flings have a way of feeling different come fall."

I don't bother to answer him with some snappy remark because I know Cooper's right. But I also know this is more than some fling and that when fall comes it's going to damn near kill me to say goodbye.

28

Lily

"I cannot believe I let you talk me into this."

"What? It'll be fun."

"There isn't some surprise karaoke or something like that is there? Because if there is, I'm going to kill you and everyone would agree it's justified." I look over at Chance's face and catch him smiling. "Seriously. I agreed to go and hang out at the bar. Nothing else, Chance."

"Nothing after?" he asks and I have to scowl to disguise the excitement I immediately feel. It's still unexpected to get that rush of heat the mere suggestion of naked time with Chance gives me. I shiver even though it's still hotter than hell outside. I can already imagine Chance's hands on me and goosebumps immediately rise on my arms.

"Nothing that involves singing in public or social axe throwing or anything like that."

Chance smirks. "I don't think Mint Springs has social axe throwing. There's a business idea for you though. We could open up one of those places. Sell beer and everything."

We. If it would keep him here a little longer, I'd consider just about anything at this point. Cat cafe? Sure. Vegan clothing store? Of course. Anything to keep this man sitting beside me in this ancient truck. Anything not to have to admit that I've gotten myself in too deep. That my feelings for him are more serious than I've been letting on.

"I think people around here consider it to be social axe throwing when you hurl your axe at a sibling while chopping wood. That market's already pretty saturated, if you ask me."

Chance laughs and turns the truck into the gravel parking lot of the Bootleggers, the diviest dive bar in the entire county. "You know, I have been thinking about a business idea." He puts the truck in park and turns that handsome face toward me. "You should think about opening an interior design business."

I stare. "Interior design?"

"Sure. You could get paid to help people fix up their houses. Like you've been doing for me."

Like we've been doing together, I almost remind him. I'm not sure how I'd feel about trying to do that without Chance.

"I've got a check for you, by the way. Don't let me forget to give it to you."

I nod. I need the money. Want the money to keep paying down those bills that keep coming to Bunny's house. The store's had its best month ever, thanks to traffic from the videos and website. I've sold more paint than I thought possible. People have been asking if I can take on other jobs, help with their renovations and redecorating. But I'm getting the feeling that Chance isn't thinking about us doing this as a team. He's got the slightest shake in his hands when he moves them from the steering wheel, and when he wipes his palms along his thighs, I know this isn't just idle conversation. He's setting things up so he can leave without worrying about how I'll get along.

He still thinks I need extra protecting. I appreciate the sentiment, but if that's how he feels, then I don't want to be talking about "our" future without him in it.

"Where would I set up this hypothetical business? Chicago?"

Chance frowns. "Sure, if that's what you want. You could combine that with the furniture refinishing and the paint. Don't people in Chicago like that upscale farmhouse vibe? You'd be like that Joanna lady from the TV show."

I keep it to myself that Joanna has Chip. I try to imagine being back in the city with a little storefront somewhere. That would have been a nice set up before, and now that I know I can do the work it's actually a possibility. But I can't deny Mint Springs would be a better place to sell my style. Not that I'd have my Chip here either because he seems to have plans to move on.

"You could stay here," Chance says, putting his hands back on the steering wheel. "Might be nice to be close to family. And the requests we're getting in the comments from the videos are usually from around here. Lots of Atlanta and Chattanooga."

"Maybe," I'm noncommittal. Why is Chance bringing this up now, right before we have to go inside and face half the population of Mint Springs, Georgia?

"Would you consider staying here, I mean, if—"

Banging on the hood of the truck makes me jump. Cooper's animated face appears in the driver's side window. "Are you guys coming in or what? This birthday isn't going to celebrate itself!"

Chance lets out a breath. "We're coming. Give us a

second." He glares at his brother through the glass and Cooper scurries off.

"We should go in." I reach for the handle of the door.

Chance nods. "We don't have to stay long, but Cooper'll get pissy if we don't come in for a drink. You'd think his birthday was a national holiday or something."

"We can stay for a bit." I'm not excited about being at Bootlegger but I'm even less excited about finishing our conversation—a conversation where Chance was pretty close to saying how ready he is to be back in his old life and away from here.

We don't have any trouble finding Chance's brothers once we get inside. They're already whooping and hollering, several empty shot glasses upside down on the table in front of them. Chance holds my hand as we make our way toward them. There are plenty of people I know and have been avoiding since I came back into town. The flashes of recognition on their faces are usually followed by what I assume is intense gossip. Heads bow together and I'm sure some of the talk is about the way Chance shepherds me through the crowd toward the back, using his body to keep anyone else from touching me. The set of his shoulders has people moving out of the way without a word, making space for us.

"About damn time," Hadley mutters once we make it to the table. I'd told her we'd probably end up here tonight, leaving out the part about it being Cooper's birthday celebration. From the looks of things Hadley's not too pleased to be the only girl surrounded on all sides by the Allens. She's got her usual glass of whiskey in front of her and slides over to make room for me on the worn bench. I wedge myself in and let out the breath I've been holding.

"I'd forgotten how crowded this place can get."

"Well, when there're only two choices for nightlife..."

Charlie swings an arm wide. "You end up with Bootlegger. Most exciting bar for miles."

It is grungier than I remember. My hand sticks to the edge of the table when I let my fingers wander. Old dollar bills with messages written on them are stapled behind the ancient bar and the wood paneling that lines the walls has to be from before we were born.

"Remember how we used to try to sneak in here during the summer?" Chance laughs. "Even Cade. And you had to be what? Thirteen years old?"

"And we'd all get so mad when they wouldn't let us just waltz on in." Hadley smiles at the memory.

"Well, Lily and I aren't staying too long, so fair warning." Chance gives my hand a protective squeeze. "I'm still not sure why you wanted to come out here tonight, Coop."

"Because we can't stay up at the farm all the time," Cooper argues, reaching for Hadley's glass of whiskey. "I need to come out and see what Mint Springs has to offer. Some of us don't have the kind of entertainment you have at home."

My cheeks heat.

Hadley swats at Cooper's hand. "Get your own drink. Better yet, why don't you see if you can get one of Mint Springs' fine ladies to buy you one? Just make sure she's got all her teeth."

"I'll go get the drinks if the two of you will stop bickering." Chance gives Cooper a glare. "What do we want? A pitcher?"

"And a lemonade. Don't forget Lily's lemonade."

I smile at Charlie.

"I wouldn't dream of forgetting that." Chance gives me a quick kiss. "Be right back." Cooper follows along behind him, slapping backs and shaking hands like he's the mayor.

"Dart board's free." Charlie and Cade scramble from their seats, running to be the first ones to the corner of the room, celebrating with high fives when they manage to grab the darts before another group of guys can.

"I cannot believe I spent an hour on my hair for this." Hadley rolls her eyes. "At least the drinks are cheap."

"You always spend an hour on your hair," I scoff. "And you know you'd just be home watching TV. This is so much more interesting."

"Maybe for you, but I've been seeing this same view forever now. The only difference is that tonight I get to watch Cooper make an ass of himself."

Right on cue Cooper leans over to get a better look at the bartender's backside. Chance gives him a slap on the back of the head and what looks like a stern talking to.

"And you get to be out with me. That's different," I remind her. I give her a little punch in the arm and Hadley's face blanches. "Come on! I didn't hit you that hard."

"Lily?"

I freeze.

"I thought that was you."

Riley.

Chance

I was so close.

So close to asking Lily if she'd think about staying.

I know that's not fair to her, trying to make her give up her life in Chicago and stay in a place that opens old wounds. It isn't fair to ask her to stay, even if I want her to. And I want her to, not because of some family obligations, but because of me. I want her to stay because she wants to be with me. And it was on the tip of my tongue to ask her before Cooper interrupted us. Stupid Cooper. Even now he's acting up, flirting with the bartender when he knows he really wants to be over with Hadley. He's making a good show of it—so good he might get us kicked out of this bar if he keeps it up.

I'd been two seconds from begging Lily to consider staying in Mint Springs. I've realized I can't go back to California. In truth I don't want to, maybe I never did. Maybe I knew that by coming back here I'd be setting myself up to stay, but I haven't been able to admit that to myself until recently. I like being on the farm, like having my aunts rely on me. Like being with Lily.

Scratch that. I *love* being with Lily. Because I've just figured out that this feeling I get in my chest every time I look at her or think about her is just that. Love. I'm in love with Lily Gentry, and I need to man up and tell her even if she laughs in my face and takes off running in the other direction. I'm hopeful she won't, but I have to lay it all on the line. To risk everything to have what I think Lily and I could have together.

Cooper's ordering way more drinks than we need, hanging over the bar to get closer to the blonde working on the other side. She slides a few shot glasses our way and goes to pour the pitcher of beer "we've" asked for. Cooper turns to give me one of his dumb smirks, probably ready to make some crack about how hot this woman is. We both know she's not the one he's been fixated on for the last few months, no matter how hard he tries to hide it. But when he opens his mouth nothing comes out. Instead, his eyes narrow and all I hear is a muttered curse under his breath. I turn, trying to figure out what's got him so annoyed. There are few things that can make Cooper stop babbling and I don't imagine any of those have walked into this establishment.

But it turns out one has, and without thinking I push away from the bar and move toward Lily. I haven't seen my cousin Riley in years. I'm not even sure where he lives or what he does for work. But I'm sure of one thing: he didn't protect Lily when she needed him. The anger from that night in the back of my truck barrels over me. I don't want him anywhere near Lily.

It's like I'm moving in slow motion as I stride across the

wooden floor, people moving out of my way like I'm parting the Red Sea. I see Travis in my periphery but even that doesn't make me hesitate. If he wants to jump in to help his brother, I'm confident I can take them both, especially with the uncontrollable rage that's started to bubble through me. I've already got one hand balled into a fist when I make it to our table and I don't ask any questions before I raise it up and let it land hard across Riley's jaw. He staggers back, grabbing at the place where I've punched him, the shock on his face only feeding my need to hit him again. I can't hear anything but the blood rushing in my ears. I grab Riley by the collar and hit him again. I get one more good punch in, my fist connecting with his face before his brother's pulling me off of him, swinging wildly at me. That gives Riley enough time to get his bearings and come running at me. He wraps his arms around my waist and we both go down, crashing into tables. Bottles shatter around us and I'm aware of the feeling of broken glass on my back as Riley and I roll around on the filthy floor. We're the ultimate redneck cliché—family having a fight in some backwoods bar—and when my brothers join in, unsure if they should be pulling us apart or trying to land punches themselves, we all end up sprawled in one giant mass of bodies until the bouncers start hauling us off each other. One of them has me by the back of the collar and I fight to get away from him, pulling to try to get close enough to Riley to hit him again.

"That's enough! You'd all better get your asses out to the parking lot before I decide to call the sheriff."

I know that's not an idle threat and as much as I'd like to beat Riley to a bloody pulp, I try to get myself under control. My shirt's ripped—one sleeve's almost clean off—and I've got blood in my mouth. I can already feel a lump rising on my cheekbone.

"We're going, no need to call the cops," I hear Cooper

tell one of the giant guys now eyeing me like I might need a few of their fists in my face as well. "Come on, Chance."

Travis is dusting Riley off, both of them scowling at me.

"I only wanted to talk to her," Riley tells me, rubbing his jaw. "You didn't need to hit me."

"Like hell I didn't." I search the crowd for Lily. "You leave her the fuck alone. You hear me?"

"Should have taken more than one wall of that barn," Travis mumbles and I see red again.

"What did you say?" I'm pushing against my brothers, nearly climbing over them to get to Travis and Riley.

"You heard me." Travis tips his chin at me, daring me to come at them again, knowing I'll be the one who gets carted out of here and arrested if I manage to land even one punch.

My brothers are pushing me out the door. "Shut up, Chance." Cade's got me by the shoulder and from the way he's squeezing he's not letting go until we're outside.

"Did you fucking hear that?" I demand as my brothers shove me through the crowd and out into the parking lot. I spit out a mouthful of blood once we make it to my truck. It feels like I have all my teeth, but Travis is about to lose a few of his if he's stupid enough to come near me tonight.

Cade releases me but doesn't let me get far. "Did you hear what Travis said about the barn?" I can't believe my brothers aren't as livid as I am.

"He's probably just trying to rile you up." Cooper doesn't sound convinced. "We'll deal with that later. Right now we've got to get out of town before someone decides you need a ride with the blue lights. Don't let him go back in there." The warning's directed at Charlie and he folds his arms over his chest, rising to his full height. He may be my younger brother but there's nothing little about him. I'm not likely to best him in a fight, especially not tonight.

"Where's Lily?" I look back over my shoulder. I don't have any intention of leaving her here.

"She's long gone." Charlie shakes his head. "What the hell were you thinking?"

"Gone? Gone where?"

"Hadley got her out of there the second you started beating the crap out of Riley. Not sure what he did to deserve that. He hadn't even said two words to her before you came out swinging." Charlie keeps his body between me and the rest of the bar patrons. They'd love to see us get back in it. Nothing like a brawl to make a Saturday night more interesting.

"I need to find her."

"Oh, no you don't. You need to get cleaned up first, and by the way she was acting she isn't going to want to talk to you until you cool off. She was pretty upset, Chance. You really scared her."

"You don't understand the situation, Charlie. I need to make sure she's okay."

"She's not. You need to leave her alone. Cooper's going to check on her. And I think you might need stitches. That cut over your eye looks pretty deep."

I touch the space above my eyebrow and wince. "It's not that bad." I'm sure it's actually as bad as Charlie thinks, maybe worse, but there's no way I'm going to the emergency room. The only emergency here is my need to get to Lily.

"Fine, if you won't go to the hospital, we're taking you home. Give me your keys."

I fish them out of my pocket and hand them to Charlie. He unlocks the passenger side door and watches as I ease myself onto the bench seat. The adrenaline's wearing off and I can clearly feel the start of some pretty serious bumps and bruises.

"I think you've started to bleed through your shirt." Charlie's face radiates disappointment at me from the driver's side. "We can take a look at that when we get back to the farm."

"I'm fine." I settle myself as best I can against the door, careful not to lean against the old upholstery. The last thing I need is to have to clean up blood in the truck along with everything else. And I've got a lot to clean up tonight. I can't believe how quickly this evening has gone to shit. One minute I'm thinking about confessing my feelings to Lily and the next I'm riding home getting a lecture from my younger brother.

"And give me your phone."

"What? No." I'm not giving up my most reliable way to apologize to Lily.

"You're only going to make things worse if you start calling and texting. You can have it back in the morning when your head's clear." Charlie keeps his eyes on the road but reaches out his hand. "No arguing. If you don't give it to me, I'm going to let Cooper take it from you. You've already got a busted lip; do you really want a black eye to go with it?"

I don't, and I know Cooper'll give me one if he thinks I'm making a stupid mistake. Maybe I should give Lily the night to calm down. It takes everything in me to hand my phone to my little brother. Knowing Lily's hurting and there's nothing I can do to fix that tonight has me physically hurting. I close my eyes and wince at the sharp pain that stabs me over the eye. I can talk to Lily tomorrow once I don't look like Rocky Balboa, once I figure out what the hell to say to make her understand why I did what I did.

If I can manage to make sense of it to myself.

30

Lily

I can't breathe.

I've got my head between my legs, but even that isn't helping me. I gasp for air as Hadley rubs my back. Thank God for Hadley because without her I have no idea how I'd be surviving this. She's driving one-handed, steering us through town, getting me as far away from the bar as possible.

"How're you doing over there?"

I let out a sob. I'm surprised I can cry in the middle of a panic attack, but I'm managing to do it. At least that means I'm still breathing.

"You just keep focusing on air in and air out. I'll have us home in no time." Hadley's voice has that fake chipper quality she uses with difficult clients at the salon, the one she uses with telemarketers on the phone. "I can't believe Chance did that."

I can. The look on his face as he stalked across the bar made it clear he wasn't about to listen to reason. I didn't want to talk to Riley, didn't want to see him ever again. But that look on Chance's face when he saw his cousin standing there? That was pure fury.

And it terrified me.

Even now I can't get the rage on his face out of my mind. He's normally so sweet, so gentle and patient with me. But in a moment he went from the man I know, the safe man I've come to love, to some sort of monster. He'd hit Riley without any warning and the melee that followed had me scrambling for the door. Luckily, Hadley had been right behind me, car keys at the ready.

"We'll get home and then we'll sort this out," Hadley's voice cuts through the rasping of my breathing. "You didn't get hurt, did you? Physically, I mean."

"No." I'd been spared any errant punches. My body's fine; it's the rest of me that's bruised right now. Chance had done what I would have thought I'd wanted years ago. He'd put his body between mine and a threat. He'd made sure no one was going to be able to hurt me.

Finally seeing it play out in real time hadn't made me feel any better. Riley wasn't really the person who'd hurt me. Not in the way that had really counted. And seeing that switch flip in Chance has me both needing space and desperate to see he's in one piece.

As Hadley puts the car in park her phone starts to ring. She's set her ringtone to one of her favorite Patsy Cline songs and I'm treated to a musical version of "Crazy" before she gets her fingers working. I hear snippets of her conversation as she gets out of the car and comes around to my side. I haven't managed to open my door or move from my seat.

"I'll take care of her. No, she's fine. You don't need to— Cooper Allen! Don't you dare. Don't—hello?" Hadley growls and shoves her phone in the back pocket of her painted-on jeans. "That man is infuriating. Cooper's on his way over here, I guess. Do you need help or can you manage?"

Hadley's outstretched hand hovers near my shoulder. She's careful not to touch me again—*had* she touched me on the way out of the bar tonight?—and I feel like I've been transported back to the beginning of all this, back when even a simple touch of my friend's hand would have me recoiling. I straighten up. I don't need to be frightened like that anymore. Tonight's a setback, but not the end of the world. I don't even care if tongues are wagging down at Bootlegger. That's what I tell myself as I take Hadley's hand and pull myself up from the jaws of this bucket seat.

"I can take it from here. If Cooper's coming over, we should make ourselves presentable."

"There's my girl. We probably could use a little lipstick." Hadley wipes at what I'm sure are mascara streaks on my cheeks. "I'll pick up the living room while you primp a little. We've got this under control."

Cooper pulls up before we even get the front door shut, bounding out of his car and heading straight for Hadley. He calls out, "Hadley Crawford, don't you dare shut that door."

And for some reason she listens. Even though she and Copper are like oil and water, she holds the door open without one ounce of sass.

Once he's inside the apartment he's checking Hadley over like she's the one who's been in a brawl.

"Cooper, we are fine. Lily's just a little shaken up, that's all." She pushes his hands away and he turns to look at me like he's forgotten that I'm even there. She nods toward the other room. "Lily, go splash your face while I get some ice for Cooper." He's got an angry bruise starting under his right eye.

I head to the bathroom to wash off the evidence of my

terrible evening. The cool water feels good against my skin, reminding me of the river and the first time this summer when Chance convinced me to go for a swim. I'd trusted him then, somehow known he wouldn't hurt me. Is tonight enough for me to forget all about that? Is one night of anger enough to have me questioning who he is? Or can I trust that he's the man he's shown me to be before, and tonight's just a blip?

When I walk into the living room, Hadley's got a bag of frozen peas positioned on Cooper's scowling face. It's hard to miss the way she looks at him and for a split second I could swear he's looking at her the same way, their eyes locked in mutual admiration.

I clear my throat and Hadley pulls away, forcing Cooper to hold the bag himself.

"Keep it there or that eye will swell shut," she barks at him and he leaves the peas against his eye, even as he shakes his head. "Better?" Hadley asks me.

"Much. I need to talk to Chance. Can you take me out to the farm?"

Cooper shoots a look at Hadley and shakes his head again. "No can do, Lily. He needs to cool off. Charlie and Cade'll get him cleaned up. After the way he acted tonight I think he's going to need a little time to think about what an ass he was. He just hauled off and hit Riley for no reason."

"I'm sure he had his reasons," Hadley interjects, standing up for Chance, knowing full well we can't really tell Cooper why he'd come out swinging.

"Reasons or not, you two are staying here. Don't make me sleep on the couch."

"You have not been *invited* to sleep on this couch."

"Hadley, if you're going to be stubborn then you're going

to find out where that gets you." Cooper's eyes glint, more than happy to argue with Hadley.

"Why don't I let the two of you work out whatever is going on here by yourselves." I reach for my bag and rifle around for my keys.

"And just where do you think you're going?" Hadley looks at me like I've decided to wear my bikini to church.

"*To the farm.*" I need to see Chance with my own eyes, be sure that he's really alright before I punch him in the face myself. Or kiss him. I'm still not sure which.

"No, you are not. I just watched you have the mother of all panic attacks not five minutes ago. You aren't driving anywhere tonight."

I scowl and put my car keys away while pulling out my phone. If I can hear Chance's voice, some of this uncertainty's sure to melt away.

"Don't bother trying to call. I had Charlie take his phone for the night—maybe longer depending on his behavior." Cooper barely looks at me. "I told him I'd make sure you were alright. He's probably climbing the walls, but it's better for everyone if he just keeps to himself. Don't want anyone thinking they need to finish what he started tonight. You know those boys are still running around."

Hadley jams her hands on her hips. "And you've unilaterally made this decision? You're not in charge of Lily and Chance, Cooper. Or me for that matter."

"We just don't need any more drama tonight. After he sleeps it off you two can talk all this out." Cooper lets out a sigh. "But it's your decision. He's just a mess tonight. You don't want to see him. I'm having enough trouble keeping Travis from running over there half-cocked."

I'm a mess, too, but the threat of running into any of Chance's cousins again makes my hands start to shake. Riley could show up at the farm and there'd be no way for me to run out of there. I'd be the reason for any new argument.

Chance and his brothers can take care of themselves but asking them to keep taking care of me is too much.

"Can you just have him call me in the morning? First thing? If I stay put tonight can you promise me that?"

"First thing," Cooper says. "Just don't expect it to be too early. He's going to be hurting tomorrow." He shakes his head, wincing as he repositions the frozen peas.

We're all going to be hurting tomorrow. Chance's face can't be in nearly as much pain as my heart.

31

Chance

"Wake up, asshole. We have somewhere to be in twenty minutes."

I pry my eyes open. That's harder than it should be, considering what time I was banished to my room last night. But I had a hard time sleeping, knowing that Lily was at her apartment most likely upset. And if my face looks half as bad as it feels I should probably not leave the house—or look in any mirrors—today.

"Where are we going?" There's only one place I want to be and I'm pretty sure Cooper and I aren't on the same page.

"You'll see. Get cleaned up and get your ass in the truck." He throws the curtains open and the morning light assaults my eyes. "You look like shit."

I feel like it too, but I still growl at my brother.

"Hurry up. I don't want to be late."

I ease myself up onto one elbow. There's blood on the pillowcase and even more caked on my knuckles. Things got out of control fast last night and I can only hope that Riley looks as bad as I feel.

I don't have to wonder long about that because when Cooper pulls into the parking lot of Ham & Eggs there he is, sitting at the counter, sipping on a cup of coffee.

"Oh, hell no. Whatever you've got planned with Riley, I'm not interested."

Cooper silently gets out of the truck and comes around to the passenger side. He opens the door with a flourish and points toward our cousin. "I don't give a shit what you want right now, Chance. You're lucky Riley didn't press charges last night. Everyone in that bar saw you come at him unprovoked. I'm not even sure what made you decide that was a great idea."

I cross my arms over my chest.

"I can understand why you'd want to punch Travis, but Riley? What the fuck's he ever done to you?"

I look away. This isn't about what he's done to me. It's about what he's done to Lily.

About what he let happen, the things he didn't do.

But I can't explain that to Cooper.

"He's still family and the two of you need to talk it out. He's not excited to see you either, but you're going in there to talk to him if I have to carry you in."

"Like you could." I'd snarl if it didn't risk opening the cut on my lip back up.

"You want to try me?" Cooper's not joking. He doesn't pull out the big brother stuff often, but when he does, he doesn't mess around. Having him physically drag me into the diner would be icing on the cake for the past twenty-four hours.

"Fine. I'm going."

"I'll be sitting here waiting till you're done."

Jesus. He's going to babysit me too. "But after this you take me to Lily's."

"We'll see. One thing at a time, bruiser. Here's your phone in case you need to call an ambulance."

I ignore Cooper's smirk and force myself to put one foot in front of the other. At the sound of the bell over the door Riley turns to look at me. He's got a black eye and a bruise on his chin that rivals mine. We really worked each other over. Everyone else in the restaurant turns to stare and I'm sure there's not a soul in here who doesn't already know all about last night.

"Coffee?" Debbie asks as I slide onto the stool next to my cousin. "You look like you could use it."

"Yes, please."

"And no fighting in here, boys. Henry's ready to throw you both out if you start anything, you understand?" She motions back toward the kitchen where one of the burly, tattooed grill cooks glares at us menacingly.

"Yes, ma'am," we both answer in unison.

"Don't forget." Debbie points an accusing finger at us. "Zero tolerance. Now, you two make up. Kin shouldn't be acting like this." She shakes her head as she walks away making that disgusted *tsk tsk* noise that every lady over forty in Mint Springs has perfected.

We stare straight ahead for what feels like an eternity. Mercifully, Riley breaks first, clearing his throat. "I didn't know you were with her." He doesn't turn to face me, just keeps looking at the kitchen.

"Well, I am."

"And I'm guessing she told you what happened."

"She did." Maybe Riley's got his own version of events, but I'll be damned if I'm going to let him turn this thing around. I may have been wrong to hit him without any warning but he was wrong to leave Lily alone with his friends. He's the reason she's been struggling. For years she's been dealing with what happened to her while Riley's been off living his life. I'm not letting him off the hook for that.

"Then you were right to punch me. Wouldn't have fought back if I'd known that was what it was about." He laughs bitterly.

I swivel on my stool. "What?"

"Might let you hit me a few more times this morning."

"Not sure what good that'll do. Probably get us kicked out before we get to eat."

Debbie slides a cup of coffee in front of me and gives us both another stern glare. "Are you two eating or did you get too many teeth knocked out last night?"

I hand a menu to Riley and we order, all the while I'm rolling his words around in my head.

"I'm sure Travis made it seem like it was Lily's fault that I left school. I'm sorry if he's been running his mouth. I'll set him straight." He massages the lump on his chin, wiggles his jaw. "You got me pretty good right here."

"Maybe you should set me straight, too. How the hell did you let that happen to her, Riley? And then why did you take off and leave her like that? You knew what they'd done and you let her face that alone." I keep my hands fisted at my sides. Even thinking about Lily broken and hurt has me seething, and I can't guarantee my brain will keep the rest of me under control.

"I didn't know what they were doing. I mean, I'd heard about their... group activities." Riley looks away. "But I didn't realize the girls weren't willing participants. I didn't know they were drugging them."

In front of us the kitchen hums along, bacon sizzling and eggs frying, and Riley takes a deep breath. "Once I realized what had happened... God, Chance, I was so angry. Lily was in shock, I guess. She didn't remember much and when she started to, well, that only made things worse. I convinced her to report it. Those guys were my friends but..." He blinks and I can clearly see the hurt on his face. Five minutes ago I would have been reveling in that pain, but now I'm feeling less like hitting him and more like walking out of here before he can tell me any more.

"But they hurt her."

"Yeah, and they weren't even sorry. Called her awful things and tried to get other people around campus to confirm that she'd been into it. That she'd agreed to everything. And when I tried to shut that down, when I tried to fight for her, they turned on me."

That ember of anger starts to get just enough oxygen to lick through me again. "So you gave up? You ran? Because your so-called friends gave you some shit?"

Riley rubs his temples, eyes closed. "It was more complicated than that. They knew things about me that I couldn't risk getting out. Things that would get back to my family. Things I wasn't ready to make public."

"So you let them tear her apart?" They'd already gotten her body and Riley'd let them get the rest of her too. "What could have been so important to you that you'd let that happen?"

Riley's eyes open in surprise. "She didn't tell you?"

"Tell me what?"

Riley shakes his head and smiles ruefully. "Even now she's a better friend than I am." He lets out a sigh. "Lily went with me to Junior and Senior prom, every one of our high school dances. I took her to every stupid hay ride. She was my fraternity date for every party, all the football games. Why do you think that is, Chance?"

"Because she's fun to be with? Because she's gorgeous? Because you were in love with her? I don't know why *you* got to take her to everything, Riley." I feel a pang of jealousy deep in my chest. I don't need my cousin reminding me that he got to take my girl around town for years. *My girl.* Because that's what Lily is now, no matter what Riley's about to tell me.

"Because I'm gay, Chance."

My jaw goes slack and stays that way even as Debbie slides our plates in front of us. "Gay?"

"Yes, gay, and Lily's known since we were twelve. But I never felt comfortable telling anyone else, and I sure as hell didn't want anyone to find out. So she was my on-again off-again fake girlfriend. For years." Riley reaches for the salt shaker and douses his eggs. "I'm not proud of it, but it was the only way I could figure to get through things until I was man enough to be myself. I'm not really out here, but I am in Charleston. That's one of the things I came home to do. That and try to make amends with Lily, if she'd let me. I protected my secret instead of doing what was right by her. I'll never forgive myself for that and I wouldn't blame her for feeling the same."

I think of Lily—strong, stoic Lily—never using Riley's secret against him. Letting people ruin her reputation instead, letting people think what they wanted without fighting back. Trying to do the right thing at her own expense.

"Does she hate me?" Riley asks and I want to tell him yes. I want to watch his face fall and to have him feel abandoned in the same way Lily was. But I know that isn't right and it isn't the right way for all of us to move forward.

"She doesn't hate anybody."

"Doesn't have it in her, I guess. She's always been like that. Think she'll let me talk to her?"

I know what he's really asking. Am I going to let him try

or am I going to rip his arms off before I let him get near her again?

"You can try. Give her a call."

"She okay this morning?" Riley shovels another mouthful of eggs in. "I imagine she was upset last night."

"Haven't seen her yet," I confess. "My brothers put me in time out. Cooper checked on her, though. I'll get over there as soon as I can and beg forgiveness." And I am going to have to do some serious begging.

"Me too, I guess." He gives me another one of those sad smiles. "But we have to try."

My phone buzzes in my pocket and I pull it out, eager for it to be Lily. A California area code flashes before my eyes. "Be right back. I have to take this."

Riley nods and continues eating. I step outside to deal with California once and for all. Time to quit avoiding the past so I can finally move into my future.

32

Lily

"We don't have to do this, you know. We could just stay home and I could make us omelets or something." Hadley looks over from the driver's side. "No harm in hanging around the house for a day."

"I know what you're trying to do." I let the breeze from the window whip my hair in my face.

"I'm not trying to do anything." Hadley acts indignant. "I happen to like making omelets."

"I'm sure you do, but I'm fine to run in to pick up breakfast."

"I could run in. You could wait in the car," Hadley offers, keeping her eyes on the road so she doesn't have to look at me.

"I'll be fine. I have to show my face eventually. Might as well do it this morning before the gossip gets any worse." And I'm sure there's been gossip. Plenty of people saw that fight last night and all of them saw me being herded out of Bootlegger like I was an invalid. It's a good, juicy story—two cousins fighting over a girl, one with a loose reputation at that—and people won't have been able to keep it to themselves.

"Suit yourself," Hadley says like it makes no difference to her, but I see her worrying her lip with her teeth.

When we pull up to Ham & Eggs the parking lot is nearly full. There'll be a bigger audience than I'd planned on for my Sunday morning waltz back into society. I square my shoulders and try to remember all the advice my therapist ever gave me about looking confident. I'm going to hold my head high no matter who's in the diner this morning, because I've done nothing wrong. I'm chanting that little mantra to myself when I see them.

Chance and Riley. Sitting side by side at the counter.

They've got matching bruises along their jaws and Riley's eye looks painfully swollen. Still, they're alive and up early enough to have a breakfast date. Chance lets Debbie refill his coffee cup and even hands Riley's over to her to make it easier for her to freshen his cup, too. Riley's tucking into his eggs like he hasn't eaten in days and Chance's plate's half empty. Neither one of them's having any trouble eating this morning. They don't seem to have the knots in their stomachs that I do.

My hand stays frozen on the door handle as I watch them talk. I haven't heard from Chance, but he's managed to get in touch with Riley. And now he's listening to whatever he's got to say, letting Riley tell him what I'm sure amounts to his side of the story. I'd spent most of my life with Riley and after all those years of friendship I couldn't believe he abandoned me when I needed him the most. But he'd run in order to protect his own skin and save his own reputation so who knows what kind of story he's spinning for Chance. And Chance went to Riley first; that tells my heart everything it needs to know.

They're family.

And what am I? I already know to Riley I'm disposable. But to Chance? Am I someone who's been helping him with a project? A friend? Just some girl he's started sleeping with? None of those things will trump family. Especially if Riley can convince him that there are holes in my story. Especially if Chance chooses to believe him.

There's no way I can trot into Ham & Eggs now. I'd rather do just about anything than face Chance and Riley in front of an audience.

"Looks like that's about it for you, Lily Gentry."

I whip my face toward the sound of Travis' taunting voice. He's still a few steps away but it doesn't take him long to be right next to me, close enough for me to see the giant bruise on his cheek and the scrapes on his knuckles. I take two steps backward, all my ideas about confident body language disappearing. I blink in surprise as Travis' mouth works its way into a sneer.

"Now that Riley's had a minute to set Chance straight there's no way he'll be messing with you anymore. What, did you think no one would tell him how you really are? That no one would tell him the truth?"

The look of glee on Travis' face only makes the pit in my stomach get bigger. I shake my head, unable to make my mouth work the way I need it to, unable to convince my feet to move and get me out of this situation.

"Nothin' to say? Not so sassy now, I guess." Travis gives me one more angry grin before reaching for the door. "You comin' in? I'm sure there are plenty of people who'd love to have a little entertainment with their breakfast this morning." He shoulders past me and into the restaurant, not giving me time to answer. Tears blur my vision as I watch

Travis head straight for Chance, probably seconds away from telling him I'm out here.

Before I can force myself to move away from the door, Chance stands. He's reaching in his pocket and pulling out his phone—the one he's supposedly had confiscated. But there it is, ringing in his hand while my own phone stays suspiciously silent in my pocket. He says something to Riley and starts to move toward the door, still looking at the screen and getting ready to use one of the fingers on his battered hand to answer the call. The threat of being discovered out here peering at him through the glass has me leaping out of the way and scurrying along the side of the building. Chance doesn't notice me as he pulls the door open and walks in the opposite direction, already engrossed in his conversation.

I speed walk back to Hadley's car and throw myself into the passenger seat.

"That was quick."

"I decided I'd rather have one of your omelets than wait. It's pretty crowded in there this morning." It isn't exactly a lie, but it doesn't hit the real truth.

Hadley looks me over. I know she notices the trembling hands and the way I'm fidgeting in my seat. "Well, then, omelets it is," she says and starts the car. She won't push me and for once I'm grateful that she thinks she knows me so well. I'm not about to explain my sudden change of heart and she's not going to ask about something she probably thinks she already understands. Of course I'm nervous about dealing with the town gossip. Who wouldn't want to avoid that for as long as possible?

But I'm only nervous about what one person in Mint Springs has to say, and I have a feeling I'm not going to like it.

33

Chance

"You're leaving now? Right now? You don't even have a bag."

I don't have time to argue with my brother. "I need to get on the first flight. Just drive me to the airport." I scroll through the ticket options on my phone, trying to choose one that will get me to Los Angeles in time to make it to my meeting. I certainly hadn't planned on showing up to see my old business partners looking like I'd been on the losing end of a boxing match, but I don't have a choice. Steven said the new investors wouldn't wait and, if I'm lucky, this will be my chance to cut ties and let those guys do what they love without me getting in the way. Then I can get back to doing what it turns out *I* love, hopefully with the person I love. That's provided all the pieces fall into place. And that Lily feels the same way about me that I feel about her.

But one step at a time.

"Can you even get on a plane looking like that?" Cooper gives me a glance. "I'd be worried I was setting myself up for a strip search."

"It'll be fine."

Cooper doesn't look so sure, but he aims the truck toward the highway. "Did you find a flight?"

"Booking it now." I'll have to go straight to the meeting from the airport, won't even have time to try to make myself presentable. It'll be unsettling to be back in my old life even for just a little while, and I'm not looking forward to it. All the things I used to love about California now seem unappealing. The bars and nightlife don't hold my interest the way the idea of a beer on the front porch with Lily does, watching her drink her lemonade while the sun goes down. I pull up her number to give her a heads up about my plans. I know leaving town right after my dust up with Riley isn't ideal, but I can't put off what needs to be done.

It rings and rings, finally going to voicemail. I listen to the familiar lilt of her voice and wait for the beep. What I've got to tell her isn't the kind of thing you leave in a message but I have a hard time keeping my feelings to myself. I'm aware Cooper's listening in too, so I keep it short. There'll be plenty of time to tell Lily all my plans when I get back.

"You'll check in on her, right?"

Cooper nods. I don't like leaving without seeing Lily first, but she'll understand the urgency even if she might be pissed at me at first. Then I turn my mind toward California and the next few days and watch Mint Springs disappear in the rearview.

34

Lily

There are some things we should talk about.

Those words ring in my ear long after I've listened to Chance's message. I can imagine that conversation isn't going to be an easy one for me. He's ready to move on and now he'll have Riley's words to help him do it. Already I feel suffocated—by the impending end of my relationship with Chance, by this apartment, by Mint Springs. Chance had terrified me with his anger at Bootlegger, but I'm almost as terrified by the things he might say to me when he finally gets the opportunity. I've heard those things before, sure, but never coming out of the mouth of someone I came to trust the way I've been trusting him. Never from someone I've fallen in love with. And he's already gone anyway, back to California like he couldn't get there fast enough. That's a blessing in disguise, maybe.

It takes me fifteen minutes to pack everything. I have to sneak out the back door because once Hadley figures out what I'm doing she's going to work hard to change my mind. She'll try to convince me to stay. But Chance might come back eventually and, even if he doesn't, I'll be reminded of him every time I turn around. I let my guard down and now I'm paying the price. There's no way I'm getting out of this unscathed, but I can protect myself from getting too many new scars. I can do what I should have done in the first place and get myself as far away from Chance Allen and Mint Springs as I can.

I can't avoid stopping by Southern Comforts. I might be able to sneak away from Hadley and try to smooth things over later with a phone call but that's not going to work for my mother and Bunny. If I can get in and out quick, I can be on the road to Chicago before lunchtime. I know that'll be a miracle but I put up a little prayer anyway before I use my key to unlock the front door.

Bunny's scooting around getting the store ready for the Sunday crowd. After church is always a good time for "looky loos" as Bunny calls them. They look but never buy much. Lately though, people have been driving to Mint Springs from all over to do more than just look at the merchandise. Sunday's become one of our best days. I can almost guarantee a few big pieces will sell and that we'll run out of paint by closing time. Paint that I suddenly realize we won't be able to restock now that Chance is gone.

"What the hell are you wearing?" Bunny yells as soon as she sees my oversized sweatshirt. "Are you sick or something?"

"Where's mama?" I ask as I push the sleeves of that sweatshirt up to my elbows. It is warm under this extra layer. I've gotten used to wearing summer clothes like a normal person. So much for that.

"In the back. You come to help set up? We could use some extra muscle to shift some furniture around. Where's that boyfriend of yours? He come with you?"

"He's gone."

"Gone?" This has Bunny's attention. "What do you mean 'gone'?" She scuttles over beside me in ten seconds flat. Probably a world record for an elderly lady with a walker.

"He went back to California."

"What happened?" She takes in my arms and legs, checks my face while simultaneously yelling for my mother. "He hurt you?"

My mother comes from the back, holding a box full of old doorknobs. "Who's hurt?" She drops the box and takes up where Bunny left off, running her hands down my arms.

I pull away. "I'm fine. He didn't hurt me. He would never do that."

"Well, we heard he got into it with Riley last night. You never know." Bunny's eyes are hard and I know if Chance had raised a hand to me, he'd be lucky not to be anywhere near here. And it reminds me about the kind of men we've all come to expect in this family—ones with hard fists and angry faces.

"You *do* know. He's got a temper, but not like that." I can't believe I'm standing up for a man who's basically run out on me, who's taken someone else's word over mine. Last night's anger might have been hard to watch, but it wasn't directed at me. My heart may be breaking, but the rest of me is fine.

"When's he coming back?" my mother asks, her face already etched with concern.

"Don't know. But whenever he does, I won't be here."

Bunny shakes her head. "You're leaving?"

"I can't stay here. It's too hard, too much. I need to get back to my own life." Even as I say it, I know it's a lie. My life is here now, not back in Chicago. "My stuff's all packed. I'm leaving as soon as I get done here."

"What's Hadley say about all this?" My mother's mouth

sets into a hard line. They aren't about to make this easy for me.

"She doesn't know. I'll call her from the road. She'll understand."

"Like hell she will," Bunny snaps. "Your boy gets into a fist fight and suddenly you need to leave town? That doesn't make any sense, Lily."

"It's more than that," I confess. "I saw him talking to Riley this morning."

"And what'd he say about that?"

"He said we had some things to talk about."

"So, did you?" Bunny asks. "Did you talk about them?"

"No, because he left." I want to stomp my feet and shake my fists. Why can't they just leave things well enough alone?

"But you talked to him before, right?" my mother prods.

"He left me a message." I don't need to hear him say the words to know where things are headed.

"A message?" Bunny rolls her eyes. "You're leaving town because of a *message*? This is a time for talking, Lily, not running."

"He ran first," I counter, not ready to give up just yet. "He left me, Bunny."

"You don't know that. You aren't heading off any heartache by doing things this way," she warns. "Might be doing just the opposite."

"I know what I'm doing." I try to sound more confident than I feel. "I'll let you know when I get home."

"You *are* home, Lily." My mother's voice is soft, pleading. "You have things here that you can't leave. What about the store? Those clients you've lined up? What about me and Bunny?"

Bunny's mouth trembles a bit when I look at her. I know if I leave here today there's a possibility I might not see her again. She's tough but human, and in this moment she looks less like the invincible force I've come to know as my grand-mother and more like the small wizened woman other people must see.

"I can't stay," I say, avoiding eye contact with either of them. "I'm sorry, but I have to go."

Then I give them both quick kisses and rush back out the front door before either of them can catch me crying.

35

Chance

I come out of my meeting with more swagger than I've had in a long time. If I didn't think I'd crush the bad boy vibe all these bruises on my face are giving me, I'd do one of those jumps with the heel click. Because I have been rocking it today and I'm about to make all that translate into *there's no place like home* in a few minutes. I take my phone out of my pocket and power it back up. I turned it off to make it through these meetings without distraction. Now, I can come back into my real life with nothing to hold me back. Good thing too, I guess, because I've got a million messages once the screen comes to life.

None of them from the one person I've been dying to talk to all day.

I dial Lily's number without even looking to see what all that other noise is about. I need to hear her voice, want desperately to tell her about how this day has gone completely according to plan. Actually, it's all gone even better than I ever could have planned it, leaving me with a clear runway to start making dreams come true. From now on it's nothing but Disney movies and fairy tales for Lily Gentry if I have anything to say about it.

Again, I get voicemail so I leave another message. Not sure why I can't get in touch with her on a Sunday night, but I don't let that bother me. I'll be spending as much time with Lily as possible once I get things here settled. It'll take me a few days to organize my apartment and get it ready to sell, but now that I've gotten everyone at the office to sign on the dotted line the rest of it all seems inconsequential.

I walk out of the building and into the California night without the weight that's been sitting on my shoulders for the past few months. The office is nowhere near the beach, but today I would swear I can smell the ocean. I take a deep breath and call my brother to tell him I'll be home sooner than expected.

"About time," Cooper snaps as soon as he picks up. "I've been trying to get ahold of you."

"Well, now you've got me." I shift the phone from one ear to the other as I unlock my car and slide into the driver's seat. I used to love this car—the tricked out exterior and the fancy leather seats. Right now, though, I'd trade it for the old Chevy in a heartbeat. It's one more thing I'll be leaving here when I go back to Georgia.

"Did you get my texts?" Cooper's agitated.

"I had my phone turned off. Is there an emergency?" My thoughts go to Mae and Sadie. Cooper'd agreed to stay for a few extra days because I hate to leave them alone.

"You could say that." Cooper's clearly annoyed. "Did you not listen to any of my messages? I've left you a million of them."

"I just got out of the meeting, Cooper. Calm down." I'm saying it more for my own benefit than for his. Cooper's obviously got a reason for the drama. I'm just hoping it's something that's easy to fix.

"Calm down? You're going to think 'calm down' once you hear what's going on over here. How soon can you get back?"

"I'm working out the details. What's going on?"

"Have you talked to Lily?"

The question shouldn't have the hairs on the back of my neck standing straight up. "I haven't been able to reach her." My stomach turns to ice. "Cooper, what's going on?"

"She's gone, Chance."

"Gone?" My mind goes to all the deep, dark places that one word manages to conjure up. "You'd better explain what the hell you're talking about."

"She packed up all her stuff and snuck out of Hadley's. Didn't say a word. Just hit the road."

I'm lucky I'm not driving because right now nothing makes sense. "Well, where the hell'd she go?" I demand, pressing my palms into the steering wheel.

"Hadley thinks she went back to Chicago. Lily called her to tell her she was gone but wouldn't give her details. Apparently, she saw you having breakfast with Riley and she freaked out."

"I'll be on the next flight back." I start the car. "Or maybe I should just go straight to Chicago and bring her back?"

"Why are you asking me? You know her better than anyone. What would she want you to do?"

I shut off the engine. I don't know if I'd agree that I know Lily better than anyone, but by now I know her better than most. I know what she'd expect me to do—what she'd want me to do—and for the past twenty-four hours I've done nothing but the opposite. I never should have left Mint Springs without seeing her first. She doesn't know how sorry I feel about the fight or what Riley and I talked about the next morning. I can only imagine where her mind went when she saw us together. She has no idea why I've rushed out here. I know Lily needs to feel safe in a way that other women might not, and I've ignored all of that to try and muscle my way through these obstacles.

"I'll be home as soon as I can," I say, already making a mental list of all the wrongs I'm going to have to right in order to fix this. "See if Hadley can figure out where Lily is and make sure she's alright."

I dial Lily's number again and again on my way back to the apartment. I leave message after message, just hitting the redial button after each one. I sound desperate, begging her to call me back, needing her to let me know she's okay and that I haven't screwed things up beyond repair. Because if there's no Lily after all this, then I'm not sure why I'm bothering. Which is why I'm determined not to let this be the end.

36

Chance

"Damn it!"

"Well, at least the driveway's gravel."

I jump at the sound of Sadie's voice coming from somewhere behind me.

"Did you get any of that on your boots? If we rinse them real quick we should be able to get most of it off."

The sun's barely up and for some reason Sadie's sneaking around the farm. I look down at the big blue splotch seeping into the gravel behind my truck. That's one more pint of paint that won't get sold today at Southern Comforts.

"I'll hose myself off, I guess." I can hear Sadie getting closer, no doubt she's going to want to help me make sure I don't end up with a pair of blue boots instead of brown. Technically this color is "faded overalls" but I don't need to tell my aunt that. There's no use in starting a discussion about Lily's paint names.

"Still bringing the paint over to the Gentrys'?"

"Yes, ma'am."

"I'm sure they appreciate it."

Lily's family appreciates it more than I would have imagined, always making a big fuss when I come by with more jars of paint or an offer to help move the bigger pieces around the shop. For me it's an excuse to see if they've heard from her, maybe find out if she's ever coming back. I've started to suspect my visits are the same for them as we all wait around to see what Lily's going to do next.

"Still no word?" Sadie asks from right next to my elbow. When I shake my head she lets out a little sigh. "Come on, let's get you cleaned up."

I follow her over to the side of the house to the garden hose and stand there like an invalid while Sadie turns the spigot. The sky's just starting to lose all the pinks and purples I love in the morning, not that I've been enjoying too many sunrises these past few weeks. I've been too busy working myself to the bone to find any enjoyment in something like the start of a new day.

"Here, why don't you roll up those jeans a little bit so I don't get you too wet, and we'll get all that paint off." Sadie holds the hose in her hand, the arc of water splashing all over me before I can get anywhere close to ready. She manages to get me again as she moves back toward the faucet. Now I'm soaked from the knees down, my socks already squishing against my toes as I try to get away from my aunt and her evil garden hose.

Sadie surveys me in the morning light, twisting her mouth up on one side like she's deep in thought. "You can't go anywhere like that," she announces. "And the store isn't open for a few hours yet. Why don't you go change into some dry pants and I'll make you breakfast while your boots dry? Shouldn't take long if we put them out here on the porch. The sun'll take care of that in no time."

"I was planning on going down to the bottoms to work on the fence this morning," I protest but I know it's no use. I'm not going to get away from Sadie that easily. "And now I have to clean up the mess in the driveway." I can't leave broken glass there for someone to accidentally drive over, or worse, step on.

"Both those chores'll keep." Sadie doesn't even wait for me to argue; she just turns her back on me and starts walking toward her house. "I'll get a few eggs from the coop and meet you in your kitchen. I need to try out that fancy stove of yours."

My shoulders slump at the thought of having Sadie inside the farmhouse. It's mine free and clear now along with the rest of it—the land, the barn, the fences that need mending—since I bought it from my father. I wish he'd been less interested in selling it and that he hadn't tried his best to gouge me in the process. But once the appraiser gave us his estimate, I was more than willing to pay market value for the farm even if a friends and family discount would have been nice. But since Lily's been gone, I've been trying to spend less time inside. I used to see my grandpa everywhere I looked but now I only see Lily. I'm not sure which is worse.

In the kitchen I run my hand over the stove top. It comes back dusty. That's no surprise. This is Lily's stove and I can't even look at it without feeling this giant hole in my chest. That goes double for the stretch of countertop where she'd convinced me to make love to her for the first time. I might not have recognized it then, but that's what I was doing. Maybe it wasn't the same for Lily. She certainly doesn't seem to be missing me the way I'm missing her.

"That is a lovely piece of equipment," Sadie says, letting the screen door shut behind her. "And they did a beautiful job bringing it back to life. Looks like new. Puts me right back in 1952. I would have loved for Daniel Rivers to have bought one of these for me."

"Who's Daniel Rivers?" I wipe my dusty hand along my thigh. I'm still in my wet jeans, dripping all over the floor.

"The man I was going to marry."

"You were going to get married?" It comes out in a sputter. Sadie? Married? I can't begin to picture it.

"Don't act so surprised. Have I never told you this story? Help me find a frying pan and I'll tell you all about it. These eggs won't fry themselves, you know."

Two hours later I know all about Sadie and Daniel Rivers. More than I would ever want to know, actually, but it's hard to convince Sadie to stick with the short version of anything. Hearing about the man she considered her one true love and knowing that Sadie ends up living with her sister isn't exactly helping my mood. If she's trying to convince me that living with Cooper until I'm old and gray is a great option, she's going to have to work harder than that. We've long since finished breakfast. Soon it'll be too hot for me to get any work done on the section of fence on the sunny edge of the pasture without risking heat stroke, so I let Sadie keep talking, telling me all about how her heart got broken into a million little pieces.

"Does he still live around here?" I move to pick up the breakfast dishes and start rinsing them, hoping this will get Sadie to wrap things up. I don't need this sad story to add to my own.

"Daniel? Oh, no. He moved away once he married. He's in Macon now, maybe. Here, let me do that."

Sadie takes the plate out of my hand as I struggle to process this new bit of information. "He's married?"

"Well, he was. Not sure if he is now. I guess he could be widowed or even—" Sadie's eyes widen. "He could be dead." She shakes her head. "Someone would probably have told me about that."

"He just married someone else?" This shouldn't be a shock to me. That's life. People move on. But here's Sadie who obviously never did and I'm not sure I ever will. Lily's it for me and if she ends up with some other guy? I don't know if I'll survive that.

"That other woman was easier. And I don't mean that in the scandalous way." Sadie gives me a sassy little tilt of her head. "She was simple to be with and there weren't as many obstacles."

"But he loved you," I protest.

"He said he did. But the timing was off."

Just like with me and Lily.

"Oh, don't make that face." She shakes her head. "That wasn't what really did us in. The fact of the matter is that Daniel gave up. He didn't want to fight for us to be together so he quit. Took the easy way out."

"But you tried. You didn't give up."

"That's true enough. And that's what you have to decide, Chance. Are you giving up?"

The answer to that question is easy. Hell no, I'm not giving up on Lily. I'm not ready to forget about the life we could have together. But if Sadie's story convinced me of one thing it's that I'm not the only one who needs to be committed to this thing.

"But what if Lily wants to give up?"

"Then that's on her and you'll have to live with it. But

you don't know that, now do you? You don't know if she's given up."

"She won't answer my calls. Ignores my texts. No one really even knows where she is." The panic that's been simmering just below the surface these past few weeks rises up. Lily could be anywhere and I'm the last person she wants to talk to.

"You're a smart boy. You'll figure out a way to get ahold of her. You know what she needs to see. Just show her." Sadie turns on the faucet and lets the water run into the giant porcelain sink Lily insisted on having me install. She'd shown me a million photos of farmhouse sinks full of flowers and puppies to convince me when all she'd really needed to do was ask. Because even then I'd have moved heaven and earth to make her happy.

"Why don't you think about it while you drive that paint over to her mama? The store'll be open now and those boots'll probably be dry."

I shuffle to the front door, turning the possibilities over in my mind. I think I know what Lily wants, the question is how to make her listen, how to let her know that I'm willing to give her all those things. By the time the sun glinting off the front window of Southern Comforts blinds me I've got an idea of how I can prove to Lily that I'm worth another shot.

And I'm going to need all the help I can get.

37

Lily

"Hello?"

"Oh my God, did you just answer the phone? Is it a full moon or something?"

Hadley's attempt at humor barely has me cracking a smile. I should have let her go to voicemail. But right now, I could use a little Hadley Crawford positivity so I'm willing to put up with the risk of an unscripted conversation. "I know how to answer the phone, Hads. I've just been choosing not to."

Hadley lets out a huff. "That's no way to treat your friends, Lily. Or your family. We all just want to make sure you're alive."

"I'm fine," I lie. I have not been even close to fine since leaving Mint Springs. Currently I'm sleeping on the lumpy couch of my one Chicago friend close enough to impose upon. I've realized my roots here aren't that deep; there aren't many people I can call in a crisis. And coming back to the realization that my sublet apartment wouldn't be mine again for two more months without a major outlay of cash is only one of my many issues. I haven't been able to walk right back into my old life in any way, shape, or form. I've come back to no job, no home, and a heart that won't let me forget how much better I had it for a while there.

"You could at least let us know where you are."

"Chicago. I told you that." I move closer to the window AC unit and let the cold air blast me in the face. We're in the middle of a heat wave, of course. I'm sweating through my giant sweatshirts and oversized tees, and unlike in Mint Springs there's no possibility that I'll be cooling off in the river any time soon. The city traps the heat in a way that makes me long even more for the front porch of the Allen farmhouse and some lemonade. Not to mention the boy I would have been looking at over the rim of my glass.

"Chicago is a pretty big place, Lily. Are you back in your old apartment?"

"No comment."

"You are so pig-headed, Lily Gentry."

I ignore that. So what if I'm stubborn? I've got good reason to be, now more than ever. "How are things with you?" If I can turn the conversation back to Hadley, I might save myself from further interrogation.

"Well, I've been stopping by the store every now and then. Checking in on your mom and Bunny."

"And?" Guilt washes over me. That's my job, not Hadley's. But I won't let her trick me into asking all the questions I want to ask.

"Things are going well. Chance has been helping out a lot, bringing more of your paint. But you probably know all of that."

"Chance is in Mint Springs? He's mixing paint? Why

would he do that?" I don't want to talk about Chance, don't want to give Hadley an opportunity to sing his praises and plant the seed that I might have been hasty in my judgement of him.

"So they can keep selling it, obviously. That's all in the videos. You saw that, I'm sure. I mean, so many of them are about you."

"Chance is still posting videos?"

"Oh, did you not know?" Hadley asks using the fake innocent voice that has never worked on anyone and will most certainly not work on me.

"No, I did not." Mainly because I've blocked his number and deleted his texts. The few times I've spoken to Hadley or my family I've made it clear that speaking his name will make me hang up faster than anything.

"I know you don't want to talk about him. We should talk about something else. Oh! Guess who decided she wanted to be a redhead for fall?"

I do not give two flips which Mint Springs woman has changed her hair color and Hadley knows it. She drones on and on about the salon and the new technique class she's been taking for highlights all while I think of nothing but Chance Allen. Why would he be helping my mother and Bunny when I've run as far as possible to get away from him? Why in the hell would he be posting videos to YouTube? And what does Hadley mean when she says they're about *me*?

"Hadley, I have to go."

"Oh? Okay." She gives up without a fight and I know I've been played. She's expecting me to hang up and get right down to the business of checking in on Chance.

Which I totally do two seconds after I hit end.

The Internet is definitely not my friend. I've been doing a good job of stuffing my feelings for Chance down deep. So deep that I thought looking at the videos wouldn't do much more than irritate me. So what if he's going ahead with the projects *we* planned? Who cares? If anything, that just proves I was right to leave. If Chance has had this little trouble moving on, and is acting like he doesn't need me, then I made the right choice. Whatever Riley told him must have made it that much easier to cut his losses.

When I pull up our account I'm slapped in the face by Chance's giant, blinding smile. *What does he have to grin about?* Oh, right. He's free of the girl with all the hang-ups.

But none of the videos are about how he's happy to be rid of me. Instead they're all about how he's missing me. How he's getting ready for me to come home. Home? Since when has Chance Allen started thinking of Mint Springs as home?

He's numbered the videos so I'll watch them in order, not seeming to care that he's putting all this out on the Internet for everyone to see. Not caring about the comments or the number of views, which, let's be honest, are extremely high.

I watch Chance hang out with my mother and Bunny at the shop, talking with them about how they need me to finish some of the pieces he's brought back from the flea market. He records himself haggling with Clifford, who seems to miss me almost as much as Chance does. When he brings up the fact that his grandson is still available, Chance nearly growls into the camera. Clifford's not scared of Chance, though, and offers to fix me up with him if I'll only come back to Mint Springs.

"Over my dead body," Chance threatens, but Clifford just pats him on the arm.

"No need for all of that, Chance. I'd hate to have to show you up for all the world to see." A wink toward the camera has Chance softening and apologizing. "Hard to control it when it comes to someone you love," Clifford says like he's been there before. And Chance agrees. "We can all see why you'd love Lily." When Clifford turns to the camera and tells me to get my butt on home I don't know if I should laugh or cry.

Sadie and Mae teach Chance how to make pickles and I get to see the Chambers stove in all its glory. They're pickling okra which makes Chance wrinkle his nose a bit. Sadie's protests that it's "all the rage in those expensive Bloody Marys," making me laugh in a way I haven't since I've come back to Chicago. When Mae lectures him that you can "pickle whatever you want" I want more than anything to be there myself, helping to wash the jars that Chance keeps nearly dropping and measuring the vinegar that he keeps sloshing everywhere. When he runs his palm along the edge of the countertop my breath catches. His face doesn't give anything away, but I see the way his hand balls into a quick fist.

Chance looks good. Still handsome even in the early videos where he's covered in stubble and looks like he's been having trouble sleeping. The ladies of the World Wide Web haven't missed the fact that Chance is attractive or that I've seemingly left him alone. There are multiple offers to come to Mint Springs to help "make it better" along with a few outright marriage proposals.

Hussies.

But Chance doesn't leave any doubt about who he wants to come to Mint Springs. He ends every video with another apology, begging me to come back. The most recent video has Chance working in the barn on a "special project." Something he's getting ready to unveil even though he claims it isn't quite finished. When he pushes through the double doors of the barn, I can see he's been busy. Not only does the building have four walls, but it's empty. There's not a trace of all the things that had been left there over the years. It's still rustic, but it's clean. The space is open and strung with fairy lights and if I look closely, I can see some shelves stocked with my paint lining the walls.

"This doesn't look like much right now," Chance begins before clearing his throat. "And really it isn't about the space, it's more about the idea." He walks through the lower level, showing off some of the same equipment I've got at Southern Comforts in the workshop. I can tell he's been over there checking out my work space.

"This is a temporary place for you to start your business. We can build something else. It doesn't even need to be on the farm, necessarily, but I want you to see that I'm making plans over here and you're in them. All my best plans have you in them, Lily. But I need you to come back home so I can tell them all to you. I want to be the Chip to your Joanna. Is that too corny? I'm in love with you, Lily Gentry and I need you here with me."

Chance Allen is in love with me.

With *me*.

He's not hiding it. He's bought the farm and moved into the farmhouse, permanently. And from the look of things he's just there waiting. Waiting for me.

But he won't wait forever. Even saints have their limits and Chance is no saint.

My hands are trembling as I slam my laptop shut. Maybe I'm making a mistake by putting all my eggs into this one basket, but in this moment this feels like the only choice. I can keep plodding along with my gray days or I can admit that I want to hear what Chance has to say. I can stay here in Chicago and try to forget about him or I can go home and let him love me.

If I'm not too late.

38

Chance

Every day starts the same way now. I roll over and look at the empty spot in my bed, the spot that should have Lily sleeping soundly in it. I curse myself for ever letting her get away, and then I spend the rest of the day doing my damnedest to get her back. I'm not known for my patience, but even though Lily's shown no interest in coming home to Mint Springs, I'm not giving up. It's taken everything in me not to rush off to Chicago and look for her, not to throw her over my shoulder kicking and screaming and bring her back where she belongs.

But Lily wouldn't be able to forgive me for that. Not if she really and truly doesn't want to be here. So that's what I need to convince her of while still giving her enough space —that she wants to make a life with me and that it's something she decided for herself. I can't force things no matter what my stubborn heart wants me to do. And it wants me to do something crazy, something we'd both regret.

Instead, I work on my farm projects, sweating in the sun even though it's September. Summer seems to be as stubborn as I am about letting go. I check in with her family, doing all the things for them that I failed to do for my grandpa. I do the same for Sadie and Mae. It's more than penance for a guilty man: it's helping to heal the spot in my heart that needs to take care of the people I love. The people I neglected for too long. The full days leave me exhausted but wide awake, longing to have Lily here to tell her all about the ideas I have for the farm and the dreams I've started having about filling this house with more than just the two of us.

I put all of those ideas into my videos, channeling all the energy I can into painting a picture of the life I'd love to have. I want Lily to see that I don't care about the past; I'm focused on our future. I send them out into the mess that is the World Wide Web and hope Lily sees them, hope she's maybe starting to thaw a little and that she'll change her mind about leaving.

Today I'm setting up in the kitchen again. Sadie and Mae have agreed to teach me how to make their famous hummingbird cake, although I have little faith that they'll give away their real secrets. I anticipate more than a few disgruntled viewers when their cakes don't turn out exactly the way they should. I set up the camera and test the lighting. Can't have my aunts looking anything less than lovely, and I always want Lily's stove to gleam in the background. If she's watching these things, I want her to see that I'm taking care of it, that I'm remembering how much she loves it and that it's waiting here for her. I tilt the camera slightly to reduce some of the glare from the countertop. I run my hand along the edge there, the memories still fresh from having my hands on Lily for the first time. If I close my eyes, I can still feel the heat of her skin against mine, smell the vanilla in her hair, taste the sweetness of her lips as I press mine to them again and again.

I've still got my eyes squeezed shut when the front door opens.

"Chance?"

I don't dare open my eyes, not if it means letting go of this hallucination I must be having. If this is all it takes to conjure up a vision of Lily then I should have been doing this weeks ago. I should've planted my feet here in the kitchen and wished for her a little harder.

"Chance? What are you doing?"

My eyes snap open and there she is. Bits of that long brown hair falling out of a messy ponytail, one of those oversized sweatshirts that I never thought I'd be so happy to see, those big doe eyes staring back at me.

"If I'm dreaming right now, please don't wake me up."

"If this is what you've been dreaming about then you need to seriously re-evaluate things." She gives me a little half-hearted laugh and one of those lopsided smiles.

"It's all I've been dreaming about."

Lily's eyes fill with tears. "You aren't mad?"

"No, baby. I'm so happy to see you there isn't room for anything else."

She lets out a sigh and her shoulders slump, her eyes closing as her head tips forward. "I messed everything up," she whispers.

"No, I messed things up. I shouldn't have made you wait to find out what was happening. I should have gone straight to Hadley's no matter what anyone said."

"I probably wouldn't have listened." Lily lifts her eyes to look at me and I want more than anything to close the space between us and wipe those tears from her cheeks. But I don't want to spook her. I've been waiting here for what seems like forever. I can wait a few more minutes.

"Can you listen now? 'Cause I've got plenty of things I need to tell you." My hands shake almost as much as my voice.

"Maybe I should go first."

Lily's voice doesn't sound like she's about to give me the kind of news I've been waiting to hear. Still, I have to take whatever she's willing to give me and learn to accept it.

"I watched all the videos." Her confession gives me a glimmer of hope. If she's seen the things I've been posting then maybe, just maybe, she's come home for good. "But I know you talked to Riley and I'm sure he..."

"Didn't tell me anything that changes things between us."

Lily's face clouds. "But if he told you his side of things—"

I cut her off. "He doesn't have a side. Riley told me you protected him and he regrets not doing the same for you. There's nothing he could have said that would make me love you any less, Lily."

Her face scrunches up and her bottom lip trembles. "That's the first time I've ever heard you say that in person."

"Say what? That I love you? I'll say it every day for the rest of my life if you'll let me. The question is if you love me too. Are you getting ready to break my heart or are you planning on sticking around, Lily Gentry?"

"I want to stay. God, I want to. But I'm scared, Chance."

"I'm scared too, but we can do this. I'm all in. These past few weeks without you, it has torn me up. I don't ever want to feel like that again. I'm ready to make a life here. With you. If you'll have me."

Lily's eyes fill with tears.

I've blown it.

I haven't said the things she needs to hear to convince her to stay. She doesn't love me enough to try. I'm turning away so I don't have to watch her leave when she comes running, jumping into my arms before I have a chance to say anything else. I instinctively wrap around her, catching her and pulling her close.

"I'll have you, Chance Allen," she whispers into the crook of my neck. "I'd be lucky to have you."

"Then you've got me. For as long as you want to keep me."

"I think that's going to be a very long time." Lily's smile against my skin has me setting her on the counter so I can kiss her properly. It's been too long since I've been able to touch her, to remind her that she's mine. And now she really is. "I love you, Chance," she whispers, already sliding her hands up under my shirt. I waste no time pulling Lily's sweatshirt up and over her head, throwing it into the living room so my hands are free to move all over the skin I've been dreaming about.

"We brought plenty of flour, but the hens aren't cooperating this morning, so we may need to run out for eggs." Sadie's voice blares through the kitchen before I have a chance to warn her about the spectacle here on the counter.

"Well, move, Sadie! I can't hold all these bags forever. And I think we forgot the pecans. I'll have to run back to the house. Can you believe that there are people who are allergic to pecans? That would be a real shame. To be allergic to pecans. I can't even imagine it. Oh, my..."

I see Mae's eyes widen as I peer over Lily's shoulder. I've got her turned in toward me but it's obvious what we're up to in here and it has nothing to do with baking a cake.

"I don't think we'll be needing those eggs, Sadie," Mae whispers as she and her sister freeze in the front hallway.

"No, I don't think we'll be recording anything today. You did turn that camera off, didn't you, Chance? I think whatever's going on here isn't something you'd want on your website. Should I check that or…"

"We'll leave you to it," Mae announces, pulling Sadie behind her. "Happy to have you home, Lily. You two come by later for supper, if you aren't too busy."

"Yes, ma'am," Lily squeaks out from against my chest. "Sorry to ruin your plans."

"Oh, you're not ruining anything," Sadie assures her and gives me a wink. "You two get back to what you were doing."

Lily lifts her head to look at me once the door shuts behind my aunts and we're sure the coast is clear. "I'm officially mortified."

"No need to be. They're probably almost as happy as I am that you're home."

"Almost?"

"I'm pretty happy. It'd be hard to compete with that." I lean down to brush my lips against hers and get back to the matter at hand.

EPILOGUE

Chance

"We don't have time for this."

"We're making time for this. Now slide over here and let me kiss you."

Lily moves over on the bench seat and turns her face toward mine. I move forward to press my lips against hers. She pulls back. My low growl makes her shake her head.

"We're only making out for fifteen minutes and then we have to get back to the barn. I don't want your brothers to come looking for us and find us out here fooling around in this truck in broad daylight."

"They know better than to bother a truck parked in the middle of a pasture. That only means one of two things: fighting or f—"

Lily slaps her hand over my mouth. "Well, there's not going to be either of those things in this truck this afternoon." She's protesting but I see how she's looking at me, notice the way her hand slides from my mouth down to my chest and stays there.

"We'll see about that. Now let me practice kissing the bride."

"I like the sound of that," Lily whispers.

"Tell me what else you like," I tease before lowering my lips to hers.

Lily's breathless when we break apart. "I like *that*. I think I'd like some more, actually." She reaches for me and pulls me close.

"You didn't get enough sugar in your coffee this morning?" I nibble a bit on Lily's lower lip.

"Must not have," she sighs as her eyes flutter closed.

"Don't think I did either, come to think of it." I give my chin a contemplative rub. "And there's nothing sweeter than this spot right here." I smile as I make my way down her neck, planting kisses on her collarbone. There's been very little privacy at the farmhouse lately, but out here it's just the two of us. This truck's maybe not the most comfortable place to show Lily how much I want her, but right now it feels damn near perfect.

Lily groans a little, her hands running impatiently down my back. "You want me to show you an even sweeter spot?" Her voice is pure honey in my ear.

I lift my eyes to hers and she raises an eyebrow. Bold Lily is making more and more appearances around here and I'm not complaining.

Not at all.

"Slide back," I growl, taking Lily's hips in my hands. The bench seat has some definite advantages at times like these. She kicks off her shoes, toes flexing against the padding of the seat. She's wearing a dress again and I run my hand up the length of one smooth leg until my thumb finds the place her panties ought to be. My head snaps up in surprise. "Are you not wearing anything under here?"

There is nothing sexier than the look Lily gives me right then, her hair cascading down onto her shoulders, her mouth open in mock surprise. "I must have forgotten this morning." Her confession is far from sincere. "Maybe you should look, just to be sure." She gives me a little wiggle.

Oh, I'm going to do more than look. I let my other hand take the same trip until I've got fingers splayed on the tops of both her thighs. Nope, no panties, just wet and warm Lily and no reason for me not to finish what I started.

I work my way down Lily's body, loving the way she squirms a little when this morning's stubble rubs against her, even with the fabric between us. I can feel her holding her breath when I reach her belly. My fingers work between her legs, sliding through the wetness to her clit. "You okay?" I ask, stopping for the check-in Lily needs less and less now.

"*Very*. Keep going." Her fingers thread their way through my hair and give it a tug.

I bark out a laugh. "Yes, ma'am, back to work." I stretch out on my stomach, careful not to accidentally nudge the horn or the gear shift. Lily giggles as I wedge myself into prime position to get my fill of her.

The material of her dress is silky between my fingers and I take my time pulling the edge of it up, revealing her to me. I hum my appreciation and plant a kiss on the little patch of curls at the apex of her thighs. Lily inhales sharply. I chuckle, my warm breath tickling her enough to get her squirming again.

"Chance." She draws my name out like a plea, impatient in a way that drives me crazy.

"Don't like waiting?" I keep my mouth inches away from her, her legs splayed open like the world's most enticing invitation.

Lily gives me another whine. "You know I don't."

"Come here then." I slide my hands underneath her ass and pull her closer, nuzzle her a bit before I lick her straight up the center. She groans, leaning her head fall back against the window and closing her eyes. By now I know what Lily likes, how to drive her wild with my tongue. She likes leisurely and so I go slow, savoring her, hitting her clit on every up stroke.

Lily settles even tighter against me, the little whimpers she's making telling me I'm on the right track. Her sighs are only happy ones and when I find her clit and give it a little extra attention, I can tell she's close.

"Oh, right there. Right there." Lily's voice urges me on and I don't stop, not even when her legs start to shake and her toes curl. I steady her with my hands on her thighs, letting her ride out her first orgasm and the surprise second one that makes her hips threaten to come completely off the seat.

As Lily catches her breath, I put a kiss on the inside of each of her knees. "Sweetest thing I've ever tasted."

Lily's laughter fills the cab of the truck.

"About damn time," Cooper mutters when I finally make it back to the barn.

"Just needed to check in with Lily," I say before picking up one of the boards propped against the wall.

"Is that what you're calling it these days? A 'check in'?" Cooper shoots a look over at Charlie and Cade. "We're here trying to help you make an honest woman out of Lily and you're off manhandling her."

"You'd better hurry up and get to work or we're not

gonna let you take any of the credit." Cade slides two more bales into the middle of the floor.

"Well, I think we've all got sweat equity in this. You'd better be sure to tell Lily how hard we've been working." Charlie slides another board over the hay bales. "How many of these do we need anyway?"

"Lily said twenty, I think. We can always add more if it looks like there won't be enough seats for everyone."

"Are these going to be comfortable to sit on? I'm not sold on these as benches." Cade plops his butt down on one of the boards and tests it out. "It's pretty hard, Chance."

"Well, nobody's got to sit there long. I'm trying to convince Lily to get the ceremony down to under ten minutes." If I had my way, I'd try to make it less than five because I can't wait another second to make things with Lily official. I'd wanted to throw her over my shoulder and take her to the courthouse but Lily wanted a wedding. So that's what I'm giving her. On Saturday I'm making her my wife and she's making me the happiest man Mint Springs has ever seen. Hell, I'm going to be the happiest man in the world when the preacher finally pronounces us man and wife.

The barn's looking less and less like a place where you'd stick a few horses and more like something out of a magazine. Lily's designed it all and I've forced my brothers to help me make it happen. We could have gotten hitched anywhere. She'd insisted on the farm. Looking out at the progress we've made I'm glad this is what we've settled on.

"Boss is coming. You guys better look like you're working," Cooper calls from outside the barn's double doors. "Shit, this is actually looking good."

"We're only following orders," Charlie says and gives a

little salute as Lily walks in. She gives a little excited dance and plants a kiss on his cheek.

"And I appreciate how well you're doing it."

Charlie's face flushes and I shake my head. These boys need to get women of their own. "Hey, don't go giving that away to just anybody."

"Chance Allen, are you jealous?" Lily teases.

"Maybe. You'd better come over here and thank me too. I'm doing most of the work." Lily runs over and gives me a kiss that makes me consider hauling her off to the hay loft. Of course, there's no hay up there now, only more wedding stuff that needs to be arranged under her watchful eye.

"That right there is why I need my own place," Cooper says and the rest of my brothers agree like they've been subjected to something horrible.

"You're just jealous. And we're starting work on your place as soon as the wedding's over. It's all in the plan." I give Lily one more kiss and then let her go. Since Lily moved into the farmhouse things have been a little crowded. There's no more sex on the kitchen counter with Cooper around all the time—and he is around all the time now that he's moved to Mint Springs full time.

"Speaking of plans," Cade says, giving Charlie a nudge with his elbow. "Charlie and I have some ideas we'd like to throw out once things settle down."

"What kind of ideas?"

"Business ideas. I know you and Lily have the design business and that you're busy with that, but Charlie and I have a few things we thought might work, especially after seeing how this wedding's coming together."

"Are you thinking about starting something here?" Having all my brothers in Mint Springs is something my grandfather would have loved. I'm willing to hear them out if it means good things for the farm. Just having them all here in one place makes something warm settle in my chest. We may fight like we don't always love each other, but I'm starting to remember how good it feels to be surrounded by family, and how reassuring it is to know they've got my back.

"Yeah. I'm finished with school soon and then I'll be ready to put that degree to good use." Cade puts another board down on the hay bales.

"And I can bring the charisma," Charlie adds with a grin. "That's pretty much all I've got right now."

"On that note, I think we should take a break. We can wait for our next set of instructions while we drink the rest of the beer in Chance's fridge." Cooper's already out the door before I can protest, my other brothers close behind.

"Don't go far! We aren't done," I yell after them but I know it won't slow them down. And I know they aren't going anywhere. They wouldn't dream of letting me down or of disappointing Lily.

She slides up next to me and takes my hand in hers. "Can you believe we're doing this?"

I take her into my arms. "Putting bench seating for eighty in the barn? No, I cannot believe we're doing that."

Lily laughs, her breath warm against the cotton of my shirt. "You know that's not what I was talking about."

"I can't believe it took me this long to find you," I say as I tilt her face up to mine. "I can't believe I've gone for this long without making you my wife."

Lily sighs and pushes up onto her tippy toes. Her lips press against mine, warm and soft. In a few days I'll have done the unthinkable: I'll have taken Lily Gentry off the market for good.

"It's going to be good, isn't it?"

"It's going to be better than good; it's going to be the

best." Because I can't imagine anything less now that I've finally made this place my home. Now that I've finally snagged the most important piece of the puzzle—Lily here with me helping me to make my dreams come true. And I'm doing the same for her, watching in awe as she runs our business like a boss. People are coming from all over to have work done, to buy things from the shop, and to soak up a little Mint Springs charm.

But this right here? This beats anything I could have wished for.

I'm home for good.

ACKNOWLEDGMENTS

Thank you for taking a visit to Mint Springs! It's a fictional town but it's close to my heart. Lily and Chance's story actually started percolating in my head as I steamed and scraped wallpaper from the walls of *my* summertime bedroom in my grandparents' house. That's sweaty work, ya'll, but it's great for getting your brain to cook up other ideas about how you could spend your time. I hope you loved reading about the farm and these two lovebirds as much as I enjoyed writing about them.

I've got other people to thank too, of course. Thank you to Tamara Mataya and Austin Ryan for their editing work on *Make It Shine*. Everything needs polish, people, and these two help me get closer to perfect.

Thank you to Kate Farlow for her fabulous cover design and for her help picking titles and putting up with, um, indecisive authors who have an idea but difficulty communicating it.

Thanks to Laralyn Doran for reading an early version of this book and helping to iron out details. As always, her suggestions were right on the money.

Just Write Salt Lake City gets a big thank you for our every other week virtual writing sessions. You guys keep me working, working, working—even in a pandemic.

And, more heaping praise for my children. For this book, you've been a captive audience quite literally for so much of the process. Being stuck together at home has made us all crazy (crazier, probably). Thanks for reminding me some things aren't the end of the world and for telling me which font color looks best. That's important stuff, right there. Kisses and hugs since we're the only ones we are technically allowed to kiss and hug so far in 2021 anyway.

ABOUT THE AUTHOR

Jessie Harper writes steamy, contemporary romance with a slightly Southern flavor. Originally from Nashville, Tennessee, she has lived all over the world—from Europe to Asia. She currently resides in Park City, Utah with her husband, three children, and more rescue animals than she ever intended. She appreciates a nice glass of whiskey, homegrown tomatoes, and well-delivered sarcasm. She hopes to never have to "bless your heart."

For updates and more visit www.jessieharper.com. Or sign up for Jessie's newsletter so you never miss a thing.